My Grandmother's Shadow

An utterly heartbreaking unputdownable
historical novel based on a true story

GW00471352

DEVORAH SHAFRIR KERET

My Grandmother's Shadow
Devorah Shafrir Keret
Copyright © Devorah Shafrir Keret

Translation from Hebrew: Idan Ben-Barak

Contact the author: shaked48@zahav.net.il

ISBN 9798863499697

To my feminine dynasty
My grandmothers
My mother
My daughters
And my granddaughters

The face I have
Is from my mother
Who got it from her mother.
My grandmother sent me her face through her,
What a long way!
Thus she sends them to her grandchildren,
Then to the great-grandchildren.
In my family,
When you're born
You get a gift – a face.

Nurit Zarhi,
The Queen Came to the King, 1971

DEVORAH'LE

The sentence my mother told me when I was seventeen was the key to my journey: "I'll tell you one thing – if I ever meet my mother, I'll kick her."

These words were the reason I placed the moon above the pine at the right spot for me to create my life's painting.

❦ 1954 ❧

"Daddy, where is mommy's family? Why doesn't she have parents like you do?" I look up to my father as we walk. Two yawns ago we got off the bus we'd boarded at Haifa's central bus station. We'd finally finished an interminable journey, the smell of gasoline mixing with that of the passengers and making me feel, as always, nauseated. Now, as we walk the path next to Adler's shoe shop towards our home in Kiryat Yam, my mother and my sister hurrying in front of us, it seems appropriate to ask the nagging question in my head. It had been bothering me all through the Passover Seder we'd celebrated with the entire family. There I had plenty of time to think, and to watch dad's brothers and my eight cousins, all sitting round the table. I checked and rechecked who belonged to whom and how come we were one family. Suddenly I was hit with the realization that all of those people around the table belonged to my father's side. Where was my mother's family?

The Seder was presided over by Grandpa Avraham. Missing a leg, he hobbled over to the chair at the head of the table from the bed he would regularly occupy by the living room window facing the balcony of the house on Binyamin street, Rehovot. Grandma Karolina wore a clean, neatly ironed dress. A very unusual look for her. To the child I was then, she looked old, and exuded an abhorrent smell of fish and poultry. Her face sported a prickly stubble. Whenever we visited, I'd prepare myself mentally for the kiss she would plant on my cheek when we said hello and goodbye. She spoke only German and always wore a cheap gown-style dress covered with a blood-spattered apron. The shop, adjoining the house, had a large concrete pool in which carps swam, happily ignorant of their imminent fate: to have their head smashed. The house was furnished with heavy brown furniture and the blankets were heavy, downy quilts that we loved hiding inside and kneading. The smell was of a house that had never been flooded with sunlight; for me it was the smell of the diaspora and of old age.

There was never a real connection between Grandma Karolina and me. It seemed that her worldview would not allow her to make conversation with her granddaughter and take an interest in her, to say nothing of expressing love. I don't recall our eyes ever meeting; I don't recall her acknowledging my existence – except for the single time I remember well: I'd tried to be quiet throughout the long, exhausting Seder and be done with the ordeal, but unfortunately, I spilled a glass of wine onto the white tablecloth and was roundly reprimanded, with and without words. Grandma Karolina saw me then.

I escorted dad, who was carrying the two over-stuffed suitcases that contained all of our small family's clothes for this trip – everyday, formal and sleepwear – to our Kiryat Yam home. I decided that it was time for me to learn the mystery of my mother's family. My intuition led me to ask dad rather than mom. I suppose even then I felt that here was a sensitive story or a big secret that my mother would find hard to reveal. Even then I knew that my father also spoke for my mother, that he was her gatekeeper and her guardian.

Dad slowed his pace but did not reply. I asked again, with a child's simplicity and innocence: "Dad, where is mom's family? Why doesn't she have parents like you do? Why do we always celebrate the Seder with your side of the family?" Dad put the suitcases down on the path and replied loudly and decisively, almost mechanically, as if the sentence was already waiting to be said: "It's good that you asked me and not mom. Never ask this question again."

I heard, I wondered, I took it in, I was disappointed and was silent. I stifled my curiosity. At that age, when my father told me something firmly, I obeyed unhesitatingly and would not protest.

We were close, but despite that, or perhaps because of that, he would sometimes hit me. A few days before that trip south, an event took place that I remember still: my neighbor Maya and I penciled a mural all over the section of wall to the right of the door of the room I shared with my sister Nurit. Instead of a small page, we had a huge wall as our canvas. We were kindergarten-age girls carried away by the joy of creation. After Maya left, my mother saw the wall. She wasn't angry with me but asked: "What were you thinking when you did that? Didn't you think dad would be angry?" Once again, she put herself on my side and against big, fearsome father. I remember her being worried, suggesting: "Since dad will be home from work soon, we won't manage to erase all this. Leave the door to your room open so it hides the drawing and he won't see it. Tomorrow, we'll clean it up and dad won't know."

The man my mother loves, the one who protects her from the world, had suddenly turned into a scary, threatening presence for her as well and she'd shifted onto my side, the side of the small, hurt child. We were two children before him.

9

My father came home and came into our room as usual, to ask how we were. Me, all of six years old, took care to lean on the door and not move. My father sensed I was hiding something. He closed the door and saw the drawings. My mother tried: "Jacob, it will be gone tomorrow. She's just a small girl, it happens. Never mind." But he wouldn't listen. She cried and begged for me, he screamed at me. I was thrashed; the pain lives in me still. In those moments he seemed like a different man altogether. The next day my mother and I washed away the scribbles from the wall and there was no more evidence of the crime, only of its punishment.

It seems that violence was the educational method my father knew from his childhood. Today I think of my and Nurit's reactions, how we didn't cry or scream when he hit us. We became skilled at hiding the truth and wearing masks. We always had each other and together we would unburden ourselves of the pain and the frustration. Sometimes I would still have red traces of a handprint on my rear and would limp for hours.

When I asked my father about my mother's family, I did not yet know that my mother, along with many of my friends' parents, were orphans. Perhaps if I'd known that, my missing piece would not cry out quite as much to be whole. I was too young to know of the decimation of Europe's Jewry and I doubt I'd listened to the words read out in the solemn Holocaust Memorial Day ceremonies. Even had I listened, I would likely not have understood. I did not know there was a heartbreaking reason why some of my classmates were living in a cluster of tin shacks called "Kamp" near the Urim elementary school.

Being prohibited from delving into my mother's past only exacerbated my need. The secret began to live within me. My curiosity, like yeast leavening dough, a family secret expanding.

The forbidden impossible childhood wish kept demanding to be fulfilled. As the years passed, fulfilling that wish became to me a defiance of fate: "I am in control of my life, I decide what is or isn't a secret in my life." This secret intrigued me: why do my parents keep my mother's secret so religiously? What does it contain? A deep shame? Unfathomable fear? Anger so profound that it made them want to ignore her roots?

With a girl's instinct, I dimly sensed that my mother was the victim of a situation that was not of her choosing. An inner feeling drove me to involve myself in this victimhood. From that secret situation I felt unconsciously that I could grow either as a wilting victim, or as a person who cultivates themselves. I realized it was up to me. I'd already had some successes at school, in sports and in painting, which I loved. This hurdle remained, but what could you do when dad said "never ask this question again"?

The hidden became present in my life; by seventeen, curiosity was beginning to make its demands heard. By then I'd begun testing the different taboos for myself. Some of them collapsed under my scrutiny. I understood that my parents were not perfect, and I specialized in criticizing what they said. I was attended by the vague feeling that my mother's secret weighed on her, that her soul was not at peace and that is why she was sometimes neurotic.

I decided that it was time to find out why my mother had no family. I remember the inner sentence that led me – "no-one will stop me. Not even my father."

I understood in a deep sense that this secret was also connected to my personal sense of identity. The need to uncover the secret became a thirst that demanded that I delve into my roots and follow their branchings to reach the groundwater. I sensed that my roots were severed, and that it was up to me to regrow them. Even then I could sense with my survival instincts that my mother carries within her a load so heavy that I must do everything to develop the tools needed to cope with it. At seventeen I did not want to bear the burden of my German-Jewish heritage: "*Benimm dich. Tu was dir gesagt wird*"[1].

I decided that my father's defense of my mother will change and I will protect her by talking to her. My mother was then a young woman of 43.

Nurit was already recruited to the army intelligence corps and stationed at a base somewhere in the center of Israel. I shared many moments with my mother in the afternoon hours, before my father would ride his bicycle home from work and during his daily nap before dinner, after which they would have their regular meetings with friends. My mother and I would chat as we weeded the vegetable patch, or sat on the front bench of the garden discussing when we should go over to Levi's nursery to buy new seasonal flowers. These are the moments of closeness, colorfully painted within the imaginary pages of the memory book I carry with me.

And in one opportune moment, as we both stood in the kitchen looking out the window at the tall white cedar tree growing in front of my astonished eyes, a moment that was a natural continuation of our conversation, a moment created just for the two of us, I gathered up my courage and asked: "Mom, where is your family? Are you an orphan?"

My mother stood unmoving. She was surprised and could not find words.

I knew my mother had heard the question and I knew that for her it was an inappropriate, very surprising question. I had touched the implicit prohibition that hung there like an invisible floating danger, intangible but fully present.

That was only the first attempt. At another moment I chose,

---

1. Behave yourself. Do as you are told.

when there was intimacy between us and I felt I could soften her rigid resistance. Her reply was brief: "I'll tell you one thing – if I ever meet my mother, I'll kick her."

I was stunned. I did not expect that answer at all. The reply was a first volley that was both short and unexpected. My mother is carrying a deep anger. I felt her vulnerability and the caustic pain.

The questions flew from my mind in rapid, confused bursts to form a list: Were you in contact? If so, when? Who was your father? Do you know him? Did your parents remain in contact with each other? Do you have a biological family? Do you have friends from Germany? Did you grow up with your beloved friends Manny and Rachael? How did you arrive in Israel? Did the horrific war in Germany reach you?

I asked these questions in silence. I was, by then, good at stifling. Maintaining control was the name of the game in our house.

"Do you have documents? Childhood photos? Anything?"

"I do and I don't want to talk about it. Enough."

I wouldn't stop. One time I said softly: "Mom, please, just let me see the papers you have from there." Another time: "Just give me an idea. Mom, please." Once I said "I'm dying to know" and another time I changed my angle of attack: "Why are you alone in the world? Tell me. Maybe it will be easier on you if you tell me your secret. What do you think?" I would harp on my rights: "It's my right to know. Your mother is my grandmother, I have a right to know who she was." I was never aggressive, always very gentle and careful.

And then, one afternoon, came the tidings. It started with an appreciative smile: "Oh, well, you're unrelenting", followed by "Come, I'll help you. I don't want to know but I want to give you what you want so much. You're right, it's your right to find out who your grandmother was. Okay, then, Devorah'le."

I held my breath, then gathered within me an imaginary oxygen container and drew deeply from it.

The smile and the loving eyes looking at me made me think: perhaps my father's taboo caused my mother's continuing distress. Perhaps she was already prepared to let go of her secret but was used to conforming to my father's understanding.

Perhaps she was used to conducting herself under a veil of mystery, but my timing gradually revealed to her that she could now dispense with the veil. The German-Jewish façade encourages the keeping of secrets; it makes everything smooth, well-ordered and clean. "Order is order" and should not be spoiled by mess.

Perhaps my mother could not understand why her daughters did not take an interest in her. She might even have been hurt by the lack of interest in her we'd displayed up to that point.

Perhaps the conversation itself freed a little of the energy she'd invested in keeping the secret.

Perhaps the heap of "maybes" would shrink if I continued to investigate the past.

She led me to the large white Formica wardrobe, custom-built by a carpenter into an entire wall of my and Nurit's bedroom, opened up the bottom left drawer, and told me I was free to root around in it. "All my papers are in this drawer."

I realized that my mother's entire history was always in my room, close to me, but I never knew it. I realized that everything my mother knew about her past could fit into one drawer, one drawer containing every connection to the world that had been hers other than the man she fell in love with.

My mother stood by my side, nervous and excited, as though I were now included in that part of her that was erased, covered, hidden, forbidden, held back. We now shared a real, unspoken bond. I had become my mother's secret-keeper.

For me, my mother's decision was more than just revealing the contents of her secret. It was also her willingness to reveal it.

We had both cracked the silence, took down the mantle of its keeping.

A simple lampshade hung from the center of the high ceiling. Just under it stood a table made of light-colored wood, its top covered with gray, marble-like Formica. Around it were four matching chairs. Nurit and my spring beds were folded to the wall, as we would make them every morning, and covered by a curtain festooned with brown flowers. This gorgeous cloth also hung over the attic door; today it is draped over the glass doors of wardrobes in my own house, providing a connection to my childhood home.

We sat together, hunched over a stack of photographs. The low window was open, and a gentle breeze blew in from the sea, so close to our home.

My mother took off the worn rubber band and lay on the table a bundle of papers. They seemed quite used to being stuck together in the darkness of the drawer of secrets. At the back end of the drawer, I noticed a bundle of photographs.

"Who are these?" I asked at the sight of a photo I took from the stack. It showed a woman and a man, young and happy, sitting at a small, square table in a very neat garden, enjoying a cup of tea and Kugelhopf cake. A bicycle was leaning on the wall of the house by them; on its rear rack lay a large bag, perhaps made of leather. By the woman's side was a wooden playpen with two babies inside. A girl aged about ten, dressed in a white dress with a wreath of flowers on her head, was swinging on a swing that hung from a thick tree branch.

Mom stopped me: "if we're going to do it, let's do it properly. If you want to understand things, this isn't the right photo to start with. Wait one minute; we've waited so many years, so let me get you the paper that will start you on this journey." In that moment, into my mother's perpetual insecurity, flowed a soft, quiet, and stable voice, a voice that came from a very private and precious place. That sweet voice merged into the beating of my heart.

The paper she drew from the bundle was clearly a formal document, a page adorned with many stamps. "Mom, translate this for me" I asked.

JOHANNA

∽ 1941 ∾

"One two three four. One two three four. One two three four," my Mia keeps whispering to herself. She is trying to get through these days by distracting herself. It seems that my child has perceived that the only thing that does not change is the fact that time crawls at a constant pace and she is trying to help it pass. My little one has another way of coping: winding the key to play the repeating tune of her dancing ballerina. Each of us has her own way of dealing with the inferno we are in.

It was promised that our personal bundle would be delivered to our new place when we arrived, so I should leave in the room everything I have. I took care to write our name on the suitcase, including the address of my small family before we moved to the ghetto: "Johanna and Mia Gerson, Latchaplezha 21 apartment 6, Riga". I know it's naïve to write that address rather than our ghetto address, but I find it hard to stop dreaming. Our entire world is packed up in a suitcase, ready to move. The term "home" moves further away from me. We were asked – oh, really, who asked me in the last few days besides me? "We were told", I should say. We were unambiguously shouted at to arrive first thing in the morning at the concentration point. Even when describing the meeting hour, I was using a word from the world now lost: they screamed "morning", but it was the middle of the night, long before first light dawns on the dark, frozen world. I can still say the year is 1941. Winter. My dreams of a celebration of my approaching birthday seem like someone else's dreams. Perhaps you can really transfer these dreams to some lucky girl living on the other side of this wall? I drive from my mind the dark thoughts that wonder if I will ever reach that day.

In these December days, daylight is stingy with its visiting hours. Last night, as darkness fell, I hugged my little Mia with all my strength. We spoke without words. I made her layers upon layers of warm clothing. She dressed by herself, silent and focused. After, we lay dressed in bed, Mia snuggling into me. In the next bed lies Diana, my childhood friend, gently sobbing. Beside her lie her two young sons, Froi'ke and Menash'ke. Her pregnant belly keeps bulging. Her sobs are the soundtrack to our experience. I choose not to comment, but once in a while I come over to her and embrace her. In the other rooms of the apartment live many other families.

This morning, I heard by my room's window a conversation between two women; they were trying to find out more details on what we all saw a week ago: "I wonder where all those from the other neighborhood have gone to," mused the older of the two.

"There were clearly tens of thousands of them. I don't think I'm exaggerating," said the other, holding two tiny children to her body, one under each armpit.

The older woman replied knowingly, as though she were sitting atop the well of mysteries:

"They moved to a new settlement. Everyone knows that."

"What does that mean?"

"Look, every person was allowed to take a suitcase, so it stands to reason they were just relocated." Her son, who looked about 13, jumped in the conversation: "Mom, are you ascribing decency to the Nazis? So what if they allowed them to take suitcases? This could be a ruse." He'd allowed himself to dispute his mother's opinions in public. Our world had truly been upended.

"You can always see the glass half empty," his mother admonished. She was, apparently, like me in her survival methods, she would like to drive away the horrible sights and sounds and thus stay optimistic. I also save the remainder of my strength for keeping myself and my last remaining daughter alive.

But her son would not let her: "Mother, we've seen it. How can you say they're human? They're the devil incarnate. Albert described to us how they..."

"Enough. I don't want to hear that," his mother cut him off, shouting.

"Mein Gott, halten uns sicher,"[2] prayed the first woman, turning her head to the heavens and clutching her babies tight.

I turned myself away from the window with a silent scream "enough!" I did not want to hear the rest of the conversation and what this boy already knew. The teenagers now take responsibility when their parents run out of strength. They crawl into all sorts of corners and steal food scraps, listen to people talking, and know.

A week ago, November 30th, I saw thousands of people marching in an endless line. I have no idea where they are now. The description I overheard was enough, and would not leave me: "children were thrown out of third story windows"

Yesterday, you could still see in the light of day puddles of blood here and there in the snow, hear frantic conversations between people, watch the children, running around in shoes made of rags after their warm, proper shoes were stolen by Latvian guards for their own children. Occasional shouting in German and Latvian is heard, with a sigh in Yiddish in response. Even when they stop, the screams keep bouncing

---

2. Yiddish: My God, watch over us.

around inside my head. I have no moment of peace. My head is exploding.

Mia is with me. Eddie the hero is gone. So is Avram. And Rennie? Where is Rennie?

What's left for Mia and me is only the putting on of shoes. I am a machine that does what it needs to do. Never mind me, nearly forty years of age, but Mia is the same. Her eight years in this world have already taught her that fate plays games with us and that her mother has no answer to even the most basic questions. She has already realized, the hard way, that she must stand on her own two feet because any support can break. I barely managed to fall asleep at night. Again and again, I thought about how my child has already ceased to expect that grownups would protect her. How could one sleep when you're trying to be a mother, simply be a mother, and must turn up with your daughter at a meeting point at four in the morning on a snowy night?

Thoughts are lucky to have no one to police them.

I can't sleep through the long night, and I feel myself in another time and place. My imagination takes me back to the time I was young and single, independent and carefree. I go back to the coffee break in the German Theater course in Riga, Latvia's resplendent capital, in late 1921. I was 19 and a full member of the theater course. Before I was accepted, I loved to dream of the day I'd be acting on a stage. I would enact scenes in my room, with Lea, my sister, two years my elder and my confidante, encouraging me, laughing and crying in the right spots. During these times, I was glad that Lea was still single and spending so many hours with me in our childhood home. Ever since I was little, whenever I was alone in my room, I would stand in front of the mirror, putting on hats and making up monologues. I would also commandeer hats from Lea and mom: different sizes and shapes, made of different materials, with a feather or a silk flower adorning them. The hats were a whole world to me. When I see them in my mind's eye, I can break off from reality and enter a world that is all my own.

During one of the Friday night family dinners, when I was sixteen, Lea rapped the wine bottle with her soup spoon to signify that she had an announcement. Dad, holding his stomach as was increasingly the case lately, gave her a wondering stare, and my mother gave him a look that was a mixture of happiness and worry. When everyone was quiet, Lea stood up and announced: "I've signed our Johanna up to audition for our well-known German-language city theater." I drowned in the brief moment of silence that followed. Lea signed me up? Did I hear correctly? I raised my eyes slowly and saw my mother's eyes glistening with tears. And then my father stood up – though bent almost completely over, as that was the best he could manage – poured a glass of wine and raised it and we all understood that the path was clear; permission had been given. Everyone applauded us both and began discussing the text I should choose for my first audition. As suggestions started flying, I felt that the burden of proof was on me. Words circled the table and merged into each other. I could make out phrases: "Maybe Gogol", "How about Chekhov?", "There's a great Ibsen scene", "Oscar Wilde has the most wonderful scene." What a family. We were always keen on culture, and this was an opportunity to express and enjoy it.

In these moments, sitting by the table with everyone surrounding me, I felt my heart thumping, I felt as if I was rising up through the air and tasting joy. An inner force made me get up on my seat, although I was no longer a little girl, and improvise an acceptance speech as would be given by an actor who'd just won the theater's annual award and is thanking each and every one in her family.

"This is my opportunity to thank first of all my grandfather and grandmother, Abraham and Shifrah Friedman, who immigrated here from Germany. They were the ones who made me understand and speak German. Danke Opa und Oma[3]. I thank my father Yedidia, our Didi, who always knows how to be with me at the crossroads of my life. My father is the strong core of our family, the one who will never let me fall," I said and blew him a kiss. "Thank you to my devoted, loving mother Etta, who keeps our home warm and comfortable and taught me to appreciate the taste of Viennese schnitzel and a properly baked strudel. Thank you to Tanny, my big sister Tanny Schidlovsky, married to her beloved Gregori Schidlovsky. She has always been my role model. Last, but not least, Lea, my beloved sister, my confidante, who initiated this, and it is due to her that I stand before you today." I added a munificent hand gesture as if to quell the deafening applause from the imaginary audience and took a bow.

Tanny laughed and grew red. "Yanni, you've overdone it. Gregori and I have only just started dating." "She foretells the future." Mother remarked calmly.

My silliness suddenly evaporated, I came down from my chair and found to my dismay that I could recall the text Chekhov gave Yelena in "Uncle Vania". I assumed a solemn expression and recited: "There is no greater sorrow than to know another's secret when you cannot help them. He is obviously not in love with her, but why should he not marry her?"[4]

In the silence, I heard the power of that moment, the consummation of my love of acting. This was the first time I'd done a monologue outside my own bedroom in front of an audience. A small audience, perhaps, but I thought this might be a more difficult sort of audition, as I would find it easier acting in front of an unknown audience in a darkened hall. The feeling of satisfaction enveloped me, but I was still wondering: why did

---

3. Thank you grandfather and grandmother

4. *Uncle Vanya*, Anton Chek hov, Act III.

Lea need to do that for me? Why couldn't I take that step for myself? Where were my determination, my inwards-turning vision? Am I even capable of being determined and consistent? The silence lasted but a short while, and then everyone stood around the table and applauded again as my mom served the pudding. Lea called out "Bravo! Bravo!" and kept calling out "Encore! Encore!" with everyone joining her. I asked myself whether I should consider Lea's act as assisting or impeding my route to independence. I felt like a feather flying on a bird's wing.

Enrolling in the theater transported me into a very intensive life. I had to combine my senior year in high school and prepare monologues for the entrance exams. Every time I returned from another level of the exams, I would tap out the special family ring on our front doorbell, dad would greet me with an inquiring look on his face, and I would announce proudly that I'd made it to the next level. During these moments dad would manage to stand up a little straighter and I knew that it was mostly for him that I would be accepted into the theater.

At the end of the long, grueling series of exams, about six months after that family evening, I was accepted. Finally. I was happy I could practice my German language skills and socialize with my fellow actors. My life filled up with interest and energy. For two evenings every week, within the beautiful theater building, I was filled to the brim with experiences. We experimented with different modes of creation. I chose to enhance my knowledge with puppetry and stage design. I was content. I managed to cram many activities into each day. I took on different characters, of different ages, and situations that were new to me. I was young and old, I spoke and moved like a little girl or even like a violent young man, I was insecure and impulsive, I was a single young woman and a desperate mother of five. I even sang. I fell in love with the theater exercises that made me act in ways I didn't know I had in me.

I surprised myself. I opened up and had a wonderful time. I felt I was improving and indeed received many compliments. I felt proud, pretty and confident. Despite my age I left no time for suitors; I felt that this was not the time for such frivolities. I became addicted to theater.

During shows, I no longer sat as part of the audience, but followed the actors, studying their movements, expressions and intonation. I attended the great Nikolai Gogol drama *Marriage* about ten times, each time focusing on a different actor or a certain interaction between the actors. I acquired skills beyond those of a regular audience member. During intermissions I would go to the small café to listen to playgoers' opinions. I wondered whether anyone in the audience sees the play and its components the same way I did.

"Mom, mommy, I need to pee," my Mial'e did not sleep as deeply as I did. When we rise from our bed, the shivering starts. It's so cold we are both shaking. The light is always on in the toilet so we can find it easily. I enter the toilet with Mia. She's afraid to be there alone. Her fears manifest in physical form as a monster that can appear when she's alone in the toilet. I taught her not to sit on the toilet seat. Our sanitary conditions are terrible. We wish we could clean, but we are not allowed.

I go back to our bed. "Mial'e, try to sleep. Sleep gives strength." Mia hugs her doll, says "good night" to me and whispers to herself "I wish you'd sleep, mommy."

Where was I? Ah, my love of theater. I will keep sailing through the world of my memories.

MY social life revolved around the world of theater, though we actors never shared details of our personal lives. We were as one being, breathing in unison. I loved my colleagues, but I didn't know where any of them lived or what their family situation was. That was how we all behaved; no point in mixing work and private lives.

Two years passed in this manner. I'd already celebrated my twentieth birthday. During one spring evening, at rehearsal, our director Andris announced: "we'll be staging 'Romeo and Juliet'. You're a wonderful team and I've decided you can handle Shakespeare." We all listened respectfully. Then Andris turned to me: "Johanna, you'll be Juliet. I've chosen you. You can do it and you'll be wonderful."

At first I felt on top of the world. Then doubts crept in: Could I do it? Will I disappoint Andris? Will I rise to the occasion?

I smiled and acknowledged my team's congratulations, but my anxieties rose, threatening to suffocate me.

"I'm still considering the role of Romeo. There are several here worthy of the part. I'll let you know when we meet again." And indeed, at our next session Andris announced: "Kaminski will play Romeo." Kaminski and me? But he's an excellent actor! His name is known beyond Riga and has even reached Germany. How could little, insecure me act with him?

That evening I ran to my friend Diana at record speed to tell her the news. Diana sat in her room, reading "Crime and Punishment" for the thousandth time. I barged into her room and exclaimed: "What more could a girl my age wish for? I'm trusted. I'm frightened, I'm happy, I don't want to let people down," and told her the news. Diana laughed: "Well, Johannuchka, maybe your newfound celebrity will bring you your future husband." "Maybe. Yes. Maybe. Think of my mother," I replied. My father died and left my mother a widow the year before and so I added that "I'll make my mother proud. Oh, how my dad would be happy if he were here."

My future seemed to everyone like a carpet, lined with colorful, sweet-smelling flowers, stretching to the horizon. I felt I wanted to share my life with a partner and experience love. Tanny, my eldest sister, was already married and I was getting a little fed up with the ritual whenever I came to their home: "Well, Yanna, what about you?" and me replying: "Lea first.

These things have their correct order." Yanna is the name Tanny gave me when I was born, and she was three and unable to pronounce my full name - Jo-han-na. Yanna is such an intimate family word that it always reminds me of our childhood years; it's a name I save for moments of intimacy.

During that period I was part of the rapidly growing group of German-speaking Jews. Many Jewish traders and businessmen were moving to Riga. The cruel Great War that had ended three years before made my city bloom with growing numbers of Jews. Riga caught the eyes of many, and I assumed that its European atmosphere – found in the cafés serving delicious pastries, the elegant outfits of the people strolling through its galleries, museums and parks –was the drawing power of our city. I assumed that Riga's surroundings also enticed many: our enormous market, where you could always find anything; the tranquility one could feel when visiting the nearby town of Sigulda, known as "Latvian Switzerland", and its majestic castles; the beach at Jūrmala, where we went every August, and the stretch of soft white sand separating the sea and the dense forest. The idle chats we had while on vacation showed me that more and more people learned to value the clean air, with its scent of pine trees intermingled with the smell of the Baltic Sea. The smell of the sea is the smell of freedom. My heart tightens, I miss it so.

My Jewishness manifested itself every week, when the whole family, often with guests in attendance, celebrated the Sabbath. These were the times I felt most keenly my father's absence at the head of the table. I would remember him, a glass of wine in his hand, announcing Sabbath's end and the start of the week. I would tear up to think of my father, wrapped in his *tallit*, on his way to the handsome synagogue on Gogol street, "Die Gogol Schule", where the city's most respected men prayed. Dad would attend the synagogue on all the important religious occasions. *Yom Kippur*, the Day of Atonement, was the holiest day of the year in our house, as it was in all Jewish homes regardless of their religiosity. The family would conduct itself quietly, and the refrigerator door would not be opened once. I was especially fond of the meals both before and after the fast, which my mother would prepare beforehand.

I remember accompanying my father to synagogue when I was little. I recall dad's voice asking "Johannuchka, are you coming with me?" and me, in my good flower-print dress and wearing red lacquered shoes, hopping by his side and reaching up so he could hold my hand. Since I was so young, I was allowed to enter the men's section with him rather than sit in the women's section, but I could not appreciate that privilege at the time. I sat beside him and marveled at my surroundings. We were a well-off family with a fairly comfortable lifestyle. We took annual holidays in lovely Jūrmala. We delighted in attending concerts and plays at the magnificent national theater while wearing our finest clothes. We enjoyed sitting in cafés with friends and celebrating birthdays in good restaurants. The Jewish society I knew, the one not so committed to religious observance, started celebrating lavish, sometimes indecent, parties. I declined all invitations to these wild parties, attended by many well-off Jews of my age or older, but I was always interested in hearing juicy details from my friend Diana. Diana would say to me: "Johanna, you're missing out on life. Think about it, these are the last days we have to enjoy this kind of life. Soon we'll be married and all of that will end." Then she would cajole: "Come with me just the once. Why not?". And I would always reply: "Each to their own. My passion is the theater." I was curious, even passionate, but also timid. I accepted what my mother passed on to me without words: that I should save my virginity for the man I marry.

In truth, I was not born into such peace, for in my teens there was a horrible war, a World War. In my childhood and adolescence I preferred to take no interest in the winds of war and in its aftermath. We went through stressful, even threatening and scary days, but I was not at all interested in the news coming from the outside world. On the contrary, in the first days of the war, my friends and I would collect and trade napkins from restaurants we'd been to, arrange empty perfume bottles, collected from aunts, on shelves, and invent dance steps to popular tunes. Before the war ended, we used to tell each other our thoughts and longings. We studied well but also fooled around with anything to do with boys. And from the age of eighteen, at the end of my studies and after half a difficult year of mourning over the death of my dear father, it was easy for me to forget the results of the war, which I already understood, and indulge in the opulence of the magnificent capital city that fate had ordained I should be born in.

Rehearsals for "Romeo and Juliet" were a complicated experience. Excitement was gnawing at my insides. On the first day of rehearsals my voice came out odd and squeaky. Andris made no comment, but the looks on my fellow actresses' faces told the truth. I thought he understood that I would gradually loosen up. My palms were sweaty. Kaminski's blue eyes made my heart flutter. I've always had a weakness for blue eyes, which are not to be found in my exclusively brown-eyed family. At night I would speak to myself: "Johanna, ease up. Your dream has come true. Breathe deep. Deeper. Great. You can do this," I encouraged myself. And indeed, at the third rehearsal I could feel the exuberance, the reason I became an actor rise within me. I felt better and better.

The theatrical life and the life of the theater became mixed up. I particularly liked rehearsing the scene in which Juliet's mother pleads with her to marry since Juliet is ready for love and is the right age for it. My fellow actor Galina, who played my mother, looked me in the eye with the gaze of a worried mother and managed to convince me that I had reached my age, which my sister Tanny had never managed to do – I'd fend her off right away. To meet the demands of the role, to feel endlessly loving, I had to be completely exposed. In the scene where Romeo and I fall in love with each other and slip into the yard, I felt my feet stumble. When Romeo climbed up to Juliet's balcony and confessed his love I could not but pray to the god of love that these would be the words I would hear soon in my real life. When Kaminski begged Friar Lawrence to marry us, I nearly ran onto the stage to call: "Kaminski, come to me. Let us love each other truly. Why not?" Two evenings a week my heart would miss beat upon beat.

I found myself fiddling in front of my mirror for a long time before going to rehearsals. I started investing my savings in more hats and sensual dresses. Lea told me that our mother, who felt I was a little out of it, had asked her if I was addicted to drink. We laughed, but I did not reveal my secret even to Lea.

The fifth time we rehearsed the scene where Kaminski kissed me longingly, he brought his face closer to mine, the blue of his eyes giving me a loving and longing look. I inhaled his special scent. My heart jumped out of place. Kaminski really kissed me. My lips responded to him on their own and joined in the celebration, and with my eyes closed I heard our director Andris say, "Well, that's quite enough now." I blushed and realized that Kaminski had noticed my embarrassment and smiled to himself with satisfaction. I felt like a little girl caught being naughty.

How does he spend time when he's not in the theater? What work does he do? Where does he live? Is he rich? These questions popped into my mind in an ever-changing order and would not let up. But all these important questions were overcome by the passion that flowed within the depths of my body, a passion that did not intend to ask questions but to realize itself.

"Gevald. Gevald." Oh no, just at such a pleasant moment I'm returned to the here and now. A woman screaming in terror.

I've never heard anyone screaming this loudly. Now more loud voices between her heart-rending screams. "He's dead." "Looks like hunger got him." "Yes, a baby has no reserves." The woman's anguished wail would not stop. It rose and fell like a siren. I held my daughter closer and wept silently. I wanted my body not to tremble so that little Mia would not feel me bemoaning our fate. I tried to fall asleep and then heard: "I'll bury him now. While it's still dark." "Come, I'll help you." "Where's the shovel?" hurried steps clattering down the stairs. The house's door opening and slamming shut. Five minutes such as these might age my eight-year-old by ten years. Quiet.

One morning I asked the educated Lea whether there are names typical of Jews. Lea was happy with the surprising topic and replied in the affirmative, and instantly brought up our own family name, Friedman, as an example of a Jewish name and added more names such as Kagan, Cohen, Levi, Einstein, Sheinfeld, Shidlovski, Gompert, and so on and on. I wasn't really listening but waited for the name Kaminski. When it failed to come up, I suggested a few of my own and asked if they were typical of Jews as well. Among these names I snuck in Kaminski. Kaminskis are usually Jewish, but not necessarily, Lea replied. There my interest in the matter ended. From that moment I convinced myself that it wasn't really important whether he was Jewish, since we're not the kind of Jews who pray daily at the synagogue and study at the *Heder*, nor are we members of the Jewish socialist and Zionist youth movements. We base our Jewishness on the Ten Commandments and those parts of Judaism we accept, and do not long for the promised land of Zion.

In my room at night, I recited, over and over again the next day's monologue. I would recite under my sheets:

"Dost thou love me? I know thou wilt say 'Ay';
And I will take thy word. Yet, if thou swear'st,
Thou mayst prove false. At lovers' perjuries,
They say Jove laughs."

Reality and acting came together. I fell asleep noiselessly
reciting part of the scene we were due to work on the next day:
"Good night, good night! Parting is such sweet sorrow,
That I shall say good night till it be morrow."

And with my eyes closing I added my Romeo's reply:
"Sleep dwell upon thine eyes, peace in thy breast!
Would I were sleep and peace, so sweet to rest!"⁵

Days came and went. My mother kept needling me about not
consorting with eligible bachelors and not seeking a husband.
Tanny's pregnant belly kept growing with every Saturday visit
with her husband. Lea was studying Russian literature at university, enjoying her studies and her Jewish friends. Each day
she would share with me what she'd read and her wonderful
thoughts. She loved reciting Pushkin and infected me with her
love for his poems.

At the end of one of the rehearsals, Kaminski said to me:
"Let's add some rehearsals so we can be at our best. I suggest
we meet at a café. Just the two of us. What do you think?" As my
heart fluttered I pretended to consider the idea, thinking about
my supposedly full schedule and... we set up a meeting.

Kaminski chose a hidden corner inside the café and when I
arrived took my hand and led me to my seat. "Here we won't be
in anyone's way," he explained. Over a glass of wine Kaminski
told me: "I travel to Germany a lot. My parents have business
interests there and they live in the sweet little town of Pirna,

---

5. *Romeo and Juliet*, Act II, Scene ii

south of Dresden. I grew up there. "Our knees touched, and I gently moved mine away. "Pirna is in Saxony. My father is a well-known architect." Kaminski's knees moved closer once more. This time I preferred not to move mine away. A hot flush came up my legs. I couldn't move. I didn't advance the conversation. I was spell-bound to the man and gave up any need to delve into details of his life. He wanted to share and I was enveloped in waves of heat.

He kept talking and I couldn't listen. I thought he too might think I was a drinker... the background music did not intrude on our conversation. "Smetana," we both agreed. "The *Moldau*," Kaminski added. I nodded. The *Moldau*, a flowing piece I knew well, fit so completely with the sweet sensation growing inside me. I whispered: "the part of the piece called 'my country'." We agreed with a smile and a look. This was a moment that told me how much the man I was sitting with was not simply an actor I happened to be playing opposite, but a man with a similar cultural background to mine. I closed my eyes and listened. My heart swelled as I thought of the name of the piece, "my country", and how impossible it was that I should leave Latvia, this wonderful place and the wonderful future it holds for me.

The rehearsal went very well. I found that, due to our meeting, I knew the text very well and Andris complimented me. It was clear to me that this was a wonderful way of assuming an acting role. We set up another meeting at the same place. When his leg touched mine again, I understood that it was not an accident on his part. After a couple scolded us "shhh... go to the theater. This is a café," Kaminski suggested we'd rehearse in the theatre's scenery room from now on. There wouldn't be anyone there during the evenings.

And then, as we sat at two ends of the scenery room table, Kaminski reached out his hand under the table and stroked my upper thigh. His hand moved further up and I started shivering. His other hand, resting on the table, touched my chin and lifted my head. His head drew closer to mine and he gave me a loving look. I heard him say "Johanna, you're not the only one who feels this way. I want to feel you with my whole body too." I started crying uncontrollably. Kaminski rose from his seat and moved behind me. His hands reached under my summer dress, stroked my breasts and hardened my nipples as he put his head on mine. He whispered: "Johanna, what will become of us?" and I cried even harder.

My priorities changed: Kaminski first, then the play. I tried to chasten myself for my foolishness, but my entire being would not concede.

Time stood still. I don't know how long we stood, his hands pleasuring me, until my crying completely subsided. He wiped away the rest of my tears with a loving hand.

He suggested we recover and recite one of the play's final scenes:

"Eyes, look your last!
Arms, take your last embrace! And, lips, O you
The doors of breath" [6]

- the lines, we both knew, connect love and death. In my mind I wondered why he had to pick these particular lines in which love demands a parting.

I nudged him away and asked in a measured tone: "are you speaking as Kaminski, or is that Romeo's voice?"

His reply was quick "I consciously chose that segment, Johannuchka."

My question remained unanswered.

"w...well?" I stammered.

"Your tears signify that we should part at once and restrict ourselves to rehearsals with the rest of the troupe."

---

6. *Romeo and Juliet*, Act V, Scene iii

I was left wondering. I couldn't add any clarification or express my opinion. I felt like a leaf blown about in the wind, a wilted leaf that can barely recall being part of a branch, part of a tree.

We packed up our belongings and walked swiftly and silently, side by side, heads bowed, toward the exit. My head was hollow. The physical excitement climbed into my head and took it over.

At the following day's rehearsal our Director, Andris, applauded: "Wonderful! Wonderful!" and complimented both of us on our convincing acting, that we were an "*Außergewöhnlich*" (extraordinary) loving couple. Kaminski and I did not look at each other and did not reveal our secret. I was both flustered and flattered, both abashed and happy.

I was afraid but also full of desire to be alone with Kaminski. A week passed, then another. During rehearsals I would hear his words of love and felt the thrilling touch of his hands on my body. The touch of his finger was enough to excite me. Diana's stories about Riga's debauched parties sounded imaginary to me, and I would not go to such. Diana would describe her sensual adventures and I would picture Kaminski and me, the heroes of every scene. My desire for Kaminski took over my entire being. As I awoke each morning I thought of Kaminski, as I dressed, I imagined Kaminski undressing me, as I ate I rolled my tongue in my mouth as if it were touching his tongue. If I listened to music I would see the both of us making love to the rhythm. When I went to bed, I felt his touch. The fantasy led me and took over my life. My body and everyday tasks separated from the longings for the future. Perhaps one could say that the heat that took me over then, was like the memories I flood my mind with right now as I lay in the cold bed, memories that can separate my body from my spirit. My body is here in the ghetto, but my thoughts fly back into the distant past. Now my head is saving me from the here and now, from this terrible moment and the terrible moments to come.

I go back to Kaminski. Don't want to think that I'm here, on this cold night.

One evening, Kaminski whispered straight into my ear. "Johannina," he said. I have a new name, I noted to myself. "Johannina, I lust after you. I booked us a hotel room. Will you come?" and added with a half-smile: "Not for any private rehearsals over a text we already know. I thought we'd do something for the first time. I can't function without continuing from where we stopped at the café. Johanna, Johannuchka, Johannina. Please. Let us free ourselves from the shackles of this world. Come to me, Johannuchka. We're not children anymore. Life is calling us." And again I found that the voice of reason has evaporated and that I could only nod wordlessly in reply.

And still I stopped him and said "No, I can't." I wanted it so much and suddenly my upbringing held me back. I said, but my eyes told a different story.

"Are you sure?"

"No," I replied honestly.

"Shall we postpone? Will you take time to think about it?"

"You've already booked?" As if that would be the decisive factor.

"I'll cancel. You need to be okay with this," he said and kissed me on my forehead.

I went through days when I was like a drop of water moving through high and low tides, there were moments of supreme energy and joy of life, followed immediately by moments of despair. Yes or no? No or yes? There was no point in consulting Diana: her answer was a foregone conclusion. Diana did not keep her virginity for very long.

I wondered what would happen to me if the answer continued to be negative and what might happen if it were positive. The day before rehearsal I decided: go with your passions.

Diana is right, you only live once. Maybe I'll end up marrying him after all.

Steps are nearing the window of the house in the ghetto, snapping me back to reality. I'm suddenly torn away from my life raft, the memories. Through all this time, the bleeding heart of the newly bereaved mother, our upstairs neighbor, translates the abyss of pain into words. I hear, but I can still manage to transfer my thoughts inside myself. The horrors here are unending and I have forced myself to learn to live with them. The front door of the shared ghetto house opens. I hear the footsteps of the men returning. Right now I cannot continue thinking of the love that I had. A baby has just been buried. I pray in my heart from the morning prayer: "O lord, soul that you have given me is pure. You hath created it, You hath formed it, You hath given it to me, and You retain it within me, and You will take it from me". A Jewish prayer, though I cannot believe its practiced words. God hath no mercy for his creations. That baby's soul was taken from him though he did no wrong.

I listened to Mia's breathing. She's fallen asleep. Great. All is quiet around me. I can go back inside my head.

I decided we'd go to the hotel, but I'll start with a question: "Kaminski, who are you?" and then add more: "What's your profession?" "Which synagogue do you go to?" "Where do you live?" He won't touch me before I know him, I told myself resolutely.

Not five minutes in the hotel room, all these resolutions, and my entire upbringing, were gone with the wind. Saving my virginity for the man I'd choose to spend my life with became an irrelevant idea. Kaminski and I found our naked bodied intertwined. Shackle-overthrower that I am. In the theater and in love.

All of Diana's stories about the obstinate hymen that requires repeated assaults until it gives up did not apply to me. I felt his practiced hands guiding me. We were insatiable. We moaned and laughed, stared in silence, on the bed and on the table and on the clothes spread on the floor. I don't know how long we were as one body. I wanted with every fiber of my being that these moments would not end. He whispered sweet nothings in my ears, kissed every part of my body and I was happy.

At first I moved to the rhythm of the *Moldau* playing in my head, sailing along with it. Suddenly there was complete silence. I flew. We are one body floating on up, away from this world and into the realm of heaven. The world around us did not exist for me. I was shocked by the feeling of holiness penetrating my being. Even now I'm ashamed to admit what I remembered during this inner flight: a Midrash to the book of Exodus that I, along with my entire class, was required to learn by heart in elementary school. I pictured a voice coming from heaven reciting the words one by one. My teacher would have been pleased to know I still remembered it perfectly, though I do not suppose she would think I'd quote it in this intimate moment:

"No bird did call,
No fowl did fly,
No ox did bellow,
No Ophanim stirred a wing,
No Seraphim did say 'Holy, Holy,'
The sea did not roar,
No creature did speak,
But the whole world was hushed and silent,
And the voice rang out 'I am the lord thy God'."[7]

Here I added with a whisper: "The God of love."

---

7. *Exodus Rabbah, 29:9*

I entered an otherworldly experience. My body, at ground level, was attending to its own affairs, while my soul floated up until I heard Kaminski's voice saying: "Johannuchka, I can't stay here all night. I have to go home. They'll be waiting for me, and I have no wish to be interrogated." I came crashing right down to the floor we were both entangled on. I was afraid to ask who it was who was waiting for him at home, and remained unknowing but in love.

When we were about to leave and Kaminski was at the door he whispered: "I didn't manage, in the heat of our first time, to make love as prudently as I should have. I didn't have time. I couldn't make it. You're something special! That's never happened to me before. Never, Johannina."

I had no idea what it was that he didn't do.

He added "That was irresponsible of me."

I didn't know what was irresponsible on his part. He put his hands together, as if in prayer, and explained: "My child, throughout the rest of the evening I was very careful. But the first time with you? I thought the sky fell on me, sparks of fire flew and a message was sent throughout the world that here was something that was never before created. Oh, Johannuchka."

He felt the same as I did. Amazing.

"From now on," he said, "I'll be more careful, though this dammed care takes away from the pleasure."

And I, like a small child who was given a splendid new toy, paid no heed to this information; only to the fact that now I, too, understood what everyone was so enthusiastic about.

By the time I got home I was a different Johanna. My mother welcomed me with a "Shhh". She was listening closely to an opera and whispered to me as if she were trying not to interrupt the singers: "Wagner. Richard Wagner, oh, what a composer!"

Our rehearsal time, from that point on, continued and we would regularly do "it", as my mother would say, at our regular hotel room. All I had to do was to show up and surrender myself. Kaminski took care of everything else. We needed no introductory ice-breakers: the fire was already lit. We enjoyed ourselves and expanded our repertoire of positions, with the skilled Kaminski guiding me like a teacher guiding a student. Our desire blossomed and we were insatiable. Every time, after about an hour, Kaminski would rise and announce he needed to go home. I carried on our lovemaking in my bed and in my dreams.

We had our shared secret. In truth, I wanted to run through the streets declaring my love, but Kaminski asked that we not talk about it, and I, so as not to lose his love, obeyed.

I only told Diana. I had to unload the emotion within me. Diana responded by telling me of the slow and gentle infatuation unfolding between her and Bera'le, a young Jewish man she'd met at the library. She surprised me by withdrawing from all the parties and being Bera'le's alone.

I enjoyed the rehearsals and enjoyed our shared secret. We began dress rehearsals. I felt very fortunate: not only was I acting in the theater, but it was a Shakespeare play, *and* I got to play Juliet, *and* I got to play opposite the great Kaminski, *and* – most importantly – be his lover.

As the days grew colder, I became aware that my monthly period was late. It took me too long to realize that.

"Diana, I don't know when I'd last had my period. It was very convenient not having one, but I understand it's been too long now."

"Oh, you silly thing. I've been with so many men. The man wears the protection. How come this had never happened to me? Well, just the once."

"I'm not the man," I tried joking.

"But you are unlucky," she said. Every evening when we meet, let me know what's going on with you. You're such a scatterbrain you might end up having birth contractions."

And so I reported every evening that nothing new was

happening between my legs. After a month went by we both concluded that I should consult a medical specialist. Diana, it turned out, already knew where to turn in these cases. I said nothing to Kaminski; I wanted our shared pleasures to continue. I was afraid my worries would intrude on what we had.

"You're definitely pregnant" said the doctor as he rummaged inside me, causing searing pain.

The news came three months before the premiere.

This was a catastrophe: How will I tell my mother? How come I didn't even know his first name? How could I get so addicted to my body? How could I have let my future be destroyed? And the most taxing question: how will my beloved react? The "How"s stacked on top of one another in a heavy and embarrassing heap. To this were added the facts that Juliet cannot be pregnant, and that luckily my father will never know about this horrible shame I bring on my beloved family. Oh well, I consoled myself, Kaminski loves me. It's a shame he won't get to propose at the time of his own choosing. Still, that's what happened. The fruit of our love came earlier than expected. My pregnant belly won't show through my wedding dress.

As we walked back from the Doctor, Diana didn't stop me from cycling through my confused thoughts. Only when we'd reached my front door did she stop and say: "We need a practical plan of action." I felt a little relieved and agreed with her. My flood of speech stopped as if it was turned off at the mains. I liked the word "we" – I wasn't completely alone in this. We decided I needed to take some time for myself: if I were to go through with the pregnancy, I couldn't play Juliet. Either that, or I'd change Shakespeare's plot so that the audience would understand that Romeo knocked me up. That might make for a very interesting play... If I were to terminate the pregnancy, I would certainly need time to recuperate.

Once again, I'd reached a crossroads in my life with me not at the wheel.

Diana came to the next day's rehearsal and quietly but decisively let Andris the director know that I was unwell and would not be able to take part in rehearsals over the next fortnight. True to my request, she looked closely at his face as she gave him the news. She said he was angry and shouted within earshot of everyone: "But, why like this? What, she's so sick she couldn't come here and say that in person? Now? After she'd mastered the part? What is this? Who does that? What's the matter with her? A two-week break?! This is a lead role! We already have a date for the premiere!" Spittle formed at the corners of his mouth, some of it hitting her. He glowered, stamped his foot and screamed at everyone that the rehearsal was cancelled.

This was an excellent opportunity for Diana to spy on Kaminski. She did not need me to describe him to her, since his image was plastered on the theatre walls. She caught up with him by the entrance to the toilets, gave him the letter I'd written him, and said she would wait for his reply.

Even now, nearly twenty years after the event, I can still quote word for word my short letter offering him to be with me during these moments.

"My dear man,

I have to see you as soon as possible at our usual place. Please, set up a time and I'll come into your comforting embrace.

With love ♥ and expectancy, Johanna."

Kaminski asked what I was ill with but Diana, at my request, kept her silence. That would be my role when we met.

Kaminski sent me a note saying he could meet me that night at our usual hotel room. I gathered he was curious and concerned. He signed "Yours, K." with no words signifying love, a fact that troubled my hyper-sensitive mind. I couldn't understand why he didn't sign his full name. The "K." signature reminded me of Josef K., the protagonist of Kafka's "The Trial" I'd just read. I was suddenly struck with the fear that I, too, might experience the vagaries of fate.

Thus rose the curtain on the second act of my life. No longer a good girl from Riga, no longer a fashionable, successful young lady realizing her dreams, but a woman fighting for her future life.

Kaminski listened and his whole body trembled. I understood his excitement: it isn't every day that a man gets to propose to his beloved. Our love will finally be made public. My man's confidence melted before my eyes. He hugged me and expressed great love. He spoke slowly, in a considered voice, as if every word that came out of his mouth had a physical weight. Sometimes he choked and even stammered. And so I heard him say: "Johanna, you never asked me about my life. I was very comfortable with that. I never understood why you chose to do so." Suddenly his body stooped. I realized that I was going to hear something that I probably, without realizing it, had prevented myself from knowing. "We cannot continue with this denial," Kaminski stated. Now I'll have to hear who he is. I knew he was right and I listened, as we both sat on the edge of the tidy bed.

"I'm a married man. I'm happily married. I'm the father of two small children." Every sentence beginning with "I" added a brick to my wall of problems, which was now reaching a height that couldn't be easily scaled. "I'm married to a Jewish woman. I'm a Christian from an atheist family. I was raised to believe that all men are equal regardless of their religion or color."

"My parents live in Germany, in Pirna. I moved here because my wife grew up here and because I accepted an offer from our German-language theatre."

I was stunned.

I felt as if a huge boulder was weighing on my head and would soon start crushing me. I folded softly into myself. My lips began shivering uncontrollably. Kaminski wasn't done yet and asked in a strangled tone: "Don't think for a moment, Johannuchka, that I'll leave you in this mess and run, but if you're fated to have that baby, I couldn't hurt my wife and our children. It's not their fault we fell in love."

"So it will be solely my problem?" I whispered, my strength ebbing.

"There's no other way. I need a little time to think how I can help you in your condition. It's time to look reality in the eye. When I met you, I understood for the first time in my life that you can love two women at once."

In those moments I came to the certain conclusion that I should have an abortion, and the sooner the better.

This was rock bottom. All the examples our teacher gave us to illustrate a fall from grace were dwarfed by my reality. Not only was my world destroyed, but I must now act very quickly so that I could still have a simple and quick abortion.

The world had changed. I couldn't believe that the beauty of the autumn colors, which mesmerized me every year, did not interest me at all now.

On the second visit to the doctor, to make an appointment for an abortion, the doctor sat me down in front of him after the physical examination and suggested that Diana join us and enter the room. The doctor added bricks to my wall of disaster and quietly announced as he leaned forward, very alert to note that I was listening to his every word –

"Listen, Fräulein[8] Friedman, listen well," he ascertained, "You're already into the fourth month of your pregnancy."

He waited two minutes and apparently only when he saw my expression change continued: "An abortion is not recommended at all, unless you're willing to take the risk of never being able to fall pregnant again."

---

8. Maiden; unmarried young woman

I froze.

Diana's soft caresses and the tears welling up in my eyes had no place in those moments, the was no room for pity and remorse. I realized I had to make a quick decision.

Kaminski suggested we meet again in four days and said he would come with practical suggestions and financial assistance for me. He sat next to me and stifled a soft, deep cry, much like the whimpering cries of my pregnant friend Diana lying in bed next to me right now. Maybe sobs that result from abysmal pain are identical twins. This time I was the one who wiped the tears with my scented handkerchief, and he said in a whisper, when a hint of a smile finally showed up on his face: "Remind me to clean my face before we leave, your handkerchief is perfumed." This time I also smiled because I understood his words. The smile was only external. Inside I wept over my fate. I was tired and defeated. The balloon of life exploded in my face and its torn parts flew at me and stabbed my entire soul and body.

All the way home I talked; I would not shut up. "What will happen to me, what will I do with the baby, what will happen to our show, maybe I could still have a secret abortion and carry on with my life. No. It doesn't make sense. If I were to go through with the abortion I might become a great actress, but I might never have children again and turn into a bitter, barren woman."

Most days I lay in my room with a blanket over my head. I counted the minutes, one by one, until the next meeting with my beloved. My mother realized that a heavy vessel was tearing at my heart. She tried to make me talk, asked me about rehearsals, brought me food to my room. Food I did not touch. I couldn't even tell my sister, Lea, the truth. Lea tried to lift my spirits with Pushkin's poems. She tried to make me laugh by putting on my hats, but I was silent and sometimes disengaged completely. I took solace in the fact that this pregnancy was the fruit borne of love. Somehow I managed to find a little consolation in that, which I raised in moments of despair.

I was ashamed of myself.

The veil of secrecy was neither colorful nor pleasant, but black and very thick. Behind this dark screen was a weak and dysfunctional woman. I understood this and could not change that reality. The number of minutes until my meeting with Kaminski grew smaller. I got tired of thinking about the essence of the practical proposal he was referring to. Would he leave his wife? Will he offer to live with two women? Will he run away with me to a distant land? Will he lovingly grow the fruit of our love?

A different Kaminski came to our meeting, a man who'd grown years older within a few days.

"Dear Johanna, I do not want to burden you. Nature has created a situation where you are the one carrying our child in your womb. I am sorry, but I cannot be a partner to that. I want to tell you that my heart aches and our secret is hard to bear."

This was the first ringing slap: he was not going to raise our child with me. I was struck by the privilege that men have in these situations. I felt the need to turn to help and found myself praying to the *Moirai*, the goddesses of fortune in Greek mythology my father told me about. They were not considered good-hearted, so I could ascribe my fate to them. I begged them for some compassion. I couldn't pray to the God of the Jews because I thought he might be on his break just now and hadn't noticed me at all.

Kaminski suggested a surprising plan: "I propose that you move to Germany until after the birth. That way you could keep your pregnancy a secret and you'd have enough time to plan the rest of your life." Out of the thick fog I could tell that Kaminski had come with a concrete plan. It stood out to me that he had planned in advance the words he would open with, and what he would then offer. I felt a hint of detachment on his part and a lot of logic that infiltrated our relationship.

He held out his hand to me with a folded piece of paper peeking out of his clenched fist. As if handing out precious treasure, he gave me the address of a Jewish lobby in Leipzig. The folded page also held one name: Flora Cohen. "Flora helps women in your situation, you can live with her and will also receive medical assistance if needed."

"How do you know a Jewish lobby? You're a Christian. What, I'm not the first one you've sent there?"

"Johannuchka, don't make it bad between us. I fell in love with you. Everything between us was real. My Jewish wife is a successful doctor who is connected to doctors in Germany and somehow, cunningly, I managed to obtain all these necessary details for you." And so, only at that moment did I realize more details about his life that I should have known before giving my heart away. He took both my hands in his, kissed me, took out his wallet from his pocket and put a very thick bundle of notes in my purse, gave me a strong hug, put his lips to my throat and kissed it softly, said some parting words that swirled round in my brain, kissed and hugged again, turned round and started to leave.

"Kaminski, what's your first name?" I suddenly whispered.

"Walter," he replied without turning, walked away and turned no more. The last I saw of Kaminski was his back.

"VAS iz di tseyt?"[9], I heard a murmured exchange by the window of my room in the ghetto. I heard every sound, like a lioness watching over her cubs. Mia keeps sleeping. Even Diana's weeping has stopped. The small hours of the night.

"Halbnakht. Punkt tsvelf"[10], comes the reply.

---

9. What's the time (Yiddish)

10. Midnight. Twelve O'clock exactly (Yiddish)

If so, I still have four hours until we are all gathered together. I will continue my journey to my past, thus continuing to ease the current burden. Interesting that this conversation came to my ears now that time has such a significant role in the world of my memories. The time allotted to us in our lives is sometimes our top priority.

I accepted that a new life was developing in my body and that I had to explain to those close to me where I was disappearing to. I forced myself out of bed. I bought travel tickets to Leipzig. I found out I could not pass by our hotel and certainly not near the theater, so the thought of getting into a conversation with Andris the director and apologizing to him – Andris, who believed in me when he chose me for a lead role in Riga's prestigious theater – I gave up on that thought. I packed my clothes in my room and even came down to eat with the family, a fact that brought my mother great joy. Some of the ruddy color returned to my cheeks. But each day I postponed the conversation I had to have; I did not dare say anything. Two days before the trip, a plan of action came to my mind.

I waited until Friday night dinner when the whole family would come to my mother's house. I tapped my drinking glass with a spoon to indicate that I wanted to say something important. "My family, dear family, the day after tomorrow I'll be leaving you for a week. I'll be going to Leipzig. Believe it or not, I received an offer to consider playing a lead role in a play that's going to come up next year. I can do that right after the Romeo and Juliet run ends. They want to interview me. Andris accepts my absence and is very proud to have discovered me." I fired the words non-stop, having practiced in front of the mirror in my room. Luckily, I know how to act. My mother's face lit up. "My talented daughter," she said proudly.

I SAW the men looking at the attractive young woman I was

as I changed trains. Who among them could have suspected the reason for my journey, who among these passers-by would have guessed that I had terminated my blooming career so that I could, in some distant hazy future, be able to raise a family. Who would have believed it, the end of love coming so close to its beginning.

"This is it, madam. Please." Said the driver when the bus stopped. He gestured in the direction I should take and added: "Fräulein, this is Brühl street, and number 7 is over there." Before getting on this bus at Leipzig Central Railway Station I glanced at the note in my hand every few minutes, though I knew every detail by heart. I'd already explained to the bus driver that I would like to alight at 7 Brühl street, and stood by the driver to make sure he wouldn't forget. Nevertheless, once I stood on the pavement, I took another look at the note.

I was standing in a busy street lined with multistoried buildings. Interesting, I'd pictured a low house with a low stone fence and a wooden gate. I walked slowly, as if to stave off reality. My feelings for Kaminski moved within me in waves alternating between hate and love, between attraction and loathing. One moment I was attacked by intense longing, and the next moment I felt hostility and deep anger. Thoughts about the cause of my condition would not leave me for a single moment. I imagined he would regret it and come for the birth. He knows where I am. This dream took seed and developed within me as the fetus grew. As I passed a woman on the street, I imagined she could hear my heart pounding. I paused, I breathed, I wanted to try and stifle a little of the storm of emotions that enveloped me. I looked left, right and forward in a searching motion, with the gaze of a tourist who is not familiar with her surroundings and wonders where she should go. In my mind I saw the moment of the long-awaited meeting between Kaminski and myself, felt him caress my belly, stared into space as he carried our baby in his arms and as he whispered in its tiny ear that he would never leave it and its mother. Once again, I found myself looking at the note with a searching, deploring look. A young man approached me and gently asked if I needed any help. I showed him the note. "Come, it's just here," and led me to the next house over.

We reached a high, grey, forbidding building. In the hallway, among the many signs, I found a small plaque in a calm shade of blue – "*Israelische Frauenvereinigung*"[11]. I climbed to the third floor step by step while holding onto the railing, as if I might drown if I let go.

11. "Hebrew Women's Union" (German)

SCHWESTER[12] HILDE REIN

⇜ 1932 ⇝

Laura came into our lives during Eastertime, about two years ago.

Laura became my Rennie's favorite.

Rennie is only seven and has already planned an outing for the both of us. She has suggested that we leave the village and walk the mountain paths, away from our nursery in our village, Gottleuba in Saxony, in the east of Germany. Oh, how Rennie resembles me in the things she likes. Who would have believed.... *gotseidank, heilige Maria*[13].

We entered the forest and walked one of the well-trodden paths. There were a lot of colors on both sides because there were a lot of flowers there. It felt pleasant. I thank God for the babies I raise here who are my world. Because, really, what can be more wonderful than caring for babies and seeing them grow? I am sure God directed me to choose this life, to forgo a married life and having children of my own. I have been working here happily for fifteen years and specialize in baby care. That's what everyone thinks. *Gotseidank, heilige Maria.*

People do not pass along the mountain path we have cho-

---

12. A nurse who is also a nun.

13. Thank you, Mother Mary (German)

sen, because the tree branches reach nearly down to the ground and strike my face. I held my veil in my hand and walked bent over the entire time. I asked not to get too far away because we would soon be unable to see the white, two-storied hospital that was the last building before the forest began. "You could get lost in the thicket," I tried to warn Rennie as I ran after her. She skipped quickly and lightly like a mountain goat. She sang in a loud, clear voice and ran to the rhythm of her song *"Hänschen klein"*. Rennie is free and it seems like the entire mountain range is listening to her *Hänschen klein*. I know that every child in Germany knows this song, the song about Hans, an independent child of Rennie's age who discovers his abilities and goes out alone into the wide world, who does not listen to his mother's sobbing voice calling him back home, but during these moments it seems like Rennie has made up the lyrics about herself. I run, limping, after her and scream "Rennie, wait for me!" while she sings and runs on ahead. "Rennie," I call out to the trees but she doesn't care. She's in her own world, and I do not exist during these moments, as if something stronger than her has taken her over, even though her obedience to me is so important to me in her education. I hope it's not a demon. Heaven forbid. Everything she does is because of my education. Although Rennie is not my daughter, I raise her as my own, just like I do the rest of the children in the orphanages in our Gottleuba. They are all children tossed about by fate. My work is to change their fate and bring them good luck. I derive great satisfaction from raising these children who are orphans or were taken from their parents when it was clear their parents could not take care of them or reached us due to an unplanned, unwanted pregnancy.

Rennie is different. She's no longer a baby and her place is officially no longer in the nursery. However, importantly, I can't part with her. I love her like a daughter. She is the daughter I never had. She is my whole world. I know and feel in my heart that God has made it so that we would be together and never leave each other's side. I am also the person she loves the most in her little world. I can look for hours into her big, black, intelligent eyes, at her pretty face. I'm very happy she has a good heart and loves our church. My child.

I couldn't stop Rennie's rapid progress toward the gentle sound of bells, chiming as if they were calling us. She stopped singing and cried out happily: "Can you hear? Can you hear that wonderful sound? Listen. So beautiful. Beautiful like the music at our church. Oh. W-o-n-d-e-r-f-u-l. I have to see who's ringing bells like that here." Luckily, I dressed her in a red dress; this way I can see her within the thicket as she moves further away from me.

"Rennie, stop. O Jesus, our Savior. Rennie, wait for me!" I commanded and my feet entangled in my scapular, now dirty and creased, which I don't like at all. I fell to my knees. I stood on all fours. I held the crucifix that hung around my neck to make sure it was still in place. I just discovered that it's not easy to raise a child who won't listen. I'm used to babies and to obedient Rennie. I lifted my head and discovered that I looked like one of the sheep we'd come upon. All of us standing on all fours. Blood painted my knees, but I was focused on Rennie's moments of joy.

We were among a small herd of sheep. I suppose you need to raise children to reach faraway-nearby places. In truth the furthest I'd ever been is Dresden, I haven't even been to Leipzig yet. I live here and require nothing more. I don't even dream about distant places. What would I do in foreign places with people I don't know? A city-dweller might find my world as narrow as the alley behind our home, but I just don't agree with that opinion because here, in my village, there live good people who help children whose world brought them to a painful, bad place. I was taught that when you help someone else, especially a child, your world becomes fuller. I like it this way.

The old shepherd, leaning on his crook, bid us a friendly greeting. I gathered that he didn't receive visitors every day. "Patrice," he introduced himself. My eyes fixed on his mouth, in which only two bottom teeth remained. Patrice invited us, with a wide motion of his arm and a big smile, to sit on the trunk of a fallen birch tree which was like a natural bench. It was a pleasant place under a huge maple tree whose shade of branches curved above us like walls. Through the branches we looked at the distant view in front of us. I enjoyed the very distant, hazy, view of Dresden and the eastern Erzberg Mountains in dark blue-green. It is not for nothing that our area is known as "Swiss Saxony". I've heard that there's a beautiful country called Switzerland, and that its landscapes are reminiscent of our own. But, these are comparisons only for people who travel outside of where they live and want more than they really need.

The maple tree was much much taller than the cypress tree I planted with Rennie in the orphanage yard. Rennie jumped enthusiastically. "Schwester Hilde, look at this interesting tree. His head is in the sky. Stunning. My neck already hurts. Look at the trunk of this tree. Do you think we can both hug it together? Look at its leaves, they are like fingers. What is? What a beauty!" She barely breathed between the words "And the log we're sitting on. God, what is all this beauty? The spots of paint on it are as if a painter used silver and white paints." She stood up under the maple tree, raised her head toward the sky, touched the leaves of a bent branch and turned them over. "Look, look, some of the leaves are yellow and some are even red." "Indeed," I replied admiringly.

My girl blossomed in those moments and went to one of the sheep, stroked it and called it "Laura", as if they'd known each other a long time. That's how she decided on the name. "Doesn't she look like a Laura?" She laughed, relieved. She put her head on the sheep's pleasant wooly back and said, "Laura. Laura. Isn't that your name Laura?" Her laughter and the bells of the herd mingled. For such moments is life worth living. *Gotseidank, heilige Maria.*

Patrice opened a tiny chest, took out a clean cloth and a small bottle, asked my permission, cleaned my knees, and put searing iodine on them both. He blew on them gently. Rennie laughed and took over from him, blowing as hard as she could. The burning sensation disappeared as if it had never happened.

Patrice kept producing surprises from his box, like a conjuror. He took out a small tablecloth hand-embroidered with a flower pattern, spread it carefully over the green grass, straightened its corners neatly and reverently laid a wooden tray with a piece of round cheese and fresh bread on it. *"Bitte schön"*[14], he said and then added "I have no cutlery or plates here, since I didn't know you'd visit. Eat with your hands. Cut yourself a piece of cheese and some bread and enjoy." The smell of fresh bread was like the best perfume in the world, it really is my favorite scent. The taste was unique. Rennie devoured a much larger helping than I was used to seeing her eat.

Since then, every warm and pleasant afternoon, Rennie asks with shining eyes that we go to visit Laura. Sometimes Rennie's good friend Ernest Winter joins us. Rennie and Ernest have been good friends since kindergarten. They have a good, even special, bond. I admire their friendship. We often walked the forest paths to Patrice and Laura the Sheep. Sometimes we collected blackberries, blueberries and cranberries in small baskets while Rennie's lips were smeared with colour. The way was hard for me, but Rennie's joy was worth the effort. I think Laura was also happy when we came, not to mention Patrice. Did he sense we were coming, or was he waiting every day for us to come? I ask this because he always brought Rennie something new his wife baked or grew: a slice of sweet cake, fresh cucumbers or juice she'd squeezed from her garden fruit. Ren-

---

14. Please, help yourselves (German)

54

nie grew excited: "How do you make this cake? Ask your wife to give Schwester Hilde the recipe." And another time: "How did your wife make this juice? Schwester Hilde, we must get these trees to grow in our garden." Rennie loves to pick green grass and feed Laura. And Laura? Laura cooperates. When sweet Ernest joins our walks, Laura eats out of his hands too.

Rennie's enthusiasm for eating everything at Patrice's and the wonderful satisfaction I felt there reminded me of other days when I had a hard time raising Rennie. During her first days at school, she would not let me leave her. She cried loudly and clung to me. She held tight to my white tunic, and I was quite embarrassed that the mothers and other nuns would see us like that. Her teacher, Fräulein Emma, whom all the children called "Fronella," would give me a smile revealing perfect teeth, but in my heart, I knew she was beginning to lose patience with the crying that disturbed the peace of the morning and the joy of everyone's meeting.

I imagined the other mothers and nuns saying, "You can tell she's not her mother," "A real mother knows how to educate and her daughter separates from her properly," "The time has come for this nun to move this girl to an orphanage befitting her age." Then a new, soothing voice came into my head: "She is a wonderful mother. The girl just can't part from her. What is it that she does so well that the girl only wants to constantly be with her?"

The voices argued within my head.

Since the beginning, I reacted naturally to Rennie's crying. I told her the truth: "Rennie, say goodbye to me. Come on, let's have a kiss. I'm leaving. You know the babies are waiting for me and Esther can't be left alone with them." I said, kissed and left. The crying grew shorter every day. After about a month when Fronella, sorry, Fräulein Emma smiled at me, I knew her smile was genuine.

One snowy day Rennie came back from school with her hands blue and aching from the cold. It was one of those days when winter descends on the world and the white snow covers everything, including the whole village. She ran over to me and asked: "What happens with Laura in snow like this? Where is she? Does her wool warm her at night too?" She calmed down when I explained that Laura and her whole family have a wooden house by Patrice's shack and that I thought that, just like her, Laura is waiting for winter to be over.

I never wanted much. I enjoy the morning prayers and then go to my babies' room with my usual greeting: "*Guten Morgen meine lieben Babys.*[15]" I like using the same words. I embrace the routine.

Every day, when Rennie returns at noon from her school, which is part of an orphanage at the other end of Gottleuba, she runs to me with such a hug that I don't need to drink wine to feel drunk. She loves helping me take care of all the babies. She's become a really great helper, but of course that's not why I left this wonderful girl here. Every night I sit at her bedside and sing her to sleep with the lullaby my mother would sing to me when I was a girl, *Guten Abend, gut' Nacht*[16]. Rennie is already accustomed to it, and it seems to me that she can't fall asleep without my voice singing the melody I love and its wonderful words: I ask her in a soft and pleasant voice to shut her eyes, float on angels' wings and wish her a new morning with sun and light.

These are the magical moments for both of us.

Every birthday I bake her a chocolate cake with *Schlagsahne*[17] on top and our dear Esther helps me lift Rennie up on the

---

15. Good morning my little babies (German)

16. Good evening, good night (German)

17. Whipped cream (German)

chair I decorated for her. My Rennie is so fond of flowers in many colors, so it's good that her birthday is in the spring and I can decorate branches with flowers on our carved white chair and make her a sweet-smelling wreath for her beautiful head. Esther and I raise her on the chair and she rolls with laughter and all the babies bless her to the extent of their charming ability.

This blessing reminds me that one really needs good luck in life, good luck without a black cat. One day, a tiny kitten with fur as black as night arrived at our yard. Rennie heard it yowling and ran to it, picked it up happily and solemnly announced: "Schwester Hilde, what shall we feed it?"

The shriek that burst out of me immediately interrupted the celebration, and I stated the obvious: "Rennie, let go of that kitten right now. Don't you know that a black cat is a witch?"

Rennie didn't know. She has much to learn yet. "I want to raise him," she insisted.

"A black cat is a transformed witch. Get it out of here!" I couldn't control the fear and was really shaking. Rennie tossed the cat away. I managed to scare her and added, so that she would know "How could we raise a black cat? If it crosses the road from right to left, that's a sign that we'll have bad luck. Why should we invite bad luck here?" The cat was gone. I really hope it grows up far away from here.

My curious girl added innocently: "What if it crosses the other way?" I was glad I had something to teach her, "Left to right is a sign of good luck. But I will not let luck play around with us all the time."

EVERY birthday a courier comes here and hands her a package wrapped in decorative paper and a colored ribbon. I'll never forget the first time eight years ago, when we celebrated Rennie's first birthday.

He'd arrived on his bicycle as I strolled in our front yard with two babies I'd put to sleep in a stroller. One of the two was Rennie. I didn't know this man, resting his bike on our wall and taking from the bike's rack a large package wrapped in multi-colored ribbons.

"Schwester Hilde?" He asked.

"Yes, that's me," I replied as I rocked the cart.

"I have a package here for you," he said, handing me the package.

"For me?" I was so stunned I forgot to shut my mouth. Who in this big wide world even knows me to send me a package? But indeed it had my name written on it.

"Jesus Christ," I said, making the sign of the cross. Only then did I open the package to discover a note. In handwritten curly, precise script it said: "To Irena for her first birthday. Happy birthday, from your father." Father? I only knew her Mother. She has a father as well? A father who knows when she was born. I found that new and odd.

On the one hand, I was very happy, since that meant this girl was made with love, not as a result of rape, *toi toi toi*[18]; someone is taking some responsibility for having a child. On the other hand, I started feeling anxious. Rich people can do whatever they feel like. Rennie belongs to someone who could, one day, decide he was taking her back.

The gift was spectacular: A hand-crafted wooden rocking horse.

And so, every year the same messenger arrived. I always take the annual photo on this important day in our life, my child's birthday. The messenger no longer asks who Schwester Hilde is. Rennie, with a wreath of wildflowers around her head, carefully unwraps the gift so the wrapping paper doesn't tear, smooths the wrapping paper as best she can and folds it gently

---

18. An expression equivalent to "knock on wood".

and with great precision. She keeps all the wrapping paper and ribbons in her little room. The wording of the note attached to the gift is always the same; only the number changes from year to year: "To Irena for her … birthday. Happy birthday, from your father." That's it. The exact same thing every birthday – "Happy birthday, from your father."

"Schwester Hilde, do I have a father? What's his name?" Rennie was quick to ask once she started understanding.

"Every person has a mother and a father. Of course you have a father. What his name is – now, that's a different matter. He might just be named Friedlander." Gossiping about Adele's rich family in Pirna I heard that they have an actor son whom everyone calls "Friedlander" even though it's not his name. I realized that Rennie wants to know as many details as she can find out about herself, so I said: "I have no idea how the father knows you're here and how he manages to send a present at the right date every year. Decide that it's fun to have someone in this world who wants you to be happy and buys you such expensive presents."

Last year Rennie got a bicycle. It was decorated in ribbons in colors I've never seen here in Gottleuba. No other child I know receives such an expensive gift for their birthday. Esther says the gifts are so expensive because the feeling of guilt is so large. She might be right. This year we had a big surprise, Rennie's gift didn't arrive. For the first time. We're sad. Really. Very sad.

At night, when I sat by Rennie's bed and sang "*Guten Abend gut' Nacht*" to her she couldn't fall asleep and just whispered "I don't have new wrapping paper this year."

Of course, my own financial situation wouldn't allow me to buy her a wonderful new gift like the ones she's become used to. I bought her pretty hair clips for her hair, which had grown lately. Luckily she quickly used them.

I wonder if children understand difficult situations even without words?

The next day the messenger came on his bike. I could see he had no parcel with him. He leaned his bike in their usual spot and said: "Schwester Hilde, I, too, have become used to arriving with a gift on the 7th of every April. I checked yesterday and re-checked this morning. There's no parcel. I'm sorry too. *Ordnung muss sein*[19], he said, and winked at me with a nice smile.

I said to the messenger: "Please come and have tea made with herbs from our garden. I've baked a *Gugelhupf* with raisins and almonds. My child had her birthday yesterday, as you know. Come, join me and we'll have a little celebration. That should make the disappointment easier." Esther took our picture with our simple camera. When we said our goodbyes, we agreed to meet for cake and tea every year on the same day, even if the parcels stop coming.

Lately, a girl from Gottleuba joined our team, so I can leave the babies and do what I like for the afternoon. Rennie and I go out during these pleasant hours. Rennie rides her bike and I walk beside her. She likes to go to the nearby garden and ride her bike around the blue pond in the middle of our village. I like to imagine we are mother and daughter, but unfortunately, we do not look it because I'm a blue-eyed blonde while Rennie is a little darker.

I'm happy she's developing well and is complimented by her teacher but I'm beginning to become concerned about her future. I've looked into officially adopting her, but I would need her mother's consent and I don't have her address.

I don't concern myself with politics. It's enough that the horrible war ended thirteen years ago. I like living in Gottleuba, where I feel as though I'm at the end of the world as well as at its center.

On Sundays, Rennie joins me for church prayers. I wear my Sunday habit, with no veil or scapular. Everything is neatly

---

19. "There must be order" (German)

ironed from head to toe. I even like that you can see the ironing crease going down the length of the sleeves. My curls are combed neatly, as befits a Sunday. For Rennie, I picked lacquered shoes the shade of the fuchsia climbing our stone wall. She's too little to understand what religion is and to know that this is not her place, that she's a Jew. Rennie loves listening to our hymns and is especially fond of our *a capella* choral singing at Christmastime. It's hard to believe but it's true: Rennie can already hum Bach's *Motetten*. I'm proud of the fact that we have here in Gottleuba a few soloists who sing in a clear, divine soprano voice and often dream that one day Rennie might join the choir.

One day Rennie herself suggested that she add a morning prayer at her bedside. I thought the suggestion might have come from Ernest Winter, her loyal friend. He's a good influence on her and I welcome it. But one evening she returned from Ernest's and demanded I buy her a mirror.

"It's really nice. I made faces in front of the mirror. I want one too!"

"No. We don't have mirrors and never will." I decreed. I stopped immediately and was sure that was the end of it.

"Why don't we have one? Why?! It's so nice just for my room on the wall it doesn't take up any space in the room," she replied to me without taking a breath.

"Rennie, if the mirror breaks it's a bad omen for your future. Come now, we don't want to invite any trouble." Ernest is putting forbidden ideas into her head.

Rennie surprised me "Schwester Hilde. No!" And started twitching her right leg nervously "No. I want a mirror! I want to see what I look like. Why does Ernest have a mirror and I don't?" She raised her voice until she was really yelling.

What am I to do now? I don't want to disappoint her, but a mirror is simply impossible. I wouldn't be able to stop being frightened of what the mirror might do to me.

Rennie kept going: "I disagree. I want one. I want a mirror. I'm not a baby. I'm a big girl. It's not my fault everyone here is a baby.

"That has nothing to do with it," I immediately corrected her. "Why would I break the mirror? I don't play ball in my little room. I play outside. Schwester Hilde, you know that!"

We fell silent for a minute, then Rennie continued – "How many things do I ask for in my life anyway?"

Rennie, please understand, there are things that are very powerful in my life and can't be in a house I live in."

Rennie twitched her leg again, quickly and nervously. "But Schwester Hilde, please."

I retorted with: "It seems there are things you're too young to understand. This conversation is over."

Rennie reacted to this unique sentence that came out of my mouth by running out the door. The door slammed shut loudly and woke baby Thomas. I spent ages putting him to sleep and now he was up again. I had to attend to him and didn't have time for Rennie who went out alone into the darkness. I was very agitated. Thomas cried harder. I was relieved when, ten minutes later, I heard Rennie going quietly back in her room. I heard her washing her face and came in for our regular bedtime routine. To my regular prayer, I added an extra thanks to Christ that this argument had ended. I entered her room as usual, stroked her head and sang our regular lullaby.

I'm proud of my daughter anyway. I still haven't decided if and when I should tell her she's not a Christian. I don't know how to reveal such a big secret to a child. Perhaps Esther also thinks Rennie is Jewish because of her family name – "Friedman", but Esther never mentioned the topic. Esther didn't usually share her thoughts or emotions with me. *So ist es*[20]. I've often been scolded during the monthly meeting that all of

---

20. That's how it is (German)

us nuns working in the Gottleuba orphanages hold: "Dearest Schwester Hilde Rein, how long do you think you can keep a growing child in your nursery?", "Schwester Hilde Rein, you must transfer Irena Friedman to a place where there are children of her age. The most annoying is Maria, the nun I call "the wrinkled nun" in my heart, who called me "egotistical".

LATELY, the name of Hitler, the new German leader, keeps coming up in our meetings. I welcome his opinions because he expresses his convictions loudly and confidently and picks the clearest words that speak to the heart of all the nuns. I certainly accept the anti-bourgeois and anti-capitalist stance he proclaims. Of course we all agree with him, humans were created equal and it's not our fault we weren't born with a silver spoon in our mouth, as they say. I read some of his speeches in the papers at the kiosk and was quietly happy that we have a German leader who sees me and Rennie. I particularly liked seeing in the paper what he said about Christianity, which is (I copied down his exact words) "The undisputed foundation of the German nation's moral and ethical life." That's the kind of leader I pick.

JOHANNA

To the right of the door, a sign in a calm shade of blue –
"Israelische Frauenvereinigung". I rang the bell. A smiling young
woman opened the door and asked "For Mrs. Flora?" "Yes.
Thanks," I replied hesitatingly.

Then a heavyset woman about my mother's age approached
me. She wore a gray work dress, no jewelry, and high boots.
Her presence telegraphed "Here it doesn't matter what we look
like, just comfort. I care that our hearts beat as one. As long as
we are comfortable with ourselves and give to others." That's
the way I perceived her from the first instant. She held out
her hand to me with a beaming face and introduced herself:
"Flora Cohen."

"Johanna Friedman."

"Johanna-- great, marvelous. I'm so happy you came. Your
room is ready. Come with me, dear." "Arnold," she called to the
lone man sitting with a glass of beer in the lobby I'd entered.
"Gustav, Gustav Arnold, come and meet Miss Johanna and
please carry her suitcase to the room we prepared for her."

The man called Gustav Arnold came at once, gracefully took
my suitcase. He walked ahead, and Flora and I, arm in arm, followed him. If I had to explain to anyone what a calm, patient,
radiant, containing couple looks like, I'd have shown them
this couple.

The house looked like an intimate family hotel. Once I
relaxed, I could see that the lobby functioned as a meeting room

with three young women sitting in it, chatting with each other but mostly checking out my small tummy. When we passed them, they greeted me with a nod and a wide grin. The oldest of them, who was about my age, said "we'll have time to meet each other. You're welcome to sit with us, if you like, after you put your things in your room."

Flora opened the door to my room. A tidy and functional room. It had a neatly made-up, inviting bed, a dresser and a wall lamp next to the bed, a two-door closet, a small table with two chairs, one picture on the wall, showing a landscape of mountainous forest and a lake. I could imagine that all the rooms in this benevolent house looked like this. Flora sat on one of the two chairs and said: "This house provides temporary accommodation for Jewish girls. What they all have in common is a need to live here for a while. I'm here to give you shelter, medical care and an attentive ear. Tomorrow we'll have a longer chat. For now I suggest you shower and rest. We have all the time in the world. Give me your laundry and I'll bring it back properly ironed. After your shower you're welcome to join us for some dinner. You could, if you want, meet the girls staying here with you. *Verstehst du?*[21]

I felt wanted and loved. The shower waters washed away the road dust and any misgivings I had over coming here.

In time, I met all the residents of the house. Each one with her own story.

There was one woman who fled an abusive husband. Fortunately, she hadn't borne him any children yet. She did not talk to us, and I can't even recall her name. I hope she had somewhere to return to after she'd left Flora. I thought to myself that sometimes a woman is so bent on marriage that she chooses not to see the true measure of the man she marries.

Two were unwanted pregnancies. There was Margot, a girl

_____
21. Do you understand?

viciously raped in a dark alley with a knife to her throat. Margot cried constantly. At mealtimes she would hardly eat and Flora would sometimes feed her with a spoon. She needed a soft embrace, warmth. We had to speak softly when Margot left her room because she was very upset by loud voices. Edith told me that Margot was afraid that her parents would find out she was pregnant. Edith explained that she and Margot have been in the house for three months together and that Margot told her that her parents believe that if a woman is raped it's her fault. Flora protects her from the world. Margot doesn't leave this house at all.

There was Sonia, fourteen, who fell pregnant to her uncle. Unbelievable, I thought, just where you think you're safe, it happens to you. Her child-like appearance with her developing belly was a rough sight for me, especially since I knew that the one who'd taken away her childhood was her father's brother. Sonia sat, impassive, biting her fingernails and the skin of her fingertips until she drew blood.

These horrifying stories make my own story sound like something sweet and beautiful. It's useless, I thought to myself, to compare and rank the personal stories and distress of the women that this house shelters. The reasons are so personal. The distress is so personal. I realized that my pregnancy was not as traumatic as it was for the others. I, at least, enjoyed the act that caused it. It was a thought that provided some solace.

ON the second day of my stay Flora invited me to have a more extensive chat, known in this house as "The Flora Conversation". She expressed interest in me, listened to every detail of my story, lingered long over the fact that my family didn't know the truth, asked about how I felt about Kaminski now and about my physical sensations during pregnancy. She just listened, and did not judge me. To my surprise, she started telling me about herself.

"I grew up in a large, orthodox Jewish family on the outskirts of Leipzig. In the winter the rain would drum on the wooden roof and wouldn't let us sleep and in summer the heat would cook us inside the house. Every night we spread the mattresses on the floor of the room and slept two or three to a mattress. Sometimes I'd go hungry for a whole week. My mother didn't give birth like a woman, she spawned like a carp," she said, a pained expression on her pretty face.

"Every year there was one more in the family. Every time the belly grew again I knew I'd get even less food and attention. We all walked around dirty and unkempt. My mother didn't know how to raise us, never asked us how we were. If any of us ever went to school, it was on our own initiative. We practically raised ourselves. My dad would come home at night drunk. Those times he didn't fall asleep immediately, we had to hear him groaning as he would rape my mother. When I was eight I swore to the sister who shared my mattress that I'd escape this cycle of poverty and misery as soon as I could. And when I was twelve I started cleaning staircases and saved money, which I stashed in a secret hole in the ground. At seventeen I volunteered at a nearby hospital. I was given unlimited food and discovered I was happy when I was giving, not when I was holding coins in my hand. I was no longer hungry and sometimes I was actually happy, especially when I could sit by a sick child and surrender myself to its needs. When I met Gustav we decided to set up a place for girls in trouble. That was the idea we had to help those who met with ill fortune."

"Flora, this is an amazing house. For me it's a great help," I thought out loud. Once again I thought where I could have been if not for this place. I asked her: "but how do you manage financially? Surely there are huge upkeep expenses, and we pay nothing."

"We get the money from charity and from the state. We worked hard for it. I discovered I had a talent for this, I discovered that when a person finds a crucial and communal purpose in life, they can easily convince others of its importance and many good people will open their wallets. I found my purpose in life. This house grew from my suffering."

I thought about purposes in life. I asked myself whether all good, useful people in society come from pain, whether suffering is necessary in order to be able to listen to another's suffering. And then I learned an important fact: "Not everyone lives here for free. Adele is paying for your stay. She has the ability, so I suggested that she do that."

Adele? Who is that? I was too ashamed to ask. Someone who is not my mother is paying for my daily life. Who is she?

Instead of asking that important question, I asked: "So you have children of your own?" "Of course. We are a small family. We have two daughters. I raised them with love. The older one has completed her university degree and the younger one is training to be a nurse. I'm proud of them. My mother is very old and demented, I help her live out her days in an aged care home."

I will never forget Flora. I thought back then that perhaps when all of this is over, I, too, could set up this kind of house in Riga. I wanted to be a good woman too.

"The Flora Conversation" went on for an hour each day, right after our nutritious breakfast. I knew that when her door was open, it was also open for me if I needed to talk more. It was only during "The Flora Conversation" that Flora's door closed. Flora the listener, Flora with her big smile and endless patience. Gustav the man at her side, an expert handyman and a wonderful cook.

There are kind-hearted people in this world. Even today I still believe it. Where are they now, in these hours when my little Mia and I need them so badly?

The woman I made friends with, Edith, was my age and came here because her house burned down, and Flora and Gustav's place was a temporary home for her. Her house also contained a hairdressing room with modern equipment, so the fire took away her living as well. Edith told me she'd had many clients and her entire future burned down within half an hour. "Luckily, I was the only one living in my house, but not really the only one. I lived with Oskar, my dog. Oskar always greeted me with happy bounds and a wagging tail and would curl down on my lap when I sat on my comfy sofa. You won't believe it, Oskar understood German and would bark in reply. My Oskar, my sweetheart, was trapped in the fire and went up in flames with the rest of the house." Edith did not stop mourning her dog and talking about his horrible death. All kinds of small, fleeting moments reminded her of him and "my sweetheart" was mentioned many times throughout our conversations. Her story deepened the black hole that formed within my heart, a hole that took the place of the theater. Oskar's cruel fate dragged me back to the death of the love that had filled my life, my painful giving up on the theatre life. Together we wept for the future that misfortune had taken away from us.

Since the onset of the winter of 1923, I wore layers that also hid the knot in the shoelace, the belly that had spung up in the middle of my thin body.

Despite the pain of parting from my familiar world, I began visiting the National Library. I wanted to fully understand what was going on in my body. I studied books dealing with pregnancy and childbirth. The books were not for pregnant women, but for doctors, and my eyes wandered over the small, busy letters and professional concepts I did not understand. I could not read with my thoughts wandering like storks in the sky. I made a pact with myself that I would let nature run its course and rely on my conversations with Flora. I went out every day to wander through the beautiful streets of Leipzig. This charming city reminded me of my uncle Chaim Yitzhak Friedman, whom

I used to call simply "Uncle Isaiah", who had been as a father to me ever since my own father passed away. I'd often hear him talk about Leipzig after he'd return from the trade fair that took place there twice a year. I remembered his descriptions of each visit and his admiration of the various sites in the city, and thus I navigated my tours.

A few days after I arrived, Flora greeted me when I returned from a short walk about town: "Johanna, you have a telegram." I read "K. has left for Argentina. Show canceled. Love. Diana." I immediately let out a scream "What?!" And blurted: "Scumbag. He ran away, and now there'll never be a father for our baby. He kicked me out of his way and suggested that I go to Germany pretending to be a loving and caring friend. The truth about a man is revealed in difficult moments. He used me and never loved me at all. Oh, oh, oh. How gullible I was. I sold my body and soul to the devil. He's stricken me and opened a new chapter far, far away from here. Scumbag." I cursed him: "Tap, tap, tap."

I didn't recognize myself thinking in such a way. I didn't recognize myself swearing like that. It seems that when I am really angry, I am no longer the innocent and pious Johannuchka. After a short pause, during which I tried to take a deep breath, a second wave flooded me again: "What a trusting fool I am! How could I ever hope he'd visit me in Leipzig? How did I believe that he didn't tell me he was married because I hadn't asked? A lover of two women? An unsurpassed lover of life and an exploiter of good, innocent girls."

I folded into myself. Images of our togetherness, forever lost, passed through my head and in a quiet and pensive voice I quoted the hurt Juliet: "*O serpent heart hid with a flowering face.*"[22] Flora took my hand, put it on her leg and pressed it warmly. All the girls surrounded me. Pregnant Margot and Sonia

---

22. *Romeo and Juliet*, Act III, Scene ii

shed tears. Edith stroked my back. I wiped away the tears and announced emphatically: "Girls, I will not be a victim. You'll see." I don't know what I meant by this, but I did not intend to stay there crying, I meant to say that I was going to choose my path and that no man would trample me.

In Leipzig, too, I homed in on one café. I was drawn to it as if by magic. As I walked down the street, I smelled a mist of fresh coffee. From the shop window, a perfect apple strudel winked at me, a fruit cake sprinkled with ground almonds, a streusel filled with red plums, a black forest cherry cake and a several more fresh and fragrant round cakes arranged on crystal plates. When I looked at them, I imagined they were calling me. Chopin's piano Nocturne led me inside. The serene atmosphere and the romantic music tugged at my heartstrings. The coffee I sipped was blended with memories that flowed into my veins and lifted my lonely soul a little. I was reminded of the naïve notion that the *Moldau* aroused in me when I first met Kaminski, that there was no reason for me to leave Riga and my native Latvia. I smiled to myself, a lot of water flowed through the Moldova river, ever since I parted from my innocence and the thought that my fate was in my own hands.

In that café I sat and wrote an explanatory letter to my family in Riga. I used up an entire block of paper, writing and crossing out. I stuck to the truth and then made up a cover story and changed it over and over again. The heap of wrinkled pages I moved to my purse grew fatter. As time went by, it became clear to me that I was not capable of telling the truth. I made up a story about a moment of revelation I'd had when seeing the theater in Leipzig. A moment when I'd realized that I did not want to stand on the stage and that I'd made a mistake choosing my path through life. I added that this inner truth had depressed me, and I realized that my acting ability had deteriorated. In order to avoid facing that truth and avoid seeing my director and my fellow actors, I'd moved to Leipzig for a time.

"I want to be with myself", my hand wrote on the paper, "and to think in this new place who I was and where I was headed". I added a few stories about the wonderful town I'd picked and once again implored them not to worry and to trust my judgement. I read and re-read the letter and finally decided it looked genuine and convincing. One heavy stone was lifted off my aching heart. Once I finished writing, I tore the letter to pieces and wrote a telegram. In an instant I decided to send a telegram that would reach my family before a week had passed since my leaving and would help my mother sleep at night. I phrased it

"My dearest, our show has closed. Kaminski has left. Rehearsals are over. Crisis at theater. Staying in Leipzig. Everything wonderful. Don't worry. Kisses. Johanna."

The secret found a space within my heart, a space that screamed "I am here."

Walking through the city slightly eased the pain of keeping the secret and the lie. My feet carried me to the cultural center and I stood, dumbfounded, in front of the impressive Opera House. Several evenings I enjoyed listening to opera and concerts. After all, Leipzig is the city of music where many composers were born and spent their lives. I particularly made sure to listen with reverence to the excellent ecclesiastical boys' choir, Thomanerchor, which even the great Bach had conducted in the past. I ate at restaurants, wandered through the market, and rested on benches in the different parks on the banks of the city's three rivers. Sometimes I would stroll together with Edith, walking arm in arm like a couple of old ladies with all the time in the world on their hands. We visited art museums and lovely little galleries. Each of us would contribute of her knowledge as we discussed the exhibits; we enriched each other.

In Leipzig's special zoo we admired the originality of the cages' structures, but when I saw a koala holding her young,

I burst into tears. Edith would have pangs of longing for Oskar, her dead dog, and grew sad thinking of her sweetheart.

It was during those days, when the hours of daylight grew shorter and my sense of longing increased, that it became very clear to me that I was no longer alone. I felt definite movements in my belly, someone was moving inside me. The emerging life told me unequivocally that I was about to experience a huge change in my life. I rejected thoughts of my life as a mother, removed from my mind the basic dilemmas that lay ahead of me: Where will I live? Would anyone agree to marry me when I am a woman with a baby? How will I bear the shame of being an unmarried mother? How do I return home with a baby in my arms? I decided that I would now prepare for the first step, childbirth, and make no plans beyond that.

The emerging winter kept me in my room. Early in April Flora knocked on my door and told me that Mrs. Kaminski had come to visit me. Kaminski? A woman? Me? The name Kaminski told me I should pretty myself up a little, and so, waddling from side to side with my stomach in front of me, I reached the lobby. A well-groomed, tall and handsome woman was speaking pleasantly to Flora, as if this were not their first meeting. She stood up to greet me, held out her and said with great confidence and a smile, "Johanna Friedman, I'm Adele. Adele Kaminski, Walter's mother."

Walter's mother. Adele. Ahh, I noted to myself. This is Adele. She'd already been here in the past, I surmised. Probably to secure a room for me and pay the costs.

The impressive and self-aware Adele took stock of my appearance, focused on my stomach, measured its size and smiled to herself. I wanted to reach out and say "how do you do" but she was too quick, and started talking as if she had to explain several things within a limited time so she had no time for small and marginal jokes such as manners: "My Walter sent us a letter. My husband and I read it very carefully. Well, there are passions and lack of control in life. Walter told us the whole truth. That's how it is with us. My husband and I decided that I would come here again to help you to the best of our ability. Well, such is life. "

I saw opposite me a woman with a radiant gaze and I was not surprised to have fallen in love with her son. I felt a kind of stab in my heart when I realized that she knew the whole truth while my mother got a tall tale.

We sat as two friends with our hands clasped together. I felt a Kaminskian sympathy that was so necessary to me these days. She conducted the conversation. She asked and I answered. I added a few necessary details about my falling in love and the irresponsible childishness with which I functioned to have reached the crossroads of my life. Then Adele threw a bomb that began with softening words: "Look, Johannuchka, your birth date is growing closer. I see that and Flora knows it too. Even by the date Walter wrote me." She knows when our first lovemaking took place. She's involved in my most intimate details and I didn't even know her.

"Johanna, well, something good must be done. The birth is approaching and you need to give birth in the best place there is, in the excellent professional and modern hospital in Dresden. That's why you will move next week to Kristina in Dresden so you can be close to the hospital I have already chosen for you. Well, she already knows."

What's going on here, I thought. This lady has already decided for me? Does money buy everything?

"I've already settled the matter with my good friend, Kristina, who's like family to me. I arranged with her to give you a room in her house. It's not exactly a house, well, to tell the truth it's an ancient castle. Oh, what a view there is. Well, well, the view doesn't really matter now. Your room will be with an *en suite* bathroom. Kristina will be with you for the birth. Everything is already settled. I'm paying her. Well, that's all fine."

I turned my eyes to heaven and addressed our God, hoping that his pause in caring for his people was over and he returned to his activities, and I asked him in my heart why Kaminski was already married, why I couldn't have been his only beloved and spared myself this whole saga.

Then, as if Adele had to surprise me even more, she continued: "You'll leave the baby pretty close to Pirna, our city, in a Christian orphanage in the charming village of Gottleuba, and then you can go back to your life in Riga and find yourself a single husband. Your secret can be kept forever and your way to a new life will be paved before you."

Adele did not leave me even a second to digest her words and continued her talk-drive: "Everything is in order, Johannuchka. Sister Hilde Reine already knows that a new baby is coming her way. A place is already being reserved for it in the best nursery, that I have picked for you. Well, everything is in order," she concluded and leaned back in her chair with a sense of well-being and victory. Everything is in order for Adele, the producer of my life, but I'm the one who has to follow this winding and difficult path. She handed me a note with the exact name and address of the orphanage. The Kaminski family hands me notes like in a game of Paper Chase.

I scratched my head to gain time, played with my hair, stroked my stomach. Edith passed us and nodded to me in encouragement with a questioning look in her eyes.

I hid the surprise of this offer and replied to Mrs. Kaminski, which I decided at that very moment is how I would address her, that I would consider her offer once I'd given birth. I clearly remember telling her "I'm not even sure I'm going to give the baby away. I might raise it."

She sat up straight, stretched the ends of her suit, checked the angle of her hat, and argued: "Naturally, a woman becomes attached to her baby. That's well-known. Well, you need to decide now. Yes, right now! If you hadn't already decided yesterday. If you don't make a decision before birth, you'll find it very, very hard to go through with it. Well, that's how it is with mothers. We get attached to our children, they come out of our body."

Come out of our body. My baby is going to come out of my body and I'm supposed to give it up?

Adele continued: "Not to mention, Johannuchka, that I need to finalize the details with the manager of the wonderful orphanage I picked for you and with the nurse-sister Hilde Reine, who's in charge of the nursery in that orphanage."

I swelled up with anger and regret. Should the fact that this lady sitting across from me has gone to so much trouble and that she has money, mean I have to obey her? At that moment I saw that Adele's approach meant that my role was to carry out what she had laid out for me. In my imagination I saw her sitting at a loom with a large cloth in front of her, she holds the loom and adds two different-colored lines to the weave, then replaces the thread and carries on with her work. I'm just a thin line in this pattern.

I hesitated again. Until that moment I did not dare think of abandoning the baby. Here I encountered a different face of the German woman in front of me, as she told me angrily: "Johanna Friedman, I do not need a grandchild from you. The two I have from my only son are enough."

These words stabbed at my heart like a poison thorn penetrating deeply and spreading terrible pain to its surroundings.

"Do not need a grandchild from you," the words echoed within me.

"Do not need a grandchild from you," and a dark pain settled within me and I felt constricted.

"Do not need a grandchild from you," made me realize, to my surprise, that this fetus was not mine alone.

And she continued without stopping for breath: "My son is happily married. A mistake occurred. Well, it happens, it happens. It can happen. Take responsibility as a mature adult. Why would you want to ruin your life with a baby who has no father? You should be ashamed! You're a young and pretty girl, you're talented and have your whole life ahead of you."

I was sitting opposite a commanding woman who could play nice when it suited her wishes, but woe betide whoever stood in her way.

I said, in a voice that barely managed to escape my throat: "Mrs. Kaminski, thank you for everything. But I need a little time for myself to think over your proposal."

She was shocked. Her head was nodding. I could see all the gold teeth in her mouth.

I was silent. I thought. I pondered. I considered. Then I asked: "Tell me where you're staying so I can reach you this evening and let you know my decision."

Her eyes blazed and her chest heaved. Her hands were trembling with anger. Her red lipstick smeared. She swiftly scribbled her hotel room details, took her overcoat and turned to leave. "I promise you I'll come to the hotel tonight and let you know my decision. I promise," I squeaked. She held up her index finger in a threatening gesture and admonished me: "think carefully", and, to herself - "you'd better." When I started walking away, she muttered: "don't you dare hurt my family." I was left alone, enormously confused.

Once she'd left, Edith jumped at me and took Adele's place. I wailed. I told her everything, speaking quickly so I would have time to make my decisions. Edith listened, embraced me, and occasionally said a word or two or asked for clarification. I concluded with my dilemmas: "Does the fact that she's not willing for me to raise my baby mean I should act as she wishes? This is mostly my life, no? Did Kaminski write asking her to find a solution freeing me from our baby, thus freeing him too? He's flown off to Argentina already. He wants us both to forget each other and for there to be no monument of the great love we had, nothing to burden his life. *Ein Schweineakt.*[23] Do I want to say goodbye to the fruit of our love? Perhaps I should raise it and content myself with one child and pleasant memories?"

Edith served as a replacement for Diana during these moments. Carrying the secret was too heavy a burden and I was struggling under the weight. Had I been at home this evening, the women close to me would have helped.

Edith suggested we consult our Flora. We waited for a little while for Flora and her husband to return from their errands, my weeping turned to spasmodic yowling, and when they came back - we both went into her room. The kicks I felt in my stomach during the conversation did not help clarify what my baby wanted. I needed my mother for the mother in me. I felt that only my mother could, if I had only allowed her, help direct me to the right path. This insight struck me at a moment when I could do nothing with it. Though my heart shrank in the face of my own maternal circumstances, I concluded that a mother is a tremendous force of life on earth. A force with basic existential instincts. "Mother. Mother," I whispered in my heart. I felt I was recruiting my mother, even my grandmother, my entire female lineage standing behind me, I really felt they were ready to help me, but I could not give them any role. At this critical junction of my life, I couldn't, and didn't want to be alone. "Mother!" I cried from the depths of my soul.

I so wanted to know what would be right for me, to make my own life choice myself and for myself. But as had happened to me in the past, I needed at least one more person in order to make a crucial decision.

Flora listened tenderly. Suddenly, a sharp pain seared across my back. "Oww!" I screamed. "Johanna, let's see. Perhaps it's labor pains. Perhaps you're in labor," said Flora in a calm voice.

---

23. The act of a pig.

"Not now. It's too early. I need time to make this decision. I can't measure time like you taught me, and feel the contractions, and make up my mind about keeping the baby or giving it away to become an orphan."

I tried my best to stay sensible. What a fateful night, I thought compassionately.

"How do you feel about the decision?" Flora tried to help me make up my mind, her eyes focused on mine.

I decided that answering "I don't know" would not be possible. I understood I must decide. "Look, I'm happy I decided to give birth. Abortion is murder. If I don't raise this child, perhaps a barren family will take it."

"That's one possibility, Johanna. So, am I hearing that you're leaning towards giving it away?" Flora tried. "Johanna, try making your decision without pressure. This is a crucial decision, my dearest. Let's see, when I tell you that you're keeping the baby, can you see yourself going home with it? Try to picture yourself one year from now in Riga. What does it feel like in your heart when you decide to raise the child?"

"Shame. Difficulty. Stuck in my life. I won't find a husband. Perhaps, perhaps I'll even become a recluse," I heard myself say before I was even aware I'd already made the decision.

"Now, dearest Johanna, check to see what you feel inside, how do you picture yourself a year from now without the baby?"

"Ow. Ow. Ow. It hurts."

They all waited wordlessly. I had the time I needed.

I said in a clear voice: "It seems like I'm leaning towards accepting Adele's proposal. That would be the right choice."

"Johanna, be alone now. Consider all the possibilities. I'm here. Edith is here too. Decide what is right for you in light of the circumstances. This is your life."

I went to my room. I laid down on the bed. I stared at the lamp dangling from the ceiling and let myself enter in my mind into the landscape in the picture on the wall. Thoughts moved like the petals of the flower at the front of the painting, leaves we plucked when we were children. "Yes, no, yes, no, yes. Yes. Yes. Ow. Ow. It hurts." The decision was made: I will hand over the baby. I will not raise it.

I went back to Flora and Edith. "I will follow Adele Kaminski's plan. I think I am starting labor pains. I will walk to Adele's hotel to expedite them."

Flora added with a loving look: "Your decision is yours. It is right for you. Embrace it. After the birth you will come back to me. I will wait for you with great love. You will recover here in Leipzig and then return to your life in Riga. You are beautiful and young, pleasant and come from a good family." That was what she said, that I was beautiful and young and came from a good family. "Many girls in your situation have given their children to orphanages and you will not be the first to do so by any means, if that gives you comfort, and you will certainly not be the last." I realized that Flora wanted to strengthen me in the decision I'd already made, for she knew that a woman who gives birth is naturally bound to her baby, and now they wanted to ease my path. Flora continued: "At most Jewish orphanages, the children come from families who don't have your economic status, and the orphanages are in pretty bad shape. You're lucky to have an offer to leave your baby at a Christian orphanage with caring, devoted nuns." Flora hugged me and I left for Adele's hotel room.

Adele was overcome with happiness. Three times I heard the sentence "Well, you truly are a smart girl. Excellent". I became "Johannuchka" again and was again smiled upon. Adele and I measured the time between contractions. "Still not regular and too far apart for birth, it's going to be a while yet," she decided as if she were a grand multiparous woman, hugely experienced in such matters. "Stay the night at Flora's. I'll take you to the Dresden hospital first thing in the morning, it's on my way home anyway."

At night I was very tired but could not sleep well. I showered again and again. I had to pass the time until Adele's arrival at the early hour we'd decided on. At breakfast I gorged myself. Flora laughed: "This might be the last time you eat for two."

On the bright spring morning, of April 7, 1923, equipped with my suitcase and having said goodbye to all my friends, and received well wishes and farewells, with Flora and her husband Gustav hugging me at the bottom of the stairs, I got into Adele's car.

Just then Edith ran to me with a tiny suitcase in her hands and got into the car. "I want to be with you at the birth. I'm coming with you," she announced.

We spent the journey measuring time between contractions, but that did nothing to lower the flood of emotion I felt. A great worry crept into my soul. Dear lord, what have I done to myself? What will happen to me? Will it hurt?

Adele acted as if she were a professional driver of women just before giving birth. "Ten minutes between contractions? Everything's fine. We'll make it in time." "Do you need to pee? What do you want us to do? Hold it in, missy." She continued like a troublesome fly: "Oh, well, Kristina won't see the baby. Well, never mind." She swallowed and again circled around: "So wonderful to give birth in the spring. When your child crawls it will be summer and it could crawl without clothes," and then: "Actually that doesn't matter to you, you won't get it." That woman left no spaces between words, which made me feel every minute of the trip. Every one of her sentences was accompanied by a smile from Edith, who motioned for me to just stay silent.

I was overwhelmed by fear of the unknown. I couldn't curse Kaminski out loud. I put my head on Edith's chest. She hugged me and we were quiet together. Her warmth enveloped and comforted me. When Adele Kaminski announced: "Another quarter of an hour and we're there." I felt like someone was twisting my spinal cord.

When Adele Kaminski announced: "Another ten minutes and we're there." the contractions started with my stomach hardening slowly and a feeling that someone was grabbing my stomach. I felt as if every organ in the central part of my body was being twisted and squeezed. Fear overtook me. I envied Edith who was able to help me and didn't need to go through this nightmare.

When Adele Kaminski announced: "Another five minutes and we're there." my contractions were coming at five-minute intervals. In five minutes my life will be turned upside down. In five minutes the hospital door will close behind me and I'll be in the delivery room. In five minutes this unknown world will begin to move whether I want it to or not. There's no way back. This baby is inside my body and it has to get out. My thoughts wandered to my theatre days, before I became romantically involved with Walter Kaminski, to my innocent, happy days. I wish I were there now.

When we entered the emergency room Adele really overdid it, making sure multiple times that their papers said that the baby would not be staying with me. She then wished me a successful birth and added, to my surprise, "In a few days I will call the hospital and ask what the date of birth was, because you will not necessarily give birth today. Well, by the time Walter came out it was two days of severe pain. It was hard for him to say goodbye to me." Tact and sensitivity were not her strong features. "Every birthday my husband and I will make sure this baby gets a nice gift." We hugged goodbye. It's farewell forever, I thought to myself, as I would soon farewell my baby.

Throughout the birth, Edith stood behind me, wiping my face with damp towels. She encouraged me with her words: "Everything is fine. You're wonderful. There you go, you're breathing right. You're a hero. Johanna, just one more minute. Soon. Keep it up. What an amazing experience. You are wonderful." I was sweating, shaking in pain, pitying myself, exhaling inhaling pushing crying weakening taking lungfuls of air taking strength from Edith wanting it all to be over pushing screaming trying to control myself bearing my terrible fate weeping listening. The midwife calmly instructed me, "When you feel a contraction, push hard." I did my best. Again and again and again. The baby would not come out. I said to Edith, "It doesn't want to leave me. It wants to postpone the separation." The midwife intervened and explained: "That's how it is, there are almost no first births where the baby just slides out. They probably know what awaits them in this world and prefer to stay inside their mother."

The intense pains and the fear of what was to come created a helpless sensation that engulfed me. When I finally felt the release, once the baby came into the world, after I'd been drained of all my strength, I heard its first cry. A new voice in our world, this baby of mine saying goodbye to me and going its own way in this world.

Mine?

So it turned out that the afterbirth was still inside my womb and had to be expelled. I was asked once more to push and felt like I was giving birth again. "Enough. I've had enough!" I couldn't stay reserved anymore and screamed my heart out. A scream came out of me that I think shook the windows of the whole hospital. I understood the old adage that anyone who had not given birth, could not know what pain is.

Within the blink of an eye the baby was wrapped and placed in a small bed that was immediately transported to another room. "Wait. Just a moment. I want to see him," I said in a weak but determined voice. The midwife did not listen to me at all and said, as she walked away: "Congratulations. You have a daughter." A girl.

How is it that all this time I didn't even think about the possibility of having a daughter and imagined that the fruit of my womb would be a son? Suddenly I realized that it would be harder for me to part with a daughter. I was left with three new and hard-to-digest facts: I am a mother, I have a daughter, I must not feel any inkling of my desire to keep this baby with me.

The crying took me over. I cried non-stop. I didn't understand how one woman could have so many tears. Edith did not cooperate with me and would not agree to go see the baby and tell me what she looked like. "No means no. It makes sense. Don't do something you'll later regret. I'm here to help you, not to make it hard for you."

That afternoon Edith said goodbye and caught the last bus to Leipzig.

I couldn't sleep and I ate nothing. The food disgusted me. The nurses were not cooperative when I asked: "Is the baby eating well?" "You shouldn't ask that and shouldn't know," they replied. The heaviness and congestion I felt in my breasts bothered me sevenfold because my breasts were telling me that I was acting contrary to nature. I felt sorry for myself and cried, whimpered and ached. For two days I laid hallucinating in bed with a fever from an inflammation that caused me excruciating pain in my breasts whenever I raised my arms. Day followed day and every day in the hospital passed in a new nothingness routine. I asked every nurse "Show me the baby from a distance" and the reply was always: "There are abandonment procedures. Everything is for your sake. Only this way can you part with it

84

without needless difficulties. These boundaries, Fräulein, are designed to ease the expected agony of separation."

The name "Irena" jumped to my head. I decided to connect the word Irena with the surname Friedman that the girl would carry. This is my name. I fell in love with the meaning of these two names: a person who brings forth peace and tranquility. I sniggered to myself and noted that with such a name I was placing spiritual expectations on her shoulders, to be the one who would bring peace and tranquility to her surroundings.

Rennie, Rennie I will call her. Soft and clear is the name. My Rennie.

My?

After all, soon I won't even be able to ask the sisters to see her for even one second.

I experienced repeated contractions in my womb, but in spite of the pain I was happy with them because they signified that soon there would be no external sign of my big belly.

On the ninth and final day of my stay in the hospital, Schwester Hilde Rein arrived to pick up the baby. She visited me in my room. A woman without makeup or jewelry, dressed in neat nun clothes. A calm and smiling woman with good eyes and *joie de vivre*. We had the introductory and separation talk.

She wrote down my details in her official papers: age, marital status, the reasons for leaving my baby, date of the baby's birth, and her name. She was even interested in my pregnancy, whether I was relaxed or nervous. She didn't ask me for the father's name, and thus I understood what I already knew: two people created a new person, but the responsibility rests solely with the woman.

Hilde told me what I already knew: "A family from Pirna has already made all the necessary arrangements and will take care of the payment for the baby." Gentle Hilde was unperturbed; it seems that I really was not the first woman to relinquish her baby. She added for my information that "this home is an orphaned baby home, not a children's home. Is it acceptable that I do not contact you, to allow you to forget the baby and return to your previous life?"

I nodded. "Yes, that makes sense. I don't find it easy, but it makes sense."

"If so, I'm not interested in your address."

The most painful but most sensible moment was when she explained the procedures to me: "You can say goodbye to Rennie only with a look from a distance. One brief look, a parting look. That's how it is. It's orderly. There must be order."

I glanced from a distance at Rennie's face, wrapped and held in Hilde's capable hands. I do not know if I was able to catch big black eyes or if I made up that sight for myself. That's all I could see. I pictured those eyes looking at me. My hands reached forward and touched nothing. "My poor dear," I whispered and didn't know who I was talking to, who's the poor one: Her? Me? Both of us?

I wanted to believe that the nine-day-old Rennie had a calm, cute look on her face as she was being carried in Hilde's hands, as if she'd come to the right place for her and to the heart that wanted to absorb her. Hilde's attitude made it easier for me to say goodbye. My whimper subsided. We separated with Hilde promising me that Rennie would receive a lot of love and grow and flourish to be a lovely and happy girl.

I was left alone. Lonely.

I summed up for myself, sighing softly, the news I had created in this world: "a huge change". Irena Friedman was born, and will grow up without a mother and father, will live in a Christian orphanage in Germany even though she is Jewish, will be cared for by a woman named Hilde Rein. I will return to recover at Flora's in Leipzig and then go home to my family. I absorbed the news and at the same time had a hard time digesting it. "Take your time," I tried to encourage myself.

The next day, I was devastated by the questions swirling in my head: Will I ever meet Kaminski? Will I be able to keep my secret even when I get home? Will I be accepted back into the theater, and if so, how will I explain myself to the director and to my friends?

"I was able to get the job to accompany the convoy leaving in an hour and a half. There were many who wanted to. Pay's not half bad."

"But won't you be tired after a night watch?"

"Maybe. But it's a pleasure I won't give up easily."

The two Latvian guards meet up near my window. In the silence that prevails in the wee hours of the night I do not miss a word.

"Oh, Justes, I really envy you. I really need that money the blessed Nazis give us. But what can you do? I have to get home this morning to take my wife to the doctor. Well...you know, she's nearly done with her needless pregnancy."

"Time flies when you're having fun. Never mind, Martins. You'll have other chances. This surely won't be the last convoy. Ha."

"I'm out of smokes. Can I have one?"

"You're always cadging. Take from the Jews. Why me. I pay for them."

Perhaps I could get a tidbit of information about the coming day.

They walk away and the conversation fades.

The return to Leipzig was as if it all had never happened. On the journey, my thoughts wandered until I found myself at Flora's house. All the girls ran towards me. I was relieved. Edith did not leave me for a moment. Emma, the new pregnant woman at the home, asked me many questions even though she had already heard details from Edith herself. She wanted to know all the details: "Was it painful? How long did it take? Did you scream a lot? Were you able to sit right after the birth? Do you have milk? Did you see your baby? Was it hard to say goodbye to her?" I answered all the questions. I understood her need.

I lay down in bed. Flora came into my room, sat down beside me, and asked quietly, just between the two of us, "How was your birth?" Tears streamed again as if they had a life of their own. "I don't know what hurt more, the physical pain or the pain of separation. My body shrank for several days, this pain shrank my heart. The milk in my breasts wanted to nourish the baby and I weaned myself off of it."

"How is it now?"

"Now my body no longer hurts. What's difficult are the constant mundane thoughts about the baby: What is she doing now? Who would she call 'Mom'? Is she well? Is she warm? Is she provided for? What does she look like? I have bouts of crying and deep depression."

SCHWESTER HILDE

⤳ 1932 ⤳

One morning the postman waved at me from a distance with an official letter we had to sign for. We receive a lot of official correspondence. The letter was for me. I held a baby in one hand and ran to Esther's office. Esther opened it and handed it to me at once.

I was flabbergasted, as they say.

The mother of Irena Friedman, born on the 7th of April 1923, has been revealed. Her name was Johanna Friedman and she was living in Riga, not Germany! Her address was apartment 6, 21 Latchaplezha street. The letter said that the search for the real mother took a lot of time because the governors of Pirna, our district city, wanted someone to pay for the orphan girl.

I was very worried because I realized they had stopped paying for Rennie. Up till now there was someone footing the bill so there was no need to find the mother. The payer suddenly disappeared. I pictured the mother receiving a letter saying she had to pay for her daughter. They wouldn't turn to the father because they could not turn to him, the father's direction was over forever. Which meant: no more payments and no birthday presents. I understood that there was a connection between the father's parents and Adele, that *Feinschmecker*[24] who brought

---

24. Fussy person (Yiddish / German)

Rennie here. I'm even sure Adele is the grandmother herself. "Maybe she no longer wants for people to figure out that this orphan girl, this girl growing up and making friends in the area, is her granddaughter born out of wedlock. That's so shameful. *Große Schande. Große Schande.*"

❦ **1936** ❧

After that concerning letter from the Pirna city council, I began to realize that a change might come. I was really worried. But the fear of hearing from Johanna Friedman, her mother, subsided as time passed and days turned into months and years, until I forgot that terrible letter and went back to my routine, the routine I love so dearly that the good lord provided for me. *Gott sei Dank, Heilige* Maria[25].

Four years had passed since. Time went by. Rennie is already thirteen. She's still my child and lives with me in my nursery. What is it that the old people say? When things go well you don't feel the passage of time. Rennie turned into a lovely young lady, already developing physically and enquiring about the world. On our walks she started asking why I didn't have any children, why she's still living in the nursery, whether my job interests me, whether I'd ever visited Berlin, what I thought of Hitler, how come no-one saved Ernest's parents when they drowned. Always apologizing: "Schwester, I'm just curious, I always want to be with you. Please don't understand from my questions that I'm looking for my real mother. Okay?" I believed her it was just curiosity and that she was happy living with me.

---

25. Thank you, Mother Mary (German),

I decided to baptize Rennie at church, as is our custom. I thought that because Rennie was growing up here, she should grow up like all the kids here and not arouse any suspicion or have any unnecessary questions asked. I knew that Rennie was not baptized when she was born, and with us Protestants the ceremony is acceptable at the age she was now, at puberty. I talked to our pastor and he was of course happy with the idea, because *so ist es*[26]. I shared this with Rennie and added that this way she would be able to demonstrate her responsibility as an adolescent and would have the right to be herself and feel a sense of belonging to our culture. Rennie jumped at my side and said that if I wanted to, and that was the usual way, then so be it. *So ist es.* Our plan was that at Easter the pastor would hold the ceremony. Then the wheel turned and the choice of the way we both go was out of my control.

My serenity was spoiled because of a letter that arrived a week before Easter, with a stamp that showed it had arrived from Riga. The letter was written in feminine handwriting in broken German and signed at the bottom by R. Gutkin. What's that woman's name, I wondered, Raya or Rita or Regina or Rebecca. Signing the first letter of the Christian name and writing the family name in full looked very formal to me, as if telling me: "We are not friends. Here important matters are arranged, official matters." She wrote to me that she was writing on behalf of Rennie's mother because the mother is ill.

I tried to think if there really was a woman named Gutkin in the world, or if Johanna the mother had invented her in order to distance her own emotions away from a sense of responsibility for this girl or for me to feel Christian compassion and a desire to help a sick woman. In any case, I was asked unequivocally to travel to the annual Leipzig commerce fair and meet

---

26. That's how it is (German)

a man by the name of Chaim Yizhak Friedman. All the details were laid out in the letter: Time and place of the meeting.

Of course I had to go. Toi toi toi, I wouldn't want anyone to think I kidnap girls from their families.

Freidman looked like a well-off merchant. He wore a three-piece suit, tailored, and wore a black felt Fedora hat. After a brief official introduction he started speaking immediately and said "Fräulein Rein, I am a representative of Mrs. Gerson, mother of the girl Irena Friedman."

"Yes, sir, I know," I replied, realizing that the mother had changed her last name.

"How is the girl? Is she healthy?"

"She's happy. She's healthy, she's a good student and she's beautiful."

"Fräulein Rein, the fact that Johanna has a daughter in this world is a secret that only four people in the world know besides Johanna herself: her neighbor Ruth Gutkin, her friend Diana, you, and me. I am Johanna's uncle who stands in for her deceased father when necessary. The four of us were exceedingly surprised that Rennie was still at the nursery where she was left at birth."

Aha, I said in my heart, the Gutkin who signed the letter is a Ruth and she is a real woman. He looked at me questioningly as he took off his hat, revealing a shiny bald spot out of which a few single hairs stood out. I learned in life that one should tell the truth and I replied: "The girl, whom I call Rennie at her mother's request, is the one and only and it would be hard for me to think of saying goodbye to her."

He looked at me with wonder mixed with anger and said: "*So was gibt's doch nicht.*"[27]

I looked at the hairs that insisted on staying on his head and

---

27. There is no such thing (German), meaning: this is impossible.

decided that I too could insist and said to him, "Mr. Friedman, I would be very happy to adopt her." I boldly expressed my dream aloud.

I realized that this was the moment that would determine my fate. But the man kicked my dream away with a dismissive motion of his hand as if I had offered to sell a brown cow instead of a white cow in the marketplace.

"Fräulein, Johanna has decided that Rennie will not grow up in an orphanage all her life. At her age she should already be getting a good education from a good family. *Ordnung muss sein.*"[28] He concluded by asking God for help, turning his face to heaven: "*Gott hilf mir.*"[29] Of course I knew he was not addressing Christ but the God of the Jews and that's why I did not share with him the plans I had for the baptism I had planned to hold for her and the truth is that at that moment I realized that the baptism would never take place. This is it. I will never forget his exact words: "Johanna is married and has two children, a son and a daughter. Her husband does not know that she is the mother of another daughter, and now, since this truth was not told to him when they first met, Johanna cannot tell him after seven years of marriage, especially since Johanna is often ill and her husband carries her in his arms. For four years I have been paying the city of Pirna for Rennie's upkeep since Johanna cannot pay for a secret child from a bank account she shares with her husband." He stressed again that I must continue to keep secret the relationship between Johanna and Rennie.

"We have decided that Rennie will find a suitable solution. The purpose of this meeting is to inform you that the state of Saxony has already begun the search for a foster or adoptive family for Rennie. I have extended my stay in Germany to advance these matters."

---

28. There must be order (German)
29. God help me (German)

I was silent. What could I say? Yell "No! No I don't agree!"? He rose. Held out his hand to say goodbye. Threw a banknote on the table and uttered the most painful sentence in the world: "The separation between Irena and you is very close at hand since several families are interested in adopting a girl her age."

The session lasted about a quarter of an hour, a short time that turned my world upside down. The sky is underground. Chaos. What I had will be no more. Before me lay a long day in Leipzig. I could use the time on this warm day to stroll and enjoy myself, but my heart would not let me do that. My footsteps were heavy and slow, my head sagged and was busy with the saddest thoughts in the world. I found myself in the doorway of a toy store. I looked around and decided to buy something for Rennie. But, on the other hand, the girl is thirteen. Buy her a toy? Wouldn't that be funny? I left the store, walked a few steps away and then came back. I told myself that this was not a toy, but a souvenir. I thought of something soft and pleasant to the touch, something that would bring the two of us closer.

I left the store with a small, soft, white, curly sheep, with a human gaze. Rennie will understand the context of this gift, a gift that brings with it memories with a smile.

On the way back I realized that I really have to tell Rennie the news: she's Jewish and she's going to have a new family.

Her young world will be turned upside down very soon, the world just beginning to develop in her. The responsibility on my shoulders is huge. It's clear to me that the way I will relay this to my beloved girl will affect her ability to absorb them.

Fate plays with us. Our prayers to Christ turned out to be to no avail. Nevertheless, I prayed and crossed myself again and again for the help of Our Lord to help me and save my soul: *"Jesus, hilf mir, bitte rette meine Seele"*[30].

_____

30. Jesus, help me, please save my soul (German).

I planned our conversation for Saturday, the day before Sunday service. We walked hand in hand between the hospital paths in Gottleuba, admired the wooded mountains around us and then, as we sat on a bench overlooking the view, I took her hand in mine and told Rennie the words I had carefully chosen: "My girl, you know you are very dear to me. The place we live in is unsuitable for a girl your age. You have a mother who handed you over to me because she could not take care of you, but your mother wants you to move in with a family."

I stopped to look at her. She did not pick up on what I told her. She remained seated upright and her gaze was distant.

"Rennie, we will both part soon and you will not live with me again, you will leave Gottleuba and be the daughter of a new family. I'm sure it will be a family that will really want you and invest their whole soul in your upbringing. Ohh, you'll have a wonderful life." I tried to sound convincing, even though my truth was as far from these things as America was from my village. Rennie scratched with her shoe at the ground under the bench. She opened her mouth in bewilderment, then said only four words: "I don't want to." She shed no tears.

She said those words powerfully. I wanted to go on and tell her about her Judaism, but I could not. I decided to stop because I realized that it was impossible to encumber her mind with two new facts of this magnitude at once. I chose this moment to hand her a wrapped package. "But it's not my birthday." Rennie said. We don't usually give gifts on ordinary days, because our economic situation here doesn't allow it.

"A parting gift. A gift from me to you. A gift that will keep you company in your room and in your bed. That way you can remember both me and our shared experiences." I kissed her on her forehead, where I tied her two braids wrapped around her head in a beautiful hairstyle. Rennie was very moved by the sheep and said with a laugh: "Laura. My Laura."

She hugged the sheep and ran her wool over her face, back

and forth. Once again I saw how Rennie, like me, controlled her emotions and put them deep down into her body. Anyone who doesn't know her as well as I do can mistakenly think that Rennie does not really care.

I handed Rennie an empty notebook with printed lines and a hard cover, and a regular pencil. I bought at our kiosk the thickest notebook they had. "Another gift?" She was amazed. I nodded and said, "Write in it what you're going through. We cannot know now whether you will have someone to tell everything to. Hide this notebook well. It's yours only. A secret notebook." The notebook is a secret and Judaism is a secret.

The secret has settled deep within my life, it is no longer a guest who will soon be leaving.

On the morning of every new day Rennie would tell me as I walked her to school the same four words: "I don't want to." Sometimes she said them out loud and sometimes silently, but I felt those words. Sometimes she added, "Please, Schwester Hilde, make it possible for me to continue to live here. Please. Please." And I always answered her, with tears in my eyes, what I must answer by virtue of my responsibility to her soul: "Rennie, you will be happy with the family that chooses you. They will choose you out of many children looking for a home with a mom and dad. They will choose you because they will want to raise *you*." I emphasized the last word. Sometimes I also added, "This change is not my decision and I really cannot change anything. I will miss you too."

I could not tell her the story of her Judaism.

The problem arising now is the political situation in Germany. Hitler, whose words I really believed at first, won the election three years ago and turned his skin, which is a phrase I'd heard. He says that Germany should be free of foreigners and that only Aryans should have the right and privilege to live in it. He has decided that our Germany should be free of Jews. His opinions are no longer mine at all, toi toi toi. I feel a great fear in my soul: I am raising a Jewish girl. Luckily my Rennie is not a boy, whom anyone can see for a Jew when he takes off his pants.

On June 17 this year, just about a month ago, Himmler became the commander of the German secret police, the "Gestapo" became an official German organization. It was only out of concern for Rennie that I began to follow the politics in my country. I read that Himmler gained full independence from the bureaucracy of the state and the Reich. We all understand that in such a situation a person can do whatever he wants and if it is true then he can be dangerous to my Jew. This Gestapo has already recruited many uneducated people from Gottleuba. It seems to me that the Gestapo is a monster that preys and consumes anyone who does not conform to its guidelines. Rennie's Judaism has become urgent, and also frightening. I was sorry that Rennie did not look Aryan and did not have blue eyes like me. I started to get scared for myself too. At the meeting of the nuns, the issue of having Jewish orphans arose. I think I spotted fear on the faces of some of the nuns. Maybe I wasn't the only one sheltering a Jewish girl in a Christian convent. Katrina summed up this painful issue in words that could only be understood one way: "If there is a Jewish girl secretly in one of our convents, we would do well to pass this thing straight to the Gestapo. That's how it should be. It's an order. Why should we get in trouble?" I lived with this sentence for several days. It's perfectly clear that I will not give the Gestapo any information about the girl I love so much, but what should I do? I'm scared for myself as well.

Adding to all my worries, Esther invited me to her office. We sat opposite each other, two nuns having an important conversation. "Dear Schwester Hilde, I'll come straight to the point.

Rennie must leave. I understand your pain. Our whole country is insane and has not been acting in the spirit of Christianity for a long time. Unfortunately, the lovely Rennie endangers not only you. Think of Natasha coming here to help. Must she also pay with her life because of Rennie? We've reached the last possible moment for action. It's a heartache, but I have to decide that Rennie should leave soon."

Esther, it turns out, always knew the secret.

I debated so much; I even considered the possibility of running away with Rennie. But the problem is I don't have money to sustain both of us. Worse, Rennie is officially registered as Jewish in Germany, so running away with a Jewish girl is not a safe option. In addition, I have no experience or knowledge in managing life outside of Gottleuba. One by one, options came up and went down like the start of pick-up sticks, our favorite game. I came to the one conclusion, the heartrending conclusion, that I hope they find an adoptive family as soon as possible. I prayed that the family would be Christian, even though Rennie's mother is Jewish. At least my education could continue in her life.

A shiny black car stopped in front of our nursery. I glanced at the emblem affixed to its front and was startled: apparently a senior priest has come here himself. On the car was emblazoned the symbol of our Holy Trinity: three silver arrows surrounded by the circle of the sky. A car with the symbol of the Father, the Son and the Holy Spirit. I crossed myself, trembling with excitement, and went towards it.

A woman and a man stepped out, calmly and elegantly. They looked about fifty, two heavy, affluent people, serious and respectable. They both wore dark, well-tailored outfits and the lady wore a large modern hat that looked a little funny on her head, and black shoes with low, thick heels. On her shoulder hung an elegant bag made of crocodile skin. I'd already forgotten the idea that a senior priest has popped in for a visit. Their driver stayed in the car, unfolded a newspaper in the steering wheel and stuck his head into it.

They approached me, the woman walking one step behind the man.

"Max and Francesca Oberlander from the city of Zwickau. We have come to take Irena Friedman to our home. All the official documents are already signed. Everything is in order."

Ahh, from now on they will be Rennie's parents.

The two entered our office and sat down facing me.

Now I could see up close that the woman had a very beautiful face. I thought that this was a couple right out of the stories, as they say: a rich man and a beautiful woman.

After the brief and official introduction Max opened things up. It was clear he was used to standing in front of an audience and deciding where the conversation should turn: "Schwester Hilde Rein, let's go through all the paperwork."

The woman tried an "Ummm," and whispered as she hid her mouth with the palm of her hand: "How about we hear a little about the girl first?"

The man silenced her with a quick imperious motion of his hand, a gesture that reminded me of the Mr. Friedman I met. "What is there to hear? A girl is a girl," and whispered to her so that I also heard: "Francesca, we agreed at home that we'd do everything here quickly. Why start with these needless questions all of a sudden?" In response, Francesca as if folded into herself, trying to disappear.

And from that moment on, only Mr. Oberlander spoke. He did not ask to hear anything about Rennie, her preferences and loves, what topics she was interested in or how she was growing up. They filled out forms. When Francesca signed her name, she whispered to herself and to me: "This girl will come to our house instead of the twins who are no more. I want to take the girl because our two daughters were killed in a car accident. We have a lot of room for another girl." I hoped that this meant a lot of room in the heart, not a lot of room in the house. The woman crossed herself as she looked up at the large cross hanging on the office wall. "We are a very respectable family in Zwickau and its surroundings. No one would dare dig into our affairs and suspect that Rennie is Jewish," Max said confidently. His wife added: "Very, very respectable." "I'm not afraid of the Gestapo. I have connections there. The fact that Rennie grew up here, in a convent, and already knows the Christian world makes our decision much easier. No one will find out she is Jewish."

Maybe despite their hard shell, there was something soft inside Max and Francesca, I hoped. "Rennie doesn't know she's Jewish," I told them. They both smiled happily at each other. It was the first smile I'd seen on their faces. It seemed to me that it was the tough man that I saw trembling from within as if he was withholding true excitement. But maybe it was just my imagination.

I knew that an adopted girl must always have a Saxon custodian appointed, whose job it is to make sure that everything goes well with the adopted one, and if so - he will see and recognize Rennie for a Jew. A small fear crept into my heart that over time became a great fear.

Then it was as if the heavens thundered and a darkness covered the world. Rennie responded like I'd never seen before. Out of the gentle child came a determined resistance. I was reminded of her first days of school, but that was as a dress rehearsal before the real thing. Now she wept and resisted, tried to escape, looked at me with pleading eyes, screamed "I don't want to!" Kicked her feet. She grabbed an electric pole, held on to it for dear life and cried out to the heavens. Her cry did not come back down from the heavens to Max Oberlander. He remained cool, collected, and serious. Rennie screamed in a nonsensical language, all the words running together. I could only make out the words "No. No. Don't want to." I started weeping uncontrollably with her as she whispered loudly: "Schwester Hilde, save me." Mr. Oberlander grabbed hold of her hand and pushed her into the rear seat of the car. His wife entered after her without moving her face, unsmiling. The driver folded up his newspaper and started the car. Mr. Oberlander took the seat beside him at the front and slammed the door.

Boom.

The car started up and left.

I couldn't see the car as it drove away, it raised so much dust behind it.

Now I could cry without interruption. I grieved for days upon days. I felt pain throughout my body, I turned into a sad woman. Only my fellow nuns understood the unbearable pain I was going through and tried to ease it with the same words I recited to Rennie, they said they were sure that Rennie was getting the best with a very rich family and that it was good for a girl her age not to live in a nursery taking care of babies every day after school. They added that the most ideal thing for any girl is to grow up in the bosom of a family with a father and a mother and suggested I find solace in Rennie's marvelous fate, a fate that not every orphan we raise gets to have. They didn't even know about Rennie being Jewish and were sure that this step was quite right and promising.

I was left with memories.

These days no one in Gottleuba and the area has a car. The Oberlanders arrived in the big shiny private car that even has an open roof. Esther wondered and said: "That symbol on the front of their car showed me it's a Mercedes! They're very rich." "Esther, in heaven's name, do you take an interest in cars?" I asked. She winked and nodded. I thought I knew her well. I laughed at myself inside that if I'd known it was a Mercedes emblem I wouldn't have thought it was a symbol of the Holy Trinity and wouldn't have become excited at the prospect of a senior clergyman visiting us. Yes, sometimes knowledge comes in handy. I tried to imagine the wealth Rennie had come into, but these images would not arise in my imagination because I'd never seen such homes.

I imagined Rennie's long hair, Mrs. Oberlander braiding her hair and twirling the braids around her pretty head like a crown. I hoped Rennie was putting the pins I'd given her in her hair. No one around her knows I'd bought her these pins and how happy she was with them. I imagined Rennie going to senior school with her uniform on. She would be a good student, because she was always obedient and bright – I promised myself within my heart. I tried to see Rennie dressed in a purple, feminine nightdress, embroidered with lace and small delicate flowers, running to kiss her parents before bedtime and them wishing her goodnight and so happy with the light she has brought to their disaster-stricken home. I imagined Rennie hugging Laura in her sleep.

I dreamed of Rennie at night. The photos I had left of her I placed on the nightstand in my little home. Every night when I came back home I spoke to Rennie, telling her about my day, updated her on new babies that came to us and those who'd moved on to the children's home. When I was about to fall asleep I wished her goodnight as well. At every daily prayer and especially during Sunday church service I always prayed for her and wished for Christ to protect her from all harm and for her future to be bright.

About a month after she left came another letter signed by R. Gutkin. She asked after Rennie. I realized that the mother did not know about the adoption. Once adoption was approved, the arrangements were made by the state of Saxony and it must be the state responsible for deciding what and when to tell the mother.

RENNIE

ᴼᴼ 1939 ᴼᴼ

Custodian.
A funny word.

I'd never heard such an odd word until I was thirteen and four months old. I had to repeat it to myself so I could remember it. My custodian will be arriving today at four-thirty, after naptime. I'm sixteen now. Yesterday Francesca Oberlander, my "mother", announced it. I like being alone in my room with the door closed so I'm waiting for him here. I've been living in Zwickau with these people for about two and a half years.

I saw this custodian when I first arrived here and now he's suddenly decided to meet me again, suddenly he'd remembered I exist. Truth be told, I've already forgotten his name.

He came as soon as I arrived at this house in Zwickau and in that whole period after that I'd not heard from him at all. If he was in touch with the Oberlanders I do not know and didn't dare ask. Perhaps there are actually many kids whose parents have abandoned them and he has a lot of work to do.

I'm debating how to pass the time until four-thirty. I will read my diary. Or rather: I will read my dear diary again, the diary I received as a gift from Schwester Hilde. I will start from the first page and maybe skip a few pages here and there.

1936. Monday, August 3rd. Middle of the night.
My diary, my dear, I really smell the wonderful smell of Schwester Hilde when I open you. I really need you here. How did this wonderful woman understand that it would be so, that you would be so dear to me and that I would need you? I have two friends here now, Laura and you.

I still haven't thrown away, nor will I throw away, the wrapping paper in which Schwester Hilde handed me to you while we were both sitting on the bench. This wrapping is like a sweater to you, that's how you will feel warm, darling. I don't care that it's unadorned like the wrapping paper of all the gifts I received for my birthdays, it is brown and the simplest.

Luckily I have a room to myself. It isn't pleasant to think that this room belonged to two girls who are no longer in this world. I really don't like it. I try to dissolve thoughts about the conversations that took place between them in this room. Do you understand me? But at least I can close the door and not see this whole house. I don't know how this Francesca would have reacted if she'd seen me turn the light on in the middle of the night.

From now on I will write here. We will meet a lot. I hope the tears of my longing will let me see what I have written. In the meantime, I see I have come to a rich family. The house is so big you can get confused in it. Yesterday I arrived at this strange house. How could I feel that these people are my mom and dad?? Schwester Hilde, I hope you know and feel that I love you. I think I will never be able to feel close to them. One moment. I will continue.

Now I'm writing after a break. The tears blur and obscure my words.

Their house is huge in my eyes. Immense. Lots of extra rooms here. It's cold here, even though it's summer now. The ceiling is so high and it really is in the sky. The many large paintings on the walls depict all sorts of people I don't know and wouldn't want to meet and make me feel like a tour of the Museum of Art in Pirna, the one I was at with my class. It feels like a museum, not a home. I have now written the correct definition: this is a museum and not a house. As if the Oberlanders want anyone who comes here to just be quickly impressed and understand that they are rich (which is true). I don't understand what there could be in so many closets with endless drawers. I can't imagine where all the staircases lead from or to. The glass chandeliers are designed to hang from the ceilings, but for them to be so shiny, Emma the nimble little maid wipes the dust with a stick with feathers tied at the end all day long, bravely standing on a ladder. I hope the feathers on this stick were plucked from the duck after it was already dead.

I'm so tired. My eyes are closing. Enough, I'll stop now. Goodnight world.

1936. Wednesday, August 5th.

Dear diary, we met yesterday. I hope you're not feeling alone hidden deep inside the drawer. My eyes are heavy. I'll write briefly, just so you don't feel lonely.

The truth is I don't know many things that people learn at school. If here and now I shouldn't wear a mask and keep silent, because I'm good at that now, then my inner truth, the one I hide as deeply inside myself as you are hidden within that drawer, is that I'm not a collector of knowledge from books. I'm a village girl. I like the freedom, the wind and the ground, the sun and the cool creeks, watching tree trunks in the forest as I notice their different shapes and colors, the smell of flowers blooming and the tinkling of the sheep in the meadows.

1936. Thursday, August 6th. A different day.

Costudian. Cusdotian. No, Custodian. That's it, that's how you write it. Custodian. A stranger came to this house today and said he was my custodian. He sat with us in the Oberlanders' guest parlor. His eyes were on me, them, the walls and the furniture, without stopping. He's the first person, more or less, who doesn't smoke while he talks. The guest introduced himself as Franz Kunstlinger. I saw a man about Schwester Hilde's age, with a colorful necktie. I've never seen a man wearing a tie in three shades of green and red spots. The tie is tied loosely around his neck in a knot that doesn't suffocate and he wears a green cap, the color of his eyes. A special man. He has good eyes with a small smile at their edges.

He said his job was to take care of me, that I'd be well and that he worked for the city. Wonderful. I'd have someone to talk to. Perhaps I could manage to convince him to return me to my Schwester Hilde.

I stop reading and really recall that Franz looked softly into my eyes and said "From now on I'm your custodian. Every child living with a family not their own has a person from the city to take care of them. I'm yours. If there's any trouble here – tell me."

Max Oberlander replied before I could understand what was going on around me: "You've left us your details already. That's fine. Great. There's no-one like the city of Zwickau and the state of Saxony."

Franz still asked me: "How are you, Fräulein?"

I was a bit excited that someone would ask me how I was and replied: "Sir, I'm finding things difficult. I miss Schwester Hilde and Ernest Winter and Laura and Patrice and even my teacher."

Franz smiled at me and nodded. "And how are you feeling in your new home?"

I'm not a fool and won't say anything against them in their presence, so I didn't tell him I felt an icy wave blowing from this couple's direction and replied: "Okay. It's all very new to me."

Franz took his leave and Emma the maid escorted him to the door.

That was the end of that short visit. That's it. That's how I remember now.

1936. Saturday, August 8th. Morning.

Children whose parents abandoned them. Children without parents. Orphans. Ernest. I even lost Ernest. Ernest, I miss you.

At school in Gottleuba I discovered the children's company suitable for me to play with and I realized what a pleasure it is compared to the company of babies. I very quickly became a girl who played ball and hopscotch, running and falling over, standing on my hands and head, climbing ropes hanging from tree branches and reaching the fruit. I have a lot of friends there, but my best friend is Ernest Winter. It's hard for me to talk about Gottleuba in the past tense. I will do this to be able to feel that I am here and not there.

My dear Ernest. I'm talking to you here. Can you hear my voice?

Orphaned at the age of two, an only child. I won't forget the place and the moment you told me that your parents were killed by drowning in the Spree River during a family vacation. You live in your aunt's house, Maria Schöne. Luckily she's a good woman. I've never seen such a beautiful house.

It's so nice to be in this house. Well, it's because your uncle is a high-level engineer and Maria has money to design beautifully. No, it's also, or mostly, because Maria is a great woman who loves people. but I only met your "father" a few

107

times because he works such long hours, into the night. Ernest, we both loved playing together after school. You became part of my life. That's how it is with a good friend. We always had things to do together and especially loved nature walks. Ernest, I have to start writing about you in past tense, I try.

Dear diary, I want to tell you that when I found out I would have to move to a real family and be their daughter because that's what the woman who gave birth to me decided, I told Ernest that very day.

Now I'll use what I'd learnt at school: when writing properly you put " (quotation marks, I remember the name) around the words of the one who's talking. Only if these are their exact words. Let's see if I can do that now. Perhaps I'm learning stuff in school after all?

Ernest was shocked and said "That's awful! How come? What right do they have to move you from your place? Everyone has a home and your home is in the nursery with Schwester Hilde. How come your mother, who abandoned you and was never interested in you, suddenly gets to decide about your life?"

I remember his words exactly. I put them in quotation marks. It was like Ernest put kindling under my anger and lit it when he told me about a really good decision made by a king in the Old Testament. He told me that this king was the smartest in the world and could even talk to animals. At this point my thoughts wandered a little and I imagined a man who could talk to Laura the sheep. "Hey, Rennie, wake up. Where are you? Listen, this story is important," he waved his hand in my face and carried on telling me: "One day, two women came to court who wanted to raise the same baby and each woman said she was the baby's mother. Do you get it? Two mothers for one baby." He said a sentence I won't forget and felt in my heart, he said to me: "And I don't even have one mother that's real." So I thought I was lucky to have

Schwester Hilde who's better than a real mother, but now this sentence is so true for me too.

The king decided that the one who got the baby would be the woman who raised it. That smart king understood that the one who counts as the mother is the one who has feelings towards the baby. I can't remember how the king realized that, but I do remember that the king decided that the real mother was the one who saw the child in its daily pains and joys. And I was cut off from Schwester Hilde who was just like a mother to me.

Midday

I had a long break from writing. Not just tears came out of my eyes, but a real cry.

Whenever I remember that story about the king, a question plonks itself at the end of my thoughts and waits for me to get to it: Why didn't my road end up with such a smart king?

Midnight. Saturday.

That story Ernest told me really annoys me about my reality. When he told me about that king a balloon grew inside me, a balloon of terrible anger and deep hatred towards that woman who gave birth to me. I decided that if I ever meet her, I'll kick her with all my strength then turn my face and leave. Now, in bed with myself, I have a name that really fits her – "shameless bint."

When I said goodbye to Ernest he actually cried and promised that we'd meet again, that he would find me. I cried with him too and I'm crying now as well. Ernest, are you asleep now or can you feel me thinking about you? Good night, Ernest.

1936. Thursday, August 13th.

My diary my dear you won't believe it today that Francesca asked me a strange request and I couldn't ask what I should have what will happen tomorrow Jesus save me please my hand hurts I wrote so fast wait I'll stop I need to breathe.

What happened was that Francesca told me, "Tomorrow our maid will not be here, we let her go. For dinner you will fetch from the cellar a jar of Powidl made last year, in 1935. You don't need to be waited on hand and foot all the time."

That's what she told me. Once her maid, who serves her all the time, takes time off for one day she can no longer bring to the meal what she needs and she thinks the best thing is that I should replace the maid. Was I brought here to be ordered around??

I probably had the look of a girl who doesn't understand because she added: "Powidl is plum jam. The year they make it is written on the sticker."

I literally remember her request word for word. She spoke to me like Mr. Schöne talks to Ernest, in a language of command. A kind of language that makes me feel small and unimportant. The three of us just sat down for dinner at a great distance from each other, just like yesterday and just like always.

On the huge table, the food was served in a set of golden dishes ornamented with sky-blue flowers. I got my eyes onto the beautiful plates and my mind took a vacation, just like Emma. I was ashamed to say I couldn't remember the way to the basement and was silent. I was really scared. The fear and the shame as if closed my mouth with a band-aid. The silence at the table was very heavy.

Now I'm with you in the room. Laura is sitting with me. You see, diary? I'm really scared about tomorrow's dinner. I have no one to talk to. Just you. Jesus, help me. Oh, I wish I wasn't here. If I could fly away...

My hand hurts. I've never written so much. I'll stop. Dear diary, good night. Here's a kiss. 💋

Night.

I can't sleep. I try. Really I do. I imagine I'm with Patrice and all his sheep, something that Schwester Hilde told me would help me when I couldn't sleep. She even suggested I count all the sheep. It always helps me, but now it's not helping at all. When I close my eyes my head sees all sorts of possibilities and they all scare me so much.

I hug Laura and we both cry.

I wish Francesca would forget about this jam. Why does she even need jam for dinner anyway? Why is such nonsense so scary to me and won't let me sleep. Why?

I'm coooooooold.

Friday, August 14ᵗʰ. I've never had a day like this.

Now I came to you limping it hurts me I don't know if it hurts more in my bottom or in my heart I thought what was more painful to Our Lord Jesus when they nailed him to the cross I've been here ten days already ten days ago I was in Gottleuba and now it seems to me so long ago it's a shame I didn't immediately ask the details I needed for the request I am disappointed in myself.

Today at school there was just my body. Well, actually this isn't new because I usually don't like listening in this school. Missing home leaves me with no room to study. Today I discovered that the fear of reprisal at home, the fear of what might happen to me, really takes over me.

My head couldn't stop seeing all sorts of possibilities that would fall on me at dinner, which was coming so soon. It seemed that my fear has become an obsession (Ernest taught me that word). This feeling reminds me of a snowball rolling and growing all the time, except my ball is black.

And so, when dinner started Francesca asked me with a crazy look in her eyes: "Rennie, where is the jam? I asked for it yesterday!" And she got up and stomped her foot on the carpet. No dust came out despite the strong stomp. Haha. I looked down, and made teeny-tiny "no" movements with my head. Not a word came out of my mouth. Max screamed: "Who are you to decide not to do what we ask? There will be no such thing in my house. Not in my house!!!" And he banged down his hand with a huge boom. I thought the table would break. He screamed at me and frothed and told me to put my head on the dining room table, took the belt off his pants and spanked me. I did in my head what Schwester Hilde taught me. I counted sheep. I went to another place and only left my bottom with Max. I was hoping his pants would fall off him when he was without the belt. I wanted his fate to humiliate him like he lets himself humiliate me. I wanted his big hairy belly to show, the one that peeks out when his shirts come out of his pants or when he wears a shirt so narrow that one button always pops open.

My diary, can you understand such a thing? Max Oberlander hit me with a belt!!!!!

While he hit me he counted out loud. One, two, three, four and so on. He counted to ten. With every blow I could hear the dinnerware bouncing on the table, making noises like the bells on Patrice's sheep. I was silent. I shut my mouth as hard as I could and didn't make a peep. I swallowed, as hard as I could, the surprise from Max and the fact that I did not understand what he was doing to me. I didn't want to let him think he'd managed to turn me into his plasticine. I didn't want to give him any satisfaction from me breaking down. Francesca didn't stop him. I got the feeling that she was also too scared to say anything. No-one in the world stood by to

watch over me. Francesca kept saying: "Rennie, I'm telling
you for your own good, you should do exactly what we tell
you. So ist est. Ordnung muss sein."
Out of the corner of my eye I saw Emma standing in the
kitchen with tears running down her cheeks. At that moment
I began to feel that there was a woman in this house who
really sees me.
I limped to my room and now Laura and I are hugging. I
wish that wouldn't have happened. I wish I didn't have to tell
you, my diary, about that.

I wish I hadn't read that just now. I think that if someone were
standing now by the cuckoo clock in the hallway they could
hear my heartbeats, despite the distance. That day I was first
spanked by Max, that day stabs at my heart and hurts me. Wait.
I breathe deep into my stomach and try to count sheep to calm
down and also stroke Laura who is hidden under the blanket.
That's it, I keep reading.

I'm getting images into my head that make me feel better
again. I'm with Schwester Hilde. Now I'm helping her take
care of the babies. That is how I get over the terrible pain and
the humiliation. I seem to understand baby language well:
their wishes, their crying and their baby babbling. Suddenly I
really miss wrapping them up in their cloth diapers and even
washing those stinky diapers with my hands, things I'd never
needed to do when I lived there.

An hour later. Night-time already.

I lie on my side in bed on my blanket while dressed in all my dinner clothes. I haven't changed into a nightgown or washed my face. The beatings hurt a lot.

I woke up from a dream where I was strolling idly through the streets of Gottleuba with a baby stroller from which three babies were smiling together at me. I protect the little babies. Now I think, dear diary, that in my reality in this house no one protects me. They are unfair towards me. What did I get spanked for? For what? What right does one person have to hit another person, even more so when the beating person should be like a father to me??? I'm alone in this world. I understand that my mother gave me up to an orphanage and I did not grow up in a normal home with a mom and a dad, but with Schwester Hilde I was happy.

Schwester Hilde loved me, talked to me, walked with me, understood me and was interested in me. So why was I handed over to an old couple who hate me? How did Hilde's promise that I would be happy in the new home become miserable and I live in fear of these two parents?

How?????

1936. Sunday, August 16th.

Today I dared to talk to Emma the maid. I went into the kitchen when the old folks weren't home. Perhaps they went to church. They didn't invite me to come. I have no idea why. I hope I can make it to Sunday prayers next week. I have a few personal things to add to the prayers.

"What are you making? Can I help you?" I asked.

Her eyes grew wide and she said "Are you sure that you, who's their daughter now, want to come into the maid's kitchen?"

Yes. Of course. I love cooking," I replied and she moved to clear some space for me.

"I've prepared the vegetable soup and main course already. Now I'm just finishing up a Cremeschnitte cake to go along with the tea for today's dessert. You see, this is the dough and that's the filling. Would you like to taste?" I scooped up a dollop of sweet cream with my finger. Emma can cook and bake anything.

I stood and watched her quick hands working and asked: "Did they hit their girls as well?"

She nodded her head. I gathered they would hit them too, their real daughters. That's how these people raise children. What a crazy world.

"I can hear them coming. Get out of here quick or we'll have trouble," she said urgently.

Emma could be my friend in this world. ♥

Sunday, September 27th.

I can't really get to you, my diary. This school demands a lot of me and I don't have much time left. I hope you're not as lonely as I am. Three times a week when I come back from school Francesca says to me "Shhhh," and not "how are you? How was school?" Like the words I would hear from the Schwester Hilde. At that hour she's in the middle of playing cards with her fancy girlfriends, while Emma the maid serves them cookies she baked for the occasion while at the same time also preparing dinner in the huge kitchen. Picture this, diary: there's one woman there who always wears a solid color and each time a different color from top to bottom. Once she's blue, once green, once yellow. And so on. I wonder if she also wears matching underwear. Hahaha. A very weird house. Well, her underpants really don't matter. Sorry.

115

There are so many rooms and pieces of furniture here that no one ever uses. So different from the teensy-weensy room I had at the nursery, where I had everything I needed in the world: just a bed and a one-door wardrobe. A room whose windows were just by the furniture and left me just a bit of room to put my feet, but that was room enough. When I wanted a table I could sit in Esther the manager's office. But what I mostly had was the main thing – I was taken care of all day and all night.

Tuesday, September 29th.

Today Max screamed at me: "Stand up straight!" I tried to do it, but he wasn't pleased and raised his voice: "What sort of girl are you!" He screamed quickly, "You don't even know how to stand up straight like someone who values her status." And summed up with: "You need to be taken back." When I heard these words I thought to myself where he meant I'd be taken back to: certainly not to Hilde because my real mother asked that I not be in a nursery and no one around me is as smart as that king that Ernest told me about, and no one thinks that the one who should be my mother is the one who loves me. I wondered if they might bring me back to my real mother who doesn't know me at all. I, in any case, don't know where this mother is in this world. By the way, my dear diary, I'll have you know that I never dared ask Schwester Hilde where my real parents were. I was very worried that Hilde would think I wanted to leave her. What I wanted every day was to be loved by Hilde and to do what she asked and expected of me.

Thursday. October 15th. A bad day.

The ten blows I received were not an isolated occurrence.

Today Max said to me with a frightening look, "What's wrong with you, you villager? How many times do I have to teach you not to put your elbows on the table?" When I had to cut the meat on my plate and tried to use the right set (there are two forks and two knives at the sides of the plate) and hold the knife and fork correctly, I accidentally placed my elbows on the table. At that moment the sky fell on me.

"There's only one way to educate you to grasp what you're told. Put your head on the table. Enough with the elbows on the table. Country bumpkin," he hissed through his teeth and splattered spittle everywhere, took off his belt and was no longer content with ten blows. I teared up but he didn't see. When he was done he said, " Fräulein, you do not leave before we get up. A bit of manners won't hurt you. Sit here." And he pointed at my chair. I sat down at the edge of the chair. My bottom burned and hurt a lot. Francesca ignored me. Emma brought the compote dessert and looked at me with a loving and understanding look. I'm lucky to have Emma here.

Monday, November 16th.

Francesca came into my room, as usual without knocking on the door, as if I too were her property and she were allowed to do with me as she pleased just as it occurred to her. I think she saw me talking to Laura the sheep. As soon as she came in I just started making faces so she wouldn't understand that I was talking to my sheep. Francesca screamed at me and stopped: "You're a crazy girl. C-R-A-Z-Y. Crazy and childish."

Oh, what's going to happen now? Will she tell Max? Will she snitch on me?

8pm.
She obviously told Max because now, at dinner, which is my daily nightmare hour, he laughed at me. He said: "Irena, you're thirteen already. You know? You should be a responsible, mature young lady, not playing with childish toys for country children." He took great pride and joy in making rings of stinking smoke from his cigar and laughed hahaha loudly. I understood that for Max, being from the country, and not a rich city man like him, was a very lowly status.

I can't let him mock me while I'm talking to my dear Laura. I don't know what to do. Really, what shall I do???

Tuesday, November 17th.

Horrible Max beat me again today and added new words to his regular ones, and they were: "I'll throw away that stupid sheep of yours if you keep behaving like this. You bumpkin!" Now I'm limping from the pain again. I've taken to wearing several pairs of underpants under my dress. That way it hurts a little less.

I skip over all the days in the diary where I got a beating. Enough, I can't read it anymore. Max developed a new indoor sport. He exercises his hand on my bottom. Sometimes he hits me without the belt. Just with his hands. I've heard all kinds of demands like "Don't eat so fast." "Why are you eating so slowly?" "How can you put the fork that fell on the floor back on the table?" "Put the napkin on your knees. We told you to spread it." "Chew with your mouth closed." "Don't lick your fingers." How dare you eat out of the main plate?" "Are you insane? You eat before the lady of the house starts eating? Where did you grow up, the jungle?" "Why didn't you greet

Francesca's friends with a smile when you came home from school and ran straight to your room?"

I can no longer remember the number of beatings I took and have no interest in remembering all their grievances. Every time he either hits me as hard as he can or sends me to the toilet as punishment. Sometimes both. I can already recite word for word the sentences that come before the beating: "We've told you not to do this. This is the only way to get some manners into your head. *Ordnung muss sein.*" I keep putting up with the pain and never ever make any sound or cry in his presence.

1936. Christmastime. An idea day.

Dear diary, are you happy to see me? We haven't met for a long time. Today was a different day that I must tell you about. I've been here for nearly half a year.

It's Christmas now. It's evening. I suddenly started having troublesome thoughts and asked Laura, "Why did such a horrible couple choose me? Maybe only this kind of people would choose me? What future awaits me in this world?" Laura didn't reply. I couldn't put an answer for me in Laura's mouth. I felt like I was becoming transparent in this world. I thought of their two daughters who passed away. Suddenly a thought came into my head, you'll excuse me for writing it, but maybe I should think it over: did these girls really die in a car accident? Maybe, just maybe, it's a possibility, maybe they wanted to die? And maybe someone beat them so hard that he caused their deaths?

My dear diary, did you notice that half an hour ago I sat in my room thinking? I'll tell you what happened to me in those moments: I felt it was impossible, impossible to feel that a large, locked gate was blocking my way. Suddenly something that came out of me lifted me on to my feet. I stood in front of the big mirror in my room (yes, I have a mirror here. What joy!!!), looked for the confident, upright stance, lifted my head, looked straight into my eyes, spoke to myself, telling the girl in front of me: "Rennie, you need to take care of yourself, don't give up, don't stay silent. Buck up, walk out of the room and find someone to help you. Go, go to the town hall." I pictured myself coming to the custodian Franz Kunstlinger because I remembered his role in my life. In front of the mirror I felt it was imperative that he knows my truth.

Tomorrow morning is a new day. A wonderful day. Good night.

An initiative day.

After my daily morning prayer and my personal bedside genuflection, which I observe daily, I ran to town hall. The way wasn't easy because I'd never been there before, but I felt a force coming out of me as if commanding me "Rennie, don't give up. Be strong. You're right. "

And I really did get there.

I returned feeling fear and disappointment. As I write this, I pray that this Franz will finally come and listen to me and maybe get me out of this house.

This was long ago, but some things are etched in memory. I remember getting dressed quickly, putting on shoes, quietly leaving my room sneaking out of the house running as fast as I could on the streets of Zwickau asking passers-by which way to town hall running again running into people shouting sorry falling on my knee getting up still running fast getting confused and going back a ways and my shoes stepping in a puddle and running and asking and finally seeing the sign getting to the window where they asked me what I wanted I said I'm feeling bad and want to talk to my custodian Franz Kunstlinger.

The clerk got up and took me to a room where a fancy young woman sat behind a table and calmly doing her nails with a nail file. She handed me a glass of water because I still couldn't breathe properly. I explained to her what I wanted. The woman explained to me, without checking, that Franz Kunstlinger was not in town hall at the moment, but said in a pleasant, smiling voice that I could tell her everything and she would take proper care of it.

I trusted her, she was, after all, a city employee. I told her everything: the beatings, my loneliness, the nastiness. She jotted things down in her notebook occasionally, and when she wasn't writing she carried on with her nails. Then, when I was done, she asked me to join her in another room: "Now wait here. We'll take care of your complaint."

A long while later, four people entered the room: the well-dressed clerk, a woman I didn't know, perhaps she was from town hall as well, Francesca and Max. My heart pounded like a drum.

Franz wasn't there.

I said to myself, "Rennie, this is probably how you these things are managed. Be strong. You did the right thing." I thought they would tell the Oberlanders that I'd be taken out of their house, but instead the woman I didn't know said, "Mr. and Mrs. Oberlander, this girl—" she pointed at me— "told us that ..." and repeated everything I'd said. I thought I wasn't hearing right when Max stepped into her words: "Is that what she told you? Unbelievable! A liar!" He said and banged the table with his hairy fist. "Can you believe me abusing a girl? Me?"

From that moment no one spoke to me, or asked why I said the things I'd said.

I felt transparent.

Max added, looking at me angrily: "What ingratitude! We gave you a house and a family and that's how you repay us? I'm stunned! What happened to you? Were you bored today?"

Francesca said nothing, just nodded her head as Max spoke.

"Now we go home," Max announced and that was the end of my complaint. Max Oberlander was an adult and a respectable man and they believed him. They were used to believing him.

They didn't believe me.

It was a long way back. They walked side by side in large, rapid steps and didn't speak at all.

I followed them. They didn't turn around once to see if I were there.

When the door of the house was locked from the inside, my nightmare began.

Whatever day this is. The day after yesterday. It's evening.

Dear Diary, what's happening in this world? Yesterday I got the roughest beating anyone has ever had in this world. My ears heard screams that could reach the houses across the road. The Oberlanders lost control of themselves. Both of them. This time Francesca also rolled up her sleeves and joined the party. The main words that were heard along with the whipping I suffered were "great shame" - " große Schande, große Schande" and also "How dare you bring out what happens in this house?!"

When I woke up I found myself lying on my bed and Emma sitting next to me.

"You fainted and fell to the floor. They left the living room with you unconscious on the floor. I took you to this room."

"How did you manage to pick me up?"

Sweet Emma stroked my hair and said: "Rennie, Rennichka, the skin on your bottom is peeled and I can see hand impressions on your back and long belt lines, but they won't allow a doctor." She cleared her throat and continued: "I promise you I'll heal you."

"Fronella, you're amazing. What would I do without you?" from that moment on I called her "Fronella", like we called our teacher in Gottleuba, Fräulein Emma. She laughed and must've thought I'd made that name up.

I've just tried to sit up but couldn't. This is my summer vacation? This is how I spend it? My handwriting is terrible because I'm writing lying down. Dear diary, I'm so lucky to have you in my world.

I can end with a true statement: today was the day I lost my innocence. Starting tomorrow, I will never trust people's promises. Does anyone in this world see me ???????????

1937. January 7th. Thursday.

Fronella visited me, just like she promised. She rubbed ointment and changed my dressings. She brought me food, left it on a small table she added beside my bed and stayed for a few minutes to sit with me. I'm starting to feel close to her. I told her excitedly about Schwester Hilde and the wonderful life I had. I told her about myself quickly because she didn't have more than a few minutes to console me and take care of me. Why was her visit so brief? Because a horrible screech "E-M-M-A. EMMA!" rang out throughout both stories of the house, followed by another question reverberating against the walls and furniture "Where are you? Why are you idling?!"

9pm.

I've never been in such pain. Fronella knows I like ice cream and brought me three flavors garnished with fruit. Fronella's kindness softens the immense pain a little, at least while she sits beside me.

It's good that I wore about five pairs of underpants. I don't know if they could have avoided calling for the doctor if I hadn't done that.

How did I get in this situation? I keep thinking in circles that make my head go round, and it wasn't very stable on my shoulders in the first place. Why did I believe anyone would want to help me? Why did I think I might have any good fortune in my life? I don't want to taint you, dear diary, with all the curses I found myself cursing the mother who'd given birth to me. Now I'll add screams that come from deep within my body: why did you have me anyway? Why didn't you have an abortion, you selfish lady? And if you decided to give birth, couldn't you raise me? What in your world made you throw away your baby? How could a mother do something like that? You know what, I never want to meet you, No, actually, I want you to look for me and I'll kick you and spit right in your face.

Middle of the night.

The bad dreams won't leave me alone. I have nightmares. I woke up just now and took you out from under my pillow. In my dream I saw myself swaddled like a baby by a garbage can, right in the middle of all the filth. I noticed that the baby understands that no-one ever goes through that place so she no longer cries. Sometimes the woman who put me there appeared in the dream. When I woke up I could no longer see that woman again although I really wanted to know what she looked like, the woman who gave me birth.

I'll try to sleep.

Friday before dawn.

Another dream. In this one I saw Francesca with horns, one moment sitting and laughing like the devil and the next moment suddenly yelling at the top of her voice and begging Jesus to save her. And again and again. Nothing changes with her, like a wind-up doll with a key in her ass.

Morning January 9th, Saturday.

I'm waiting for faithful Fronella. Francesca hasn't been in the room yet. In my dreams I get back at Francesca: I saw her tied to a pole at the center of Zwickau with kindling alight at her feet. She screams at the top of her voice to be untied. The people who pass by her take no notice of her whatsoever.

Now I remember another dream: Ernest drowning in the river, he moves his hands and feet like the wings of a butterfly and swallows water until he disappears. I stand on the bank and look at him but I can do nothing.

Fronella has more time to be with me today. She brought mountains of ice cream and we sat together on my bed. I told her about my life. Fronella knows how to listen.

Since I learned to use quote marks I like writing the conversations as they were. I can do it very well.

"Tell me why you work here. They're terrible people."

"Look, Rennie. They're horrible to you because they want to educate you. That's how they educate. They treat me pretty well. Why I'm here? They pay me well above market rate. Here I get a room and food. I have no expenses. My entire salary goes to the bank, I'm saving up for school. My family can't afford tuition and I want to take off. To be a success."

"What will you study?"

I want to be an engineer who designs airports. My parents always told me about my uncle who was a pilot and died in the Great War, and ever since then I've been interested in aviation."

This time my mouth dropped open. Fronella surprised me.

January 13th, Wednesday. A week since the beating. Morning.

Still in great pain. The nightmares keep coming. A minute ago Francesca left the room. No, if you say "left" one might think she entered my room. I'll be precise: she reached the door, opened it without knocking, kept one foot out of the room so the door wouldn't shut and asked me without saying my name or looking at me: "How much longer do you think you'll be staying in bed?"

"Excuse me, how can I tell? I'm not a doctor," I hinted at the doctor ban. I no longer mind being cheeky. I'll cop it anyway.

"I need to fill out forms about your injury. We'll get money for it. Oh well, never mind. I'll put down a fortnight in bed," she said and left. Witch. I have no other words. An evil witch. All she needs is the broom.

Evening

I fell asleep for the whole day. It's probably better for me to sleep and not be here. In my last dream I saw people kicking me as I lay on the road and one of them put his knee on my neck. I try to say I can't breathe. Max and Francesca stand to the side and watch. I try to shout, to make a sound and I cannot. I shout and the voice doesn't come out. When a sound finally came out of me, Fronella came over and woke me up and said: "You were screaming in your sleep again." "What did I say?" I asked her. "I didn't understand. Go back to sleep."

The dreams come even during the day, when I am not asleep. I intentionally put a different reality into my nightmares, in which I'm loved and wanted. I picture myself as a girl running in an open field with my long hair blowing free in the wind, I skip lightly forward and there right in front of me stand two young and beautiful parents with their hands outstretched towards me like the breadth of their hearts so that I can curl up into them.

At the end of this exciting scene I return, disappointed, to reality.

I've lost faith in human beings and I've lost my place in this world.

1937 Thursday, January 21ˢᵗ.

Two weeks have passed. I can already sit up. I wanted to go down to eat, Francesca informed me, through Fronella, that for now I was not allowed to leave my room to any room in the house. "You're in disgrace."

I'm nearly out of space in this notebook.

Sunday, March 7ᵗʰ.

Today I received an announcement. Not only was I humiliated with the beatings, but the old folks announced it at dinner. These parents announce. I'm never asked my opinion. The announcement was that I was quitting the vocational school I was sent to when I first came here, and that they had enrolled me in a sewing workshop. In the middle of the school year. That's what they decided. The reason for such a change I still don't know. My most painful difficulties are being separated from "Our Kitchen" classes, where we learned to cook and bake, and from a few friends in my class.

I'm a stone the Oberlanders kick around the hopscotch squares marked in chalk on the playground. But the playground is the playground of my life.

Monday, March 8th.

Saying goodbye to my classmates was very awkward. I didn't even know why I was leaving. Frida and Masha promised they'd keep in touch. I don't know how they'll do that.

Leon came over to me as I was gathering up my things and said to me in a weak, quivering voice: "Rennie, I'm really sorry you're leaving. Every morning when I woke up I knew I could look at you. Because of you I was happy to come to this crap school. I never had the courage to say anything. I suppose it's a bit late now to tell you that."

I felt his excitement. He spoke from the heart. My heart quivered with him. Leon is a kid who doesn't stand out, a quiet one. Rather cute actually. The pimples on his face smiled at me at that moment.

"Leon, yes, it's a little too late now. I'm going now." I felt sorry for him. Really.

His eyes welled up with tears. I don't think I'll forget this goodbye.

Wednesday, March 9th. Morning

Dear diary, dear friend. I need to go to the sewing workshop today. Max will drive me in his fancy car and show me the way there.

What will it be like? My heart is all aquiver.

After dinner.

Finally, something good. The workshop was very pleasant. Nine girls of different ages. They were all happy to see me. I'm beginning to learn how to do the work. The atmosphere is light and pleasant.

I think this is a wonderful change for me. Dear diary, are you happy to hear the news?

1937. Sunday, April 11th.

Today I had my 14th birthday celebration because it's Sunday so all the guests can come. I did my best to be well-behaved and make the Oberlanders proud.

I showered well, washed my hair, Fronella braided my hair in two braids for me and wrapped them around my head. She bought me a fabric flower and attached it with my pins to my temples. I wore the new dress that Francesca asked me to wear and wore matching lacquered shoes.

I welcomed each guest with a wide smile. I ate with the napkin spread on my lap, my elbows were not on the table, I ate at a moderate pace and did not speak with food in my mouth.

I felt that everyone was examining me to see if the Oberlanders' acquisition had been successful.

I received a lot of very expensive gifts, most of which I don't need at all. Only one gift is worthwhile and arrived just in time: a blank, lined notebook for writing a diary. A notebook with a red leather cover with a pattern of flowers decorating each corner of every page. This will be the notebook for the next diary that I will need very soon.

Wednesday, April 14th.

Dear Diary, this is the last page in my diary, which will now be called "Diary Number One". I will write briefly since there's not much space, and end on an optimistic note:

In our small sewing shop I feel cozy and free. I talk quite a bit there. I have friends there. For now I only do manual work with needle and thread; I still don't use a sewing machine. I have another way of professional advancement in the sewing shop. I sew buttons and make an invisible inner seam to alter dresses and pants.

Sewing the buttons on requires precise expertise ,which

I was taught very patiently: I pass the needle through the buttonholes ten times, from one side of the fabric to the other, then twist the thread on the outside of the fabric around the ten threads where the button meets the fabric, then to the inside of the fabric. There I make two cross stitches over all the threads and make a knot. It's the same thing every time, one button and another button and again and again. What's important to me is that I'm more comfortable here than at school or at home. The conversations with the girls pass the time pleasantly. I love our breaks, where we get together for a cup of coffee and a sandwich, laughing and enjoying the companionship, and play great music on a gramophone whose handle we all love to turn so we take turns operating. I listen to different and complex life stories. We are honest with each other. Sometimes we cry together and sometimes we burst out laughing.

♥ *End of notebook number 1* ♥

I've finished reading an entire notebook, skipping lightly. What should I do now, until the custodian arrives? Ah, I'll keep reading. The cover page says "Notebook number 3. Do not read. Strictly private." At the center of the cover page, I wrote in large, ornate lettering "Property of Rennie Freidman". I folded the left-hand corner of the page, wrote "Please no peeking" on the front and under it I wrote "You peeked". Under the right-hand corner I wrote, in red, *In allen vier Ecken/ soll Liebe drinstrecken.*[31]

---

31. "Love should stretch into all four corners" (German)

The moment he appeared in the doorway I recalled his name: Franz Kunstlinger. I didn't even have time to open notebook #3. I tucked it into the drawer under the red diary, my second diary.

Now that I'm sixteen, this custodian is sitting alone with me in my room. He's still a stranger but I feel like he brings with him some kind of calm that you just can't buy at the store. Those so-called "parents" of mine, Francesca and Max, know about this, of course. They would never in a blue moon let me bring a stranger into their house and certainly not to meet alone in my room if they've not confirmed his arrival a few days in advance. The truth is, none of my girlfriends ever come to this house. I don't invite friends here. I could be proud of the splendor of this house, but the walls and furniture never spoke to me or moved me. That's not the point of my life. I want the best for the few friends I have and that's why none of them are invited to the Oberlander house. This is a cold castle and not a warm home for me.

Franz looked around and I remembered him looking in our previous encounter, the first visit. He looked around my whole huge room. At the carved dresser with drawer buttons that look like violets, at the rug spread out in the center of the room, at the boxes of games that Fronella put on top of each other inside the two-door glass cabinet, at the red wooden desk with the shelves over it and my textbooks on them, on the desk covered in brown glass, and the upholstered chair standing next to it that's nice to the touch, at the wide bed, with its bedspread made of pieces of fabric artfully sewn together. He could not have guessed that under the blanket, my sheep Laura is waiting for me. I don't know if he admires the size of this room, its abundance or its perfect arrangement.

I wanted to continue his thoughts and told him like I was revealing a secret: "This is their girls' room. That's why it's so big. They were killed in a car accident before I got here." Franz nodded his head with a somber expression on his face and I realized he knew about it.

Although it's not easy for me to talk about myself, and certainly difficult for me to speak my truth, I decided that this conversation will be my last option to get myself out of here and that I will tell everything as honestly as I can. Could I do that? Enough, no masks now. The truth is I want to leave this lopsided house, but don't know where I might end up. I'm afraid that I might fall into a deeper pit than this and then I won't even have Fronella and the sewing shop.

I hope my decisions and my execution won't be like the distance between two parallel lines that will never meet. This is a very clever fact I learned from Ernest Winter when he drew two parallel lines in the snow with his finger. I think to myself, with a bitter laugh, that the distance between my decisions and my execution is also like the love between Francesca and me.

Franz asks me to tell him about my life in this house. I hold in my hand the red-bound diary notebook, perhaps so as not to miss anything important. But the truth is it's funny to me now, I remember everything that happened to me and don't need the notebook. I just don't know how to behave with a stranger who told me over two years ago with a grown-up seriousness that he was the man who wanted to help me with settling in with this family, then disappeared when I needed him most in the world.

"So, what's been going on with you here since we first met?" He tries to start the conversation, but my mouth won't open. All kinds of sentences go through my head as good opening sentences, but I can't begin to tell. I can no longer talk about myself with a stranger who'd let me down for so long and because of whom my skin on my bottom had peeled. Why should I believe this man?

"I feel bad here," I managed to say.

"You must tell me. If you're not doing well and you want to get out of this house, then let me know, so that I can help you right now. But you need to talk to me. It's very difficult to get a girl out of her house, her family, if she loves the place and if she's feeling good there. Tell me everything," he said over and over again.

Silence. Only my eyes tell him a story.

"If you do not speak, I cannot help you."

And suddenly, as if someone flipped a switch, the words spill out of me as if I'm not the one speaking. My mouth pours out my words like the water coming out of a mountain spring.

"When I was forcibly taken out of the house I loved and grew up in, Schwester Hilde's house, when the Oberlander couple virtually kidnapped me, I could not stop the sadness. I allowed myself to cry only when I was here, in my room. All day and all night I thought of Schwester Hilde. I felt a big black hole inside my heart. I couldn't laugh, I couldn't get along in this house at all. My anger at being taken from my place grew as the days passed. The whole world seemed lost to me. I wrote a diary. This notebook became my best friend, it's stained with tears. Look," and I open it before him at a random page. "You can see my tears even there." I read the sentence "Ernest, what are you doing now? Do you have a new girlfriend? Do you still remember me?" And close the notebook.

"The heaviest moments were my moments of falling asleep. Oh. I went to sleep with my door closed and the whole room dark. *So ist es.* I imagined mountains of roses, white lily flowers, red maple branches and fragrant carnations growing near my bed, close-up. I imagined Schwester Hilde sitting next to me singing only to me in her gentle voice, *Guten Abend, gut' Nacht.* I was only able to fall asleep when I felt Hilde's breathing next to me. "

I tell him about Hilde, but he stops me: "I just want to hear about this house." He too, despite my feeling that he could be my lifeline, is not interested in hearing my voice the way I want to make it heard and knowing about the warm place I had. I feel like he, too, is directing me and trying to control me.

And yet I choose to continue as he asks, because I have no better option: "I've never understood why this couple wanted to be my parents. They never asked me how I was, never smiled at me, they only speak in commands. The words I hear every morning and every evening are "Be upstanding. We don't want you to disgrace us. "

"Irena, now you're starting to tell me about your parents in this house. Keep it up." The custodian looks deep into my eyes. "Please, now just tell me about the relationship you have in this house. You're running away from the story I want to hear."

You're running away. You're running away, I think to myself. I immediately get to the story, I stroke my thoughts inside my head. Yes, I'm running away. Oh, you will hear soon enough. You will soon know what it means to flee. I shift my legs and place my left foot on my right. I tell myself that I find it hard to describe the truth because it hurts deep in my heart and my spring doesn't really flow like they do in the mountains. I take a deep breath.

I tell Franz about the daily beatings and about running to town hall. I take time to go over the "mother of all beatings" in detail. I take care to tell him I looked for him. I tell him nothing about Laura. That's my own business and he'll understand everything without knowing about that. That's a secret matter between Hilde and me. Even when I open myself to him I leave myself corners that are mine alone.

Franz looks increasingly more surprised and attentive. He's serious and makes notes in a small notebook he takes out of his shirt pocket, and then puts the notebook back and takes it out again for more notes, again and again, all through my story. I finish my tale with mixed feelings of fatigue and satisfaction.

"How did you get over the pain?" Franz asks. Perhaps he's

hoping to hear that Francesca came to me afterwards and helped me.

Now the story just came out of me, real and flowing.

Franz listened intently. I've learned to know people by the way their body moves. I can look at the world without showing the world my inside. I know how to control my body and my expressions. Since arriving at Zwickau I've learned that it's better for me to seem like I'm strong and know what I want and leave for myself, in my room, the weakness and hardship.

"I'm stunned. Such a distinguished family all throughout Saxony. Not all that glitters is moral and kind-hearted." He hangs his head. He's embarrassed. "Only now, from your mouth, do I understand your running away from a year ago. I read in the file that you were at town hall and that Max reported that everything was all right. They are the best-regarded couple in town. Max donates to orphanages and his wife sends Christmas presents to many families. I didn't think I had to read everything in your file. I trusted that couple. I didn't know you were going through such suffering. I truly didn't know," he repeats with a very serious expression. "I need to question the adopted child, not just the adoptive parents," he notes, to me or to himself.

Before he leaves, Franz tells me that he will come next week at the same hour. He asks me to leave all details of our conversation secret. "You are skilled at keeping secrets and keeping your expression so it doesn't reveal what you're going through, so do the same with the conversation we had now." I nod my head in agreement.

A second after he leaves my room he comes back and says, "This time you did the talking. Next time, I'll talk."

And he left.

I remained curious.

I decided that if Franz Kunstlinger arrives next week at the agreed-upon time, then maybe there were still good people left in the world around me.

This week is passing slowly, really creeping along. I wanted it to pass already so we could meet again in my room and hear what he had to say to me. The time after my sewing job is broken down into hours, and the hours into minutes. I make myself laugh thinking that the world has probably extended the time allotted to one minute. It's true that every hour has sixty minutes, but now every minute has been extended. I look, doing nothing. at the annoying cuckoo clock that hangs in the hallway in front of my room. I listen to every minute passing, counting the cuckoo calls every hour and every half hour. Again and again I see that the cuckoo is not wrong...

Throughout these moments I want to know only one thing: What does Franz Kunstlinger want to tell me?

Sometimes on Sundays Francesca and Max became ordinary, even happy, people. Anyone looking at us from the outside might think they were looking at a father, mother and daughter. I was lucky this Sunday too, the long week I waited for to end. The three of us went to a concert where we listened to piano works by the great composer Schumann, who was born in Zwickau and is a source of great pride for the city's music lovers. It was actually my time with the Oberlanders that exposed me to the world of music and learned to appreciate and enjoy it. I close my eyes when I hear music and drift to imaginary places.

Discipline and obedience were their first priority in my education, love of music came second. I don't know if they really love music, if they are at all capable of loving anything in the world, or if they go to concerts only to appear cultured.

After the concert was over, we took the family car to the nearby valley and walked under the red brick bridge. As usual I counted ninety-eight arcs there. Max – who loves the "most":

the richest, the most well-connected, the most fashionable, the owner of the newest car, the best concert, the most delicious meal and also the most rustic, undisciplined girl – told us again that it was the tallest railway bridge in the world. It's not at all clear to me how humans built it. This passed the time. These Sunday outings were the bright spots in my life. If there's a place in Zwickau that I'm willing to be in now, this is it.

I began to believe that there were people left who were as good as their word... Franz arrived as promised. I was flooded by the pleasant feeling I'd already forgotten: that there was someone who cared for me and wanted me to be well. We sat like two adults around the dining table in my room. Fronella served coffee with cheesecake topped with sweet cherries. She snuck me a friendly wink. I felt very grown up.

"Would you like to stay here and officially become their adopted daughter? I must know before we continue the conversation."

"I want to get out of here. Obviously. I... I... I hate them," I stated decisively.

"In the previous meeting I had to learn everything about you. I had to be confident in my steps. I hold a big responsibility for your future."

I marveled and explored without a sound.

"There's a possibility I'll get you out of here."

"And where will I live?"

"I will help you reach Palestine."

"What is this Pasteline? A new orphanage? Another family?"

"No. It's the Land of Israel. This is the place the Jews dream of reaching."

"Jews? What do I have to do with Jews?"

Franz did not immediately reply. There was a long pause that seemed to me as long as my longing for the real Laura and the maple tree.

"Irena, you are a Jew."

"What???"

"Everyone who raised you knew it but chose to keep it secret. It really is a big and important secret."

It was as if he put my whole life in a glass, quickly stirred it in one direction, changed the stirring direction and then turned it over and shook it over and over again and then served it to me to drink. Now I have something new to manage, something that fills the entire space of the room and pushes hard against the shuttered windows as if it wants to spill out onto the street and throughout the city.

I think my heart stopped beating.

"Is that true? Are you sure?"

"Yes. Absolutely."

"Do they know in this house that I'm Jewish? Did Hilde also know this truth?"

"Yes. They do and she did."

We fell silent again. Only the cuckoo in the clock carried on as usual. For it, nothing had changed.

And we remained silent.

"Ummmmm. So everyone lied to me? Why? What's going on here?"

"You understand that in the current situation in Germany we won't turn any Christian into a Jew, right? Being a Jew today is dangerous, as you know."

"Certainly. How can one not know and feel the reality in Germany, even at my age? For some reason Max taught me right after I came here about the Nuremberg Laws that our Reichstag enacted for racial purity. If Max knew I was Jewish, why did he tell me this news? Why? What did he want to convey? That he would save me? Nonsense! He wouldn't bend over to help me, he would bend over to beat me. And now I understand why he took the time to explain that the state clearly declared that 'the designation 'Jew' would be determined by race and blood and not by religious affiliation'. I like going to church and listening to the heavenly music there. I like to look at the stained glass in churches. It's my world. What will happen? What's going on in my world? How come I'm Jewish? Me? Me?! Jewish? Are you sure about this? How do these things happen in my life? What is this? Is everyone allowed to play around with my life? What are these lies? I was raised by nuns. I pray a Christian morning prayer and cross myself every day. Enough. Enough. Enough. Leave me alone, all of you. Let me be me. It's my right."

I couldn't stop talking, as if my speech could put off facing the facts.

"Look, Irena. You understand that they took a Jewish girl into their home because they don't care what a person's religion is. Everyone was born equal. You can keep loving church music. But because there are so many in Germany who are keen to know who is or is not Jewish, it is very dangerous for Jews these days. Keep up your normal lifestyle, keep acting like a Christian for now. Do not reveal your secret to anyone in the world. "

There was silence again. A deep silence where my inner voices tried to overcome each other. I received a secret as a gift.

"Palestine??" I asked, my voice trembling.

"You'll get there with your friends, who would also be travelling there without their parents. Francesca and Max know what we are discussing now. They are ready to say goodbye to you. From now on I will guide you through all the steps until you reach Palestine."

"And when will you tell me about this place? And who will I live with?" And- And-?

I was awash with so many annoying question marks. So many that I didn't know where to begin.

"Next time," he said. "In the meantime, come to grips with your new identity. Easy does it."

We said goodbye.

I was left alone, with the knowledge that my "parents" also shared this secret.

JOHANNA

It seemed to me that I hadn't been to Riga for ages. The telegram announcing my homecoming arrived on time and I was greeted with joy and abundant love. My room was as I'd left it and made me understand, when I ascribed a soul to it, that there were those who accepted me as though nothing had happened. My life carried on from the point at which they stopped.

Tanny arrived with her happy baby, which brought much joy to our Saturdays. My mother's concern for that baby shrank my heart and flooded me with guilt. I was afraid to hold Tanny's baby, I was afraid of my own feelings. My mother used to ask me half-seriously and half-sarcastically "Well, did you enjoy Leipzig? Didn't you miss your theater after such a long time?" And "When will you be back to the theater?" and "Did you take the exams at the Leipzig Theater?"

The next day I popped over to sweet Diana.

"Johannuchka, you're back? I'm so happy to see you!" And she gave me a warm hug. "Let me look at you. I can't believe it! What a beautiful body. How did you do it? Did you actually give birth or was it all a dream?"

I twirled like a model. "What's new in my arena?" I asked. "There's actually something new," she ignored my question and passed the answer to her arena as she showed me her finger. With an engagement ring.

"Who with?"

"Don't be silly. What kind of question is that? With Bera'le, of course. You know I'm also done with all these wild parties. That's it, I've been domesticated. Bera'le is my one and only."

"Wonderful. Exciting," I said and was envious.

"Diana, you will remember that my secret must remain strictly confidential?"

"Johannuchka, what's up with you? Of course."

"How did you find out about Kaminski? Did the show really fold?"

"Let's leave Kaminski to the side for now. First, tell me how you feel. What's it like giving birth? How is the baby?"

I related everything in detail. Then I questioned her again about Kaminski and the show. "I wonder why Andris didn't replace us both in our roles, rather than cancelling the entire show."

Her face grew gravely serious. She sat down by my side and told me with a husky voice a fact that absolutely floored me: "Kaminski's departure was in all the papers. There was an absolute flood of gossip around here. You're lucky that your name wasn't mentioned at all; you were mentioned as one of the people who paid the price for the show being cancelled because of him."

"How come my mother and sisters never told me about that?"

"That is strange."

"No, actually it's not strange at all. I understand. I'm the one who wrote them the telegram about the show getting cancelled because of Kaminski leaving. They realized I knew and didn't want to hurt me."

If my life is divided into acts, this was the curtain rising on the third act. I'd left Riga as a woman with hopes of motherhood and a couplehood with my beloved and came back a bitter woman. The hopes fading away stung me and announced decisively that they belonged to the past.

The new facts made it clear to me that I would not visit the theater and would certainly not go back to being an actress. I had become *persona non grata* in the world I loved so much.

At home I felt that my mother knew my secret and chose to cooperate with me, to make it easier for me. Perhaps her maternal instinct explained my urgent journey and my failure to return to the theater reaffirmed her maternal senses. My suspicion arose because she stopped wondering why I was not going back to the theater.

As the days passed, I learned that Riga had changed before my eyes. Many Jews flocked to it. Its cultural life flourished and many possibilities opened up in this city. Trade flourished, new banks opened, all of them owned by Jews, many Jewish schools were added, and the numerous shades of Judaism in this city lived together in impressive harmony.

In Lea, unlike for Diana and me, there was no change.

I started passing the time by preparing special and particularly delicious dinners. I loved going to the market and buying fresh vegetables and making colorful and unconventional vegetable combinations. I loved to spice dishes in original ways. My mother and Lea loved my creativity. These meals allowed us to sit together and talk to each other. It's a wonderful memory of being together with my mother, who had always cared so much for us.

"My Lea, is it not a pity I will have no grandchildren from you?" Mother asked in a hesitant voice, as if she wasn't sure the question was in place. This conversation, in one variation or another, repeated itself every few days.

"Mom, how many more times will we discuss this? No, you will have no grandchildren from me," Lea replied angrily.

"Lea'le, you don't have to get upset. I'm just saying how I feel," Mom said and continued eating my salad. "Mom," Lea straightened up and pounded her fist on the table "Mom, I'm fine as I am. I'm not looking for a husband. Get that expectation out of your head."

I was silent. An image from the past floated into my head: Lea going into her room with a friend, a woman I didn't know, and locking the door from the inside, which was hardly ever done in our house.

Lea remained single and lived with mother at home. She'd already started her final year of graduate school. She sounded so determined and happy, that no one expected anything to change. My mother stopped wishing for her other grandchildren to come from Lea, and so I became the object of family expectations. Mother begged me with explicit statements and with hints, both clear and subtle, to get out there and find a husband, get married and have children. According to her, I was already a bit old because at the age of twenty-one and a half most of the women are married and the worthy men have already been caught in the net.

As the days passed, when much water had flowed even in our Daugava river, as they say, I discovered that mother's words had seeped into me. I realized that I was in a rut and it became important for me to find a Jewish husband, to experience a real relationship and not just fall in love, to build my nest and pad it with the unfulfilled love that was bubbling inside me. The decision to take the initiative grew within me day after day. As the boredom swelled and took hold within me, the need to get out of here and build a home for myself grew.

I longed to not be stuck within the memories of Kaminski and the girl I abandoned.

I began hatching plans to find a husband for life. I wanted a rich man. I traveled several times by first class train from Riga to St. Petersburg and back, sat in the best restaurants and attended concerts. I wanted to catch the eye of an eligible man when I was looking attractive. Sadly, I did not stop comparing every man to the handsome, charismatic Kaminski, and the holes in my net widened every trip until the whole program failed.

One spring evening I put my makeup on, wore my favorite

dark green dress fastened with a brooch, fine, delicate pant-yhose, high-heeled shoes in a matching color, and a small, unique hat elegantly placed over my brown hair, and went with much determination to the Jewish social club to hunt my future before it escapes forever.

I couldn't find the entrance and accidentally entered the hall next door. I realized that this was the place Diana described to me where weddings took place, and that this is where I will come to celebrate her wedding to her Jewish beloved, her Bera'le. I wished in my heart that I would come to this hall intentionally and that the reason for my arrival would be myself. I regained some composure. Right in front of me stood a bright, ornate sign directing me to the café. How had I not seen this sign before? I asked myself. I adjusted my hat, shook some imag-inary crumbs from my dress and walked upright and deter-mined thrusting my chest forward, though my heart told me to back off. I sat down at an empty table. I looked around my charming surroundings, the polished wooden furniture, the chandeliers dangling from the ceiling, the bar with the counter and high chairs beside it, I heard the background music that made the stay pleasant and I smiled inwardly. It's nice here, I noted to myself. The languages spoken around me were Latvi-an, of course, German and also Yiddish. People laughed, chat-ted, shook hands, drank, raised a voice and someone burst into song with a drink in his hand. They sat in pairs and groups, here and there a woman or a man alone. I ordered a glass of vodka and sipped leisurely. I felt very ambitious.

This is how I behaved the other times I visited the Jewish club. I was hoping someone would invite me to their table even though everyone seemed to be busy with their own. I didn't give up immediately because I realized that the patron-age changed every evening. I still had hope. It did occasionally happen that someone would sit next to me or buy me a drink, but I didn't like any of them. This one spoke only Yiddish and thus made it clear to me that he was not in tune with Western culture, that one was too fat for my taste, another was very old and yet another had a shrill voice that hurt my ears. Even that was a reason for me to reject a guy. Every detail, even the most inconsequential, disqualified men immediately. I became very critical. I persevered with these visits for a considerable time, before finally, utterly giving up. I realized that my mission had failed and would continue to fail. This wasn't the way. I had to find different stones to pave my way with.

Throughout these mission-directed days my friendship with Diana, helping her choosing a dress and shoes for her wedding was like a warm ray of sunshine on a cold day. We used to meet and walk from one bridal salon to another. Diana tried the outfits on and I expressed my opinions. I felt like I was in training for my own future.

One day, after we finally chose the fabric from which her dress would be sewn, and the cut of the dress from the French *Vogue* magazine with the help of her seamstress, I announced: "Diana, would you agree for me to sew your veil for you? I would be so happy to do that."

"My dearest. A great idea. Surprise me," she jumped happily.

There was no end to the sense of creative renewal I felt as I designed the veil, but at the same time as I sewed, my tears sometimes soaked the sheer, wavy white fabric. Roses were woven into the fabric of her dress and in her hair I interlaced white roses, with one wine-red rose among them.

Diana got married in the hall I stumbled into, the one next to the club. I spent the minutes before the ceremony at her side. She was radiant with happiness in her beautiful lace dress with the special veil. It was both a happy and sad evening. I sat with my family. Tanny couldn't come because of the baby. Opposite us sat two friends who were very communicative. They got up, held out their hands to Lea, my mother and me for an introductory handshake. The more attractive one of them introduced himself as Abram. He had a captivating smile. I forced myself not to stare at him and shifted my gaze to the hall. The tables were laden with good food. There was a happy atmosphere in the air. To this was added the moving Jewish music playing and the wine that filled with glasses without pause. Diana looked happy; she and Bera'le were a couple in love.

When the dancing began Abram chivalrously invited me to dance the Waltz with him. I relished Strauss's music. I had a bit of a hard time dancing after those dry years. I hope I didn't leave my heelprints on his shoes... but the main thing was to be held in his masculine arms.

Immediately afterwards Abram surprised me when he got up and informed the occupants of the table: "We need to leave now." He approached me, only me, and added, "It was a pleasure to meet you." I noticed my mother watching me very carefully. "It was a pleasure to meet you, too," I replied. That concluded this short relationship. I noted to myself that Abram was a man after my own heart. I loved his clever, beautiful blue eyes, his full hair, his shapely body. Even his mustache - and I had previously stated more than once that I hated mustaches - even his wispy mustache was to my liking.

I enrolled in a hat sewing course, my great love. I decided to be a hatter. All my creativity burst from me through my designs. I found a sewing shop to work in and went there six mornings a week, happy to meet with my colleagues, and in the evenings I came home again. From time to time, I agreed to go out to concerts, but I did not dare go to the theater. I was afraid of meeting my director, the talented, committed Andris, and I did not know what I would do if we'd met.

I must get back to the here and now. Two boys walk on their toes by the door of our room. Silence. The middle of the night.

I'm in my bed. Mia is sound asleep. I try not to think about tomorrow. Odd that we are all to be gathered in the square at four in the morning. It's a snowy winter and so cold. There's a sentence that keeps coming back to me: Mia is with me. Eddie the hero is gone and Abram has disappeared. And Rennie? Where is Rennie? Time passes. It's two o'clock. I have two hours ahead of me.

I celebrated my twenty-second birthday with my family. I went to several weddings of the last girls to be married from my class. During these celebrations I was flooded with my special moment, my birth. Sadness took the place of the expected happiness. I sometimes left the festivities.

I celebrated my twenty-third birthday and kept making hats and went on the occasional date with an enthusiastic suitor. Rennie would come to my mind at night. When it was cold outside I hoped she wasn't cold. When it was hot I whispered to myself "Wear a hat."

I was twenty-four and the main thing I can remember now from this year is the guilt of leaving my girl, melancholy and exhausting reflections on walking in my expected groove.

I was twenty-five and still single. The internal tortures of punishment and reward in the world have taken their place and evolved from night to night this year. I realized I was paying for abandoning my baby. I got to the point where I came to terms with the fact that this was my destiny. My mother is getting older, Etta is becoming a Zionist, and me? No external change. A renowned hatter and a good friend of Diana. I did not connect with other friends, but was content with attending birthday get-togethers or a joint friend trip. I was too melancholy to enjoy deep friendships. I found it enough to carry my secret in my house in front of the people closest to me in the world.

When I celebrated my twenty-sixth birthday Rennie was already five. Soon she would start going to school and learning to read. I wondered where she was. She must have already found herself in a different orphanage. The disturbing thoughts would not confine themselves to night-time; they snuck into my waking hours. I wondered whether Kaminski's parents were still sending her birthday presents, as Adele promised, or whether they'd long since forgotten she even existed, and whether they still pay for her upkeep. I tried to push these thoughts away because my hands were tied in this matter. I thought to myself that the woodpecker inside my head had already drilled a large enough hole and should probably let me be. My birthdays, the marking of another year passing, were the hardest. I missed being loved by a man; I was worried about my girl; and most of all I was wracked by guilt. I longed to stop thinking about Rennie, but usually couldn't manage. I hoped life was smiling on her despite her growing up with no parents and being a Jew amongst Christians.

During my twenty-seventh birthday celebrations, with an apple strudel made of paper-thin dough expertly prepared by my mother, when she hinted again that I was quite old for marriage, a thought came into my brain to go to Gottleuba and take my daughter back. At least I won't be alone and my daughter would have a mother and the incessant annoyances would finally stop.

That idea haunted me at night, accompanied me while I made my hats. I fell in love with it. I couldn't find a reason not to go through with it. I felt weak faced with my lack of practical initiative. I saw Rennie looking at me with a piercing, begging look. I heard her whispering in my dream "Mother. My mother." These thoughts became nightmares. Instead of being an old maid I could be the mother of my girl. What could be more right than that? In my waking dreams I imagined the conversation with my family, gathered the right words and watched my mother's mouth drop open and longed for her to be happy for having a ready-made granddaughter. I tortured myself for my decision to abandon my baby, for allowing myself to listen to an egotistical woman and her son who knows what abandonment meant, since he'd abandoned me, the theater, and Riga. I had sold my baby to wealthy people who, because their money allowed them to arrange things as they like, made me give up my own flesh and blood. I felt sorry for myself for not allowing my maternal voice to emerge from me and declare that I would raise my child no matter what. I wondered about myself, for being so spineless and impressionable. At night a dream came back to me in which I would drive to the orphanage, meet Rennie, and just as I was about to see her gaze, the dream would end. I never finished it and could not deduce from it if my girl would like to move in and live with me or would rather stay with Hilde. I rejected the possibility that she'd already been adopted by a family. I lived in an alternative world that increasingly existed inside my head. At work I functioned and was creative and sociable, but at home I became eccentric and detached. I knew that my mother was very worried and that the constant worry had turned her hair white.

I had a strange dream that I could not forget: in my dream I'm riding a bike in the mountains. I rest my bike on a tree trunk and take a walk. I can't remember the purpose of the walk, but when evening falls I have to find the bike and can't remember where I'd left it. I walk on and on until darkness falls. I change directions until I meet a young man who tells me he saw a bike on the way. A wave of joy floods me. He walks a long way with me. I believe he's going with me to the bike, but he leaves me unexpectedly and I am left with only a direction. Here I woke up.

I thought a lot about the dream and began to realize that the bike expresses a ride that I have to make and that I must be very attentive to the path and not lose it. I then determined that the bike was Rennie who'd been abandoned and that now I could no longer find, even if I find help on the way. On third thought the bike was me, me who had abandoned myself and I can't use myself in the right way and had already lost myself somewhere. At any rate, this dream showed me that I needed to find my own way, and that I couldn't get help for my personal right path.

I internalized a deep realization that would stay with me for the rest of my life: a woman must listen to the small voice inside her showing her the way by instinct. No-one else, not even the father, can show her her own way of motherhood.

I was dreaming, even when awake. I lived in two parallel worlds. I became the subject of whispers and concerns.

I readily accepted Tanny's invitation to dinner at her house. There, with no prior notice, Tanny introduced me to their guest. It was Abram, the man I'd Waltzed with at Diana's wedding. When I came into the kitchen to help Tanny serve the main course, she asked with a hint of a smile: "Well, Yanna, how do you like Abram? What say you?" "Give me time," I replied sharply and went out to the living room, taking care to look my best. Abram was interested in me, would not take his eyes off me. I wanted to dive into the blue of his eyes, through which I'd seen his kindness at Diana's wedding. I realized he'd already received the relevant information before this evening and he seemed to like me. The conversation flowed in German and Latvian, all four of us moving easily between the two languages.

"I served in the Latvian military. I enjoyed being a soldier and a commander. I found it interesting to move from place to place. A military man's life is not confined to the one spot, so I never found the time to start a family." I thought he was only saying this to me.

The more he spoke, the more I relished every additional sentence because it was becoming clear this guy was a bachelor. Not a divorcee or a widower, heaven forbid.

The next sentence made me feel even better: "I've settled in

Riga recently and I deal in flax," he said modestly. "It turns out I can be a trader, even a good one, though I started pretty late in life. My situation in business is improving very nicely. This is an interesting world where I have to be attentive to all the business winds."

I felt very free in his company and spoke about the theater, about my rapid rise in accepting roles. "I loved the different characters I played. It was challenging and satisfying to be for a moment a femme fatale, and the next a nice, opinionated girl, to play the tough one and to also play a carefree little girl with a squeaky voice."

He looked at me appreciatively.

"My advice, Abram - beware of this actress." Tanny made us all laugh. "She can pretend. She can be the ice queen and look sensitive and in love."

"Tanny, hey, he might believe you. No, it's not like that. I've left the game. I don't act anymore," I said and started weaving my big pretense, and put on the mask of my life. "My life turned around. A turnaround that landed on me three months before the premiere. I traveled to Germany to audition for a role at the Leipzig Theater and ended up staying there. It was just *Wunderbar*[32]. I felt that I was not in the right place in my life and that I didn't want to continue to be an actress. I felt an inner need to drive a stick into the wheel of my bike and stop the ride. I stopped and got off. I left it all, from one day to the next."

No one interrupted my story. Tanny and her Gregori wanted Abram to admire me and to wish to meet me again, so they cleared the stage for me. Now my secret began to be constructed in front of Abram as well. "My time in Leipzig was extended because I wanted to find what I wanted to do. I heard lovely concerts and operas. When I returned I found my destiny, I am a hatter. I really enjoy watching my creations live on the heads

---

32. Wonderful (German)

of the women of the city. Millinery is a very creative job and I enjoy it so much."

When I heard the story of my life, I was afraid for a moment that Abram would fend off any continued acquaintance with me. Leaving the theater three months before a premiere sounded like the story of a very unstable and capricious woman. But Abram listened calmly and responded in the most wonderful way possible: "Life can be full of upheavals; it's great that you caught yourself before the last minute." I smiled and he added: "I could have carried on in the military, but sometimes we have to stop everything and put the considerations for our moves on the balance. Every move in our life has advantages and disadvantages. One can't rush forward without occasionally thinking about the future in light of the past and the present. When I stopped and thought about being a military man, I realized I was erasing the possibility of being a family man. I decided to stop this situation I was already used to, and leave the military. I, too, got off my bike even though I had a good salary and excellent working conditions."

With these words Abram found a common denominator between the two of us, except that mine was built on shaky ground. I realized I had to continue with my lie.

The evening continued pleasantly and towards midnight Abram approached me and said as he looked casually into my eyes: "Johanna, how about we both meet in a café or at a cultural event?"

His suggestion sounded like it flowed on naturally from what was beginning to form between the two of us and I replied, "A café is a wonderful idea. We can continue to get to know each other."

I suggested the café Kaminski and I used to frequent. I felt that Abram could be the correction in my life that would erase the memories I carried and allow me to tread wherever I wished. Then, with Kaminski, I experienced a frenzy of passion. Today

I know it was immature love, which was less welcomed by my palate of memories.

When we sat down, I whispered in the waiter's ears and asked them to play the *Moldau*. The waiter happily agreed. I wished to recreate the excitement I felt in this place in the past, this time with the man being worthy of my thrill, and the music in the background to be chosen by me. Even now, whenever I hear the piece in my imagination, I get excited. The flow of the river matched the flow of our relationship. In the movement where two springs flow, one hot and the other cold, I wondered for a brief moment which of us would take the cold role.

Tanny told me that in a marital relationship one person complements the other, and that sometimes you change without meaning to, because the behavior of the other person leads you to it. She drew the Chinese yin-yang symbol to illustrate her point.

Yes, there were days when I could choose the man, the location, the music. Days when the option to choose was clearly present in my life. I did not know then that there would appear a long-armed monster that would take over and overwhelm us, leaving us no individual choice, and would keep biting until it wiped everything out.

This time I did not neglect asking about my man's family and opened with: "Tell me about yourself, about your life." Abram smiled, sipped his vodka and willingly shared his story.

"I am a native of the Latvian city of Ventspils, on the Baltic coast, at the mouth of the Venta River. We have the largest port in Latvia. The city is small, certainly compared to Riga. Nowadays the Jewish community in the city numbers only a thousand."

"And where are your parents? Siblings?" I continued. After all, he'd already met part of my family and could have found out more details about my family during the evening at Tanny's. I was determined to know who this man was. I treated this as a very significant task.

"I'm an orphan. Both my parents passed away when I was young, a fact that made my decision to enlist easier. I had no-one to say goodbye to. At the age of twenty I was left alone. My older sister immigrated to New York. She's married there and feels at home in America. University was never an option for me. I like learning, but not in a formal institution."

"Do you see your sister? Are you in touch?" I kept up the interrogation while enjoying the wonderful background music and the exquisite coffee.

"We correspond occasionally. I'm actually a man with no family," he summed up, then changed the topic: "Johanna, I know how old you are. You should know I'm fifteen years older than you." "Abram, what the birth certificate says doesn't matter to me. The fact that you're an older man doesn't bother me at all. On the contrary, I'm happy to meet a man with some life experience." I don't understand why I felt that way, perhaps it was his military man's demeanor that made me feel safe and secure. I was convinced that he was really interested in building a family. He gave me a winning smile. A handsome man, I mused, I'm still lucky such a man stayed single as if waiting for me to be ready for a real relationship.

I recalled my father's saying: "If we wish, in life, to walk fast, it is better to walk alone, but If we want to walk far, it is better to walk together."

Walking together with Abram seemed like a very inviting proposition.

I felt Abram and I were meant for each other. I wondered whether everyone has a predetermined fate and I had to walk my cruel path to get to this moment. Abram voiced my thoughts in an original way when he said out loud: "If I were twenty years old, I'd take my time, but since I'm forty-two I'm ready to jump in the water with you right now." A month later, while we sat in a café after a show, Abram did it chivalrously. He kneeled beside me, took a small ruby-red box from his pocket, produced a golden ring with a small, delicate white diamond and asked: "Will you marry me?". Four words. Four words that encompass a world. Four words I'd longed to hear for nearly ten years. The smallest things can sometimes be the largest. I think a tiny shiver of excitement rushed through him. I looked at him with love, with supreme happiness. At that moment I pictured my mother when she finds out I was to be married and replied: "Yes, my love. Yes, I will marry you."

I was happy to wear a ring, a small ring that managed to stop my night terrors and enabled me to start dreaming about the future ahead. This ring is now stowed away in the inner lining of my suitcase. If I wore it, the Latvians would rip it off my finger.

I wanted to be wrapped in Abram's arms every moment of the day. He did not expect me to be a virgin at my age and was happy with the rich experience I had brought to our bed. I loved the fact that our acts of love were so mature and varied. Abram allowed me to untie the reins of responsibility and control over my life and return to being pampered like a little girl. He blended generosity, punctuality and compassion for others. He was Rigan in character, but also enjoyed the Western culture he so admired, and was open to the winds that blew from it to us. He integrated into the diverse Jewish community that had formed in our city. Abram found a common language with everyone. It was nice for me to be around a person that people connected with so readily.

My whole being was subject to him, I was completely immersed in my love for my future husband. Rennie popped into my mind ever more rarely. Sometimes I thought I was unfair; she was lonely in the world and I'm feeling so wonderful. And Kaminski? Kaminski faded in the light of this wonderful man who filled my life. I moved into his house at 1 Weiswalze Street.

I was so free from the oppressive past that we watched 'Romeo and Juliet' in my theater together. My lips moved soundlessly throughout the entire show. It turned out I still had the play committed to memory. All my fears disappeared.

When we left the theater, I faced him and felt comfortable addressing him in the name of Juliet speaking to her beloved Romeo. I looked at him and recited with feeling: "O gentle Romeo, if thou dost love, pronounce it faithfully".

I was sure Abram recognized the quote and was enjoying the scene, so I continued, adding gestures and a fitting facial expression: "Or, if thou thinkest I am too quickly won / I'll frown and be perverse and say thee nay / So thou wilt woo."[33]

Abram's eyes shone. He came closer and sealed my mouth with a warm, long kiss. My feet left the pavement and I hung on to him, flooded with ardor. Abram became Romeo when he quoted back: "I am no pilot, yet wert thou as far / as that vast shore washed with the farthest sea / I would adventure for such merchandise."[34]

Today I am certain that true love is the greatest gift anyone could wish for.

Before our wedding, Abram bought us a large flat in the center of the city, in a corner block, quite close to the lovely market at 21 Latchaplezha street. Even now, if I close my eyes I can clearly see the entrance to the building, decorated with a mosaic of brown stone. My home, and the entire neighborhood, was special in that its outer wall was cylindrical and looked like a corner tower raising its proud head to the sky. Then, in the first days of my love for Abram, I felt this house expressed Latvian romanticism. The floor of our apartment was laminated with wood, so our footsteps were nearly silent. The notable advantage I loved so much were the large windows that let in plenty of light, even on the dark days of Latvian winter. We used to stand by the windows in the evening with a glass of drink in

---

33. *Romeo and Juliet*, act II scene ii
34. ibid

our hands and watch life buzzing about on the main street and at the nearby park. Our hearts beat and Riga beat with us.

"Half an hour to go. We'll see them come out like mice from the holes soon."

"I'll stay a little longer just to see."

I can already recognize the voices of the two Latvian guards.

"I can hear they the toilet flush again. What do they have to shit when they're starving?"

"Hahaha."

"We're lucky, eh?"

Despite it being our first marriage, we decided on a small wedding, with only those closest to us attending. Abram was quick to invite his sister in a letter he sent to America, saying that this wedding was an opportunity to strengthen his family ties. She sent us heartfelt wishes, but apologized for not being able to travel from New York to Riga.

Rennie was forgotten from my heart for long periods of time during those days. I no longer tried every day to calculate how old she was; one time I even forgot about her birthday. Only the future lay ahead. When I remembered this girl, I thought to myself that I'd done well not to marry Kaminski and how fortunate it was that he was married, because now I realized that Abram's Judaism was important to me and that I was now building the nest that suited me.

I sewed the wedding dress and the veil myself. If I shed any tears on the fabric, they were tears of happiness. Etta accompanied the sewing with advice and cries of admiration. Ah, those were wonderful days.

My mother looked radiant as she shook the hands of all the guests. She stood beside me under the Chuppah[35] and beside

---

35. Ceremonial cloth canopy under which a Jewish couple gets married.

her my dear uncle Isaiah. Tanny and her family, Etta and Diana stood very close to the Chuppah. Close by, my fellow milliners and those classmates I'd kept in touch with. Abram's four friends from the army held the canopy poles. There was, of course, Ben-Zion Colin, who was an old friend of Abram, Misha whom I met at Diana's wedding, Dima and Alexander. Those who occasionally popped in for a drink at our apartment.

In the middle of the meal, Etta tapped on her wineglass, but the gentle tinkle could not be heard over the din. She stood up and thundered. Everyone fell silent. The wonderful Lea blessed us on behalf of the family.

In my great excitement I did not absorb all the clever references to Jewish lore that were woven into the blessing, but I remember its end: "I will conclude with the words of Rabbi Akiva: 'If they are blessed, the divine spirit rests between them.'" Then she picked up the glass in her hand and shouted "Mazal Tov" and everyone echoed her blessing.

The last time we'd danced was at Diana's wedding, and here my wish came true in those magical moments when we danced at our wedding. The whole crowd stood around us and we floated to the beat of the sweeping Hassidic music. This time I did not step on Abram's feet.

We decided that I would try to get pregnant as early as possible. One of Abram's friends was already a grandfather. But to no avail. I knew I was not barren. This difficulty clouded our relationship and Abram could not understand why I refused to be examined by a gynecologist. I asked that we wait a little longer and let nature take its course. But inside me I feared that some kind of providence had decided to punish me for abandoning my firstborn. Abram thought that maybe at the age of twenty-eight I was already too old for a first pregnancy. I was silent. What could I say? My secret intensified within me and tormented me with excruciating guilt; I felt like I deserved this. The goddesses of fate would not allow me to get what

I want while at the same time an innocent girl has to grow up in orphanages. In the Torah I learned "An eye for an eye and a tooth for a tooth." I remembered the quote "Fathers ate unripe fruit and the teeth of the sons will erode." I thought it could happen in the opposite direction too: when the girls eat of the unripe fruit, the mothers' teeth erode.

Our failed attempts to conceive damaged the attraction between us. As we continued to try, they turned intercourse into a single-purpose tool. On those days my secret bubbled inside me: "Hey, what were you thinking? That you could keep a secret from your husband and live with it in peace?"

Diana agreed with me that it was too late to tell Abram the truth. I can't come to him after a year of a loving relationship and say to him: "Oh, I forgot to mention, I have a daughter." This secret grows in its inner presence like a snowball.

Only after about a year and a half of repeated, exhausting attempts did my body inform me in its own way that we had succeeded. I carried my pregnancy with pride. From the start I wanted my belly to be prominent. Abram was very busy with his business and I continued to work in the small millinery.

Pregnancy was a prelude to childbirth, but sadly not in the usual sense. Abram woke me up several times and told me I was screaming in my sleep: "Give her to me. Do not take her from me. She's mine." "Who is yours?" He tried to interrogate me. "I don't know what I dream about," I replied. The actress in me could lie without my facial expressions betraying me. Every night I fell asleep praying inwardly that tonight I wouldn't scream, but the prayers did not help me. "Don't take her. She's mine! "I shook the walls of the house.

I felt a fear that expressed itself in the from the book of Samuel - " For thou didst it secretly." This is the explanation the prophet Nathan gave to King David who lay with a married woman, Bathsheba, and was punished for it with the death of the fruit of their love.

I was afraid of disaster striking with the birth of the baby. The words "For thou didst it secretly" thundered inside me up until the moment of birth.

A good link formed between Lea and Abram, which I was very pleased with. Every time Lea visited the row of cherry wine bottles sent by my mother grew longer. Lea was getting better at Hebrew, the language of our prayers, and had even started to teach it.

One evening Lea rang our doorbell at a later hour than was customary for visits. She arrived excited with a huge need to unload an experience she'd had: "Don't ask. Tonight we met the poet Chaim Nahman Bialik. I worship him."

"How did I not know of this? I would have joined you." Abram instantly replied. He clearly admired my sister.

"It was a meeting with Riga's Hebrew teachers only. He recited his poems to us and spoke of life in Zion. Oh. I could listen to him forever."

She stood in front of us and gave a lively rendition of the first verse of Bialik's "To the Bird" in the strange, polished Hebrew language:

"Welcome thee back, lovely bird
From the warm climes to my window
For your pleasant voice my soul did yearn
Over winter when you left my abode."

The poem sounded odd to me. I understood a few of the words in it, especially the opening word "shalom", which meant "hello", "welcome" or "peace". "This poem makes me long for the Land of Israel. Oh, it's hard to explain this wonderful emotion," Lea exclaimed.

"How can you miss a place you've never been to?" I asked. No one addressed my question. In this room, with those two present, my question had been a mistake. From that moment on, Abram and Lea tried to read the poem together from Lea's page. They burst out laughing together as Abram tried to pronounce the words "only keening, and laments, and sorrow." "What is that? Such strange words in Hebrew?" He asked. And Lea? Lea was having a great time explaining.

I realized that my husband identified with her words with his eyes all a-twinkle. Abram told us that one of the reasons he'd decided at the time to quit the Latvian army was the connection to Zion that was beginning to bud within him. "Wait," I said to myself, "is Abram now adding another reason for leaving the army? Now he suddenly remembers that it wasn't just the desire to build his nest that made him stop his bike ride?! If so, then maybe, maybe I, too, can take my secret load off myself and tell him the real reason I'd quit the theater? Maybe if I tell him I can go back to acting?" From that moment on I no longer listened to their conversation and went off into the kitchen to wash the dishes. They did not seem to notice my absence. "No," I argued to myself, "my secret must remain a secret. It's not at all like the other reason he told tonight. I lied; I didn't merely forget to mention a fact. I told a substantial lie. "

When I returned to the living room, they'd already agreed among themselves that the national future of all Jews is in Zion, on the banks of the Jordan River and not on the banks of our Daugava.

I realized they were two wheels of a bike that was running pretty well, and I was the third wheel. After Lea left, despite the late hour, I seduced Abram into lovemaking. I wanted to make sure he was mine.

As September of 1931 approached, Abram, who'd integrated himself into the family as if born to it, booked seats at the Peit-av Synagogue in Riga's old city. "So we'd have a good place for Rosh Hashana and the High Holy Days," he explained. I was so happy, especially for my mother who was getting back to her roots in her old age.

My son Eddie's birth was an excruciating nightmare. It took place on the 1st of November 1931. When the transitional labor contractions started I became hysterical and screamed "No-one will dare take this baby away from me!" Nurses came in and out of the room with me brazenly telling them "Get out," "don't try to get near." None of them could shut me up, least of all myself. A demon sprouted from within me, one half of it inside me and the other half assailing the entire outside world. The nurses admonished me "Shhhh, you're disturbing the other women!" and though I was so weakened, I screamed "Go away. Leave me!"

I gave birth without helping myself through breathing, without paying any attention to what was going on around me. The birth took many hours. I sweated, turned crimson, wailed. I inhabited some alternate world within my being.

When the baby finally emerged, I yelled at the top of my drained lungs "Let him go. He's not yours!" and slumped back completely exhausted and unable to move. Then three words came from me: "Rennie. My girl."

Now we'll move your baby to the nursery. That's the procedure. This baby is yours alone. We are doing what we do for every woman. You will use this time to rest and gather your strength." But I kept commanding: "This baby is mine!" a sentence I repeated over and over again.

Abram came to visit immediately after the birth, and grabbed his head in despair. I saw him struggle but couldn't help. The screams emerged from me until I fell asleep, hoarse and completely spent.

I had no milk for breastfeeding and made no effort to produce any. I didn't smile, didn't speak to anyone, not even Abram or my family. Half-asleep, I heard one nurse whispering to another: "What a mess. If I were her, I'd rather not marry and certainly not have a baby. So shameful!" The other sprinkled oil on my fire: "The poor husband." Abram did not leave my side. He stroked and soothed me: "Johannuchka, we have a son," and would place the child in my arms. He soothed me with words, took all my capriciousness in stride, stroked, loved. With the help of this dedicated man, and sedatives, my insanity subsided. My strength returned and I held my infant son. I embraced him, but the embrace was mechanical. I couldn't feel. The words "eye for an eye" returned to run around in my head.

At the Brith, eight days later, we announced that our son's name is Edward-Solomon, the first name after Abram's departed father and the second after my departed father Yedidia. Yedidia-Solomon was the name of the baby born to David and Bathsheba after their first baby, conceived in sin, had died. Since Solomon went on to become the wisest of men, we thought it would be fitting for our son. King Solomon famously ruled that the mother who raises the baby is the real mother, even if she was not the one to have given it life. She who abandoned the baby is not worthy of receiving the honorific "mother". I swore to myself that I would raise this boy with all of my being and will escort him on his wedding day. I prayed that my fits would never come back.

"I suggest we call our baby Eddie in daily life. What do you think? Short and sweet," Abram said after the Brith.

"A wonderful idea," I replied. "Eddie, my Eddie," I addressed my sweet baby. But at that moment I felt a shiver course through my body: was it a coincidence that Eddie and Rennie were the same meter? Would Rennie never let me go?

At home I wanted no physical contact with my husband. Abram didn't know what to say and how to act. I took care of Eddie like an automated machine. Abram tried, more than once, to understand the meaning of my screams at the hospital, why I was so afraid they'd take the baby from me, what had happened. "Who's Rennie?" and I just looked at him dumbly and said nothing, or brushed him off with "I don't know."

Abram did his best to come home from work as early as possible each day to take care of our baby and let me sleep, and I slept like a log.

Boom. Boom.

My riffle through my inner diary is abruptly terminated by dreadful explosions. The shots sound so close by.

And once again the silence of the night.

Boomboomboom. A burst of firing.

Mia my daughter grabs me and whispers: "Mummy, what is that? It's here, right by us." I hold her as powerfully as my love for her, reaching to the ends of the earth, and attempt to give her confidence and warmth. A scream punctures the night. Probably someone in the Ghetto tried to steal food under cover of darkness, and was caught and shot. Hopefully not murdered. My Diana has started her weeping again in the bed next to ours. She rose and said she had to go to the toilet. Our toilet is used by so many people and its stink is not something a pregnant woman should endure, especially since leaving this room means going out into sub-zero cold. Her sons woke up and started groaning: "Mummy, mummy."

"Mummy, I'm so hungry. It hurts."

"You know that if I had a morsel of bread I'd give it to you, my girl," and I spread warm kisses on every exposed spot of her small body. We were both pretending to sleep. The truth is I can't sleep in this inferno.

I will keep thinking. That would pass the time, at least.

RENNIE

∽ February 1939 ↷

From that day onwards everything proceeded at an extraordinary pace. I was being moved out of Germany with the utmost speed. Throughout the final month of my stay, the Oberlanders treated me well. Normally. Perhaps they were afraid I'd tell someone I was Jewish. If the Nazis found out they'd hidden me in their home, they would lead them to prison or execute them by law. Or perhaps the Oberlanders decided they had no further need to educate me since I'd be vanishing from their life shortly. At least the final period was okay.

The beatings stopped. Finally.

One spring evening after dinner, Max asked me to join him in the living room, an unheard-of request. He blew smoke rings from his fat cigar and the smell in the room was unbearably disgusting. Max said. "Rennie, we know you're a Jew. You already know we know. I want to make sure you understand how dangerous it is to be a Jew in Germany today and how very dangerous it is to hide Jews here."

I nodded my head and allowed myself to reply with a few sentences: "We knew that even back when I was at school. Our Jewish teachers were kicked out of school and we all talked about it. Our music teacher, the wonderful Sara, left for good in the middle of the day, two of the math teachers and the German literature teacher and the bearded Geography professor were dismissed one by one. We all knew why. You couldn't not know that being a Jew was dangerous."

Max told me about what happened six months prior, on a night called "Kristallnacht" because the pavements by the Jews' shops sparkled like crystals from the glass shards of the broken shopfront windows. This was when I learned the word "pogrom". He spoke, and I saw my own private tragedy, Max the beater, Francesca the abuser.

"Did the church do anything to stop that?" I asked what I thought was the right question.

"No. after Kristallnacht the church was too frightened and horrified to speak out. No-one dared organize protests. I'm telling you this terrible story because you're a Jew and your real records are kept at town hall. Every day I pray that no-one will find out these facts. We are extraordinarily fortunate that Franz Kunstlinger understands the situation and will never tell on you and on us, but he says there might be another copy of your papers somewhere he cannot see. You must leave Germany as fast as possible. This is the moment after the last moment."

"Yes, I know that many children my age are disappearing lately. Now I understand they were Jewish and escaping Germany."

He agreed. Our frightening conversation stays with me till this day, a conversation that ripped away my childhood and adolescence, which weren't that innocent even without it, and catapulted me into the adult world. It was like jumping head-first into an empty pool.

Max leaned toward the small wooden magazine rack, and picked out a newspaper from the 30th of January of this year, 1939, about a month ago, and read out to me in a quiet voice a small part of the Führer's speech: "Yes, Europe will have no peace as long as the Jewish question remains. It may well be that, sooner or later, Europe will reach consensus about this problem, even among nations who would normally not easily see eye to eye. There are in this world many places to settle, but it is time, once and for all, to dispel the notion that it was God's intention that the Jews would live as parasites in the bodies of other nations, exploiting the fruits of their labor." He stopped, looked into my eyes, saw that I was taking all of that in, and read out another sentence from that speech: "Nations are not prepared to die on the battlefields only for that international, rootless nation to profit from the business of war and satiate its biblical lust for vengeance. The Jewish slogan 'Workers of the world, unite!' shall be overshadowed by a more exalted awareness: that workers and producers of all nations would recognize their common enemy!" He wished to point out to me seven words from the lecture that he believed best expressed Hitler's ideology, so he repeated them three times: "extermination of the Jewish race in Europe."

In these moments he was no longer Max the Terrible, but a sensitive, humane Max. Hahaha, I already know, he only cares for himself. He hadn't suddenly turned into a wonderful father. I couldn't forget then and cannot forget now the beatings and abuse I'd taken in this house. He's acting like a progressive father calmly explaining the national news to his daughter, but I've already been through two and a half years with him and know all too well that tigers don't suddenly turn into housecats. When they beat me they said that "Ordnung muss sein" and now he thinks the same: there must be a new order in Germany, so the Jews need to go away. And if so, then it follows that I must bugger off as well, I thought bitterly to myself.

Max continued: "Hitler believes and is convincing everyone that the Jews are an inferior race sullying Germany and the world. We added a Jewish girl to our family because religion changes nothing in the human character. It's important to us that everyone would be a proper human, a *Mensch*." I didn't know whether to believe him. If he's saying what he thinks is true, then a *Mensch* is someone who maintains proper German manners and doesn't cause embarrassment. What I call a *Mensch* is someone who loves people and animals and really wants for everyone to be happy.

At that moment I realized that from his perspective, all the shouting and the beatings were intended to make me into a *Mensch*, a civilized girl who's worthy of a groom from a good family, as the Oberlanders like to say. In these minutes of closeness I almost managed to justify their horrible behavior toward me, the girl who grew up in their house. But just almost.

Francesca joined us and sat on the foldable couch next to us. She said nothing. The three of us sat in silence.

The next day Franz gave Max a printed form and explained that this was my boarding certificate for the ship that would take me to Palestine. He added that my age was a stroke of luck, since these permits were available for fifteen- to seventeen-year-olds only, and I was turning sixteen soon. Some siblings were separated because one of them was out of that age bracket, he added a dramatic fact that touched my heart.

But I couldn't keep listening to him. I'd learned that I had to ask the moment anything was really relevant to me, because if I didn't ask now, I'd miss my chance. Some things have their moment.

"One moment, I'm not going to Palestine," I declared and stamped my foot on the Persian carpet. "You told me I was going to the Land of Israel. Please don't switch destinations."

They all burst out laughing and started speaking at once. Despite the racket I managed to gather that these were two names for the same place.

I took a deep breath.

Franz moved on to the specifics: he formally announced that on the 27th of March, at 6pm sharp, I had to be at the Berlin Anhalter Bahnhof railway terminus. I was allowed two suitcases only. I liked his instruction: "when you pack, remember it's a warm country with no snow". "At the station, go to the Palestine Bureau counter and hand them the permit, and they'll sign you on. The organization responsible for this entire formidable operation of getting young people out of Germany is called 'Aliyat Ha-Noar.'"[36] The three grownups agreed that this was the last legal way of saving Jews from death in Germany. I didn't know what the words "Aliyat Ha-Noar" meant, and didn't know that throughout my life I'd remember that name. Franz added that the next morning a train carrying the young people who'd signed up for the voyage would travel from Berlin to the port of Trieste in Italy, and we'll travel by ship from there.

I started getting excited. Here, finally, was a way of leaving this family.

A strange way, I thought. A bit tortuous and special, I even laughed to myself about it. My imagination never came up with an idea that was even slightly similar to this strange possibility. Admittedly I wasn't the one who chose this path, but perhaps fate nevertheless sometimes does me a good turn as well. The world around me is on fire, but I am saved.

Incredibly, Max later announced that on this occasion he and Francesca would drive me in their car to the meeting place in Berlin. This would allow us to have fun together before parting.

We said goodbye to Franz with great excitement. He wished me good luck and explained to me what I was already beginning to understand: "You are very lucky to have grown up as a Christian."

The excited Fronella gave me a farewell gift: a wooden box engraved with colorful flowers.

On the trip to Berlin we looked, for a few hours, just like a normal family.

---

36. Youth Immigration (Hebrew)

We arrived in Berlin and visited the office above which was written "The Israel Office". Hundreds of girls and boys stood in the long queue for registration. "Hundreds" is not an exaggeration. This sight removed one stone from my path and made it more comfortable to cross: I was not alone. I was like all the others. Almost. I now have with me hundreds of children without parents, a bit like my perpetual situation. A little bit.

The clerk announced, with eyes agleam, that I would arrive at a place called "Nahalat Yehuda Workers' Farm." He explained that there I would study and work, sleep and eat, enjoy various classes and a social life. In short, it will be the new home where I will have a wonderful time. "I guarantee this," he declared as he handed me the note with my next place of residence and a ticket for the ship, passport and immigration certificate. I noticed the two girls standing in front of me in line, because I overheard that they too were directed, each in her turn, to the same place I was.

As soon as I said goodbye to the Oberlanders, my heart twinged. Because the last days with them changed my memories of them a little, and also because every change demands an internal strength that, in my case, had started dwindling away. Francesca actually trembled and acted as if separation was not easy for her. Max was as matter-of-fact as ever and gave me final instructions: "Do not lose the envelope with all your certificates. Always, always, take care of it. Also take care the money I gave you. Twenty marks is a large sum. Be careful around young men. Write us a letter when you can." He sounded both authoritative and hesitant, which was new to me. Max added a surprising sentence, very out of character for him: "We will not forget you." Francesca agreed with him and suddenly, for the first time in my life, she walked towards me and kissed me on the cheek. I managed not to wipe away the kiss. I was educated in German cultural behavior, properly...

I was standing in line for the office, together with the two girls whom I earlier saw on the platform, when Max suddenly appeared, breathing heavily. He grabbed my hand and pulled me away from them: "Rennie, now I can tell you," he whispered in my ear and paused for a long second, "I'm a Jew too. At least you survived."

He hugged me and I felt his trembling all over my body. Now I understood the hesitation I'd heard in his throat before; he was considering whether to tell me. Having spoken, he turned and walked briskly back to his car. I didn't have time to reply. I was left standing alone stricken with astonishment. Max, a Jew? Was that why they chose me? The threads of destiny are twisted and sometimes they form knots and lumps, I thought to myself and wiped away a tear that rolled down my cheek.

I need to recover, I informed myself. I decided to open a new page of my life, with courage and resourcefulness. I held on tightly to my beautiful wicker suitcase, with a large, elegant handbag hung over my shoulder, my hair professionally trimmed to the shoulders by the hand of the best and most expensive barber in Zwickau and wearing a splendid dark blue beret. Hidden away from prying eyes was Laura.

I approached the two girls, who were standing quite close to each other. I said with a hesitant smile: "We should get to know each other. We'll be together in the same place, so I heard," I spoke, of course, in German, our native language. The three of us talked one after the other, even though we did not know each other. I introduced myself: "Irena Friedman, Rennie." The shorter of them, curly-haired one, answered loudly and with a quick speech like an express train: "Mannie Guttman, Mannie." Mannie radiated cheerfulness and I immediately felt comfortable around her. The second girl was more serious, thin and handsome, with a deep voice and a worried expression: "Gisela Kornitzer."

It seemed that I was not the only one in need of some support;

both of them did as well. And so from that moment we did not part from each other. Mannie and Gisela became the sisters I never had. In time, everyone knew us as a trio.

We sat together on one cramped seat on the train. Most of the way Mannie, who lived in Berlin, told us about their family decision to accept the Aliyat Ha-Noar proposal and send her to Palestine. She talked a lot and very quickly. She took a long time to tell the story of her painful separation from her parents.

I learned that they both had parents, but Aliyat Ha-Noar suggested to their parents that they send them to Palestine to save them from the laws and the barbaric behavior of the Germans ever since the Nazi party took over Germany. Their parents could not leave with them. We didn't notice the train and time moving, and soon we arrived at Trieste. There we stayed in the house of a Jewish family for one night and one day.

At precisely eight o'clock in the evening we boarded the "Galilea". A large white ship, which I thought was beautiful. The three of us commandeered three beds close to each other. We transferred our luggage to the belly of the ship, as requested, and cheerfully went out to the deck to watch the light of Trieste recede. We acted like we were on a school trip we were looking forward to. Something within us told us to be what we were, without worrying too much, to be sixteen, cheerful and looking ahead to the path opening before us. Somehow we managed to get rid of the sadness of separation. Maybe because we became a trio.

We kept telling our stories. My insides were churning, my face not showing my inner considerations, what I would like to tell and what I should hide inside me. I didn't want them to know that up until a month ago I was a devout Christian and went to church on Sundays, I was still not ready to tell all my secrets.

I wanted to be like them.

I stayed silent a lot and gave only the details about the family in Zwickau. You could really think this was the family I'd been born into. Gisela told us that her brother would also immigrate to Israel soon and that she feared that she might never get to see her parents again. When Gisela showed us a photo of her handsome brother Albert, Mannie snatched the photo from her hands with real excitement and said with prophetic determination: "This will be my husband."

As the ship left the Aegean Sea and sailed into the open Mediterranean the sea turned rough, the ship tossed and turned, and many vomited. But the three of us felt young and healthy and weren't bothered. I remember Gisela saying a beautiful sentence, the kind you remember: "Even though *Galilea* is swaying like a drunk man, we are intrigued to be tumbling on the ship of our lives towards the new day tomorrow." The stages of getting to know each other spiced up our sailing days with curiosity and joy of life and helped us forget the pain of separation.

What weighed heavily on me was a whole new concept I had learned – "Kabbalat Shabbat". On Friday evening, March 31, 1939, all the young people sang songs in Hebrew together. Everyone was very excited. I didn't know any of the songs; I didn't know one word of that strange language, Hebrew. After a few songs a bearded man, who looked like the Jews I sometimes saw on the streets of Zwickau, with a very long and unkempt white beard and a small, round covering on his head, prayed, and a woman with a handkerchief on her head lit two white candles and added a prayer in Hebrew. This evening brought to my mind that from now on I was Jewish, and that Judaism has its own prayers and blessings. I must get used to the new situation. For the first few days I had a hard time giving up my regular Christian morning prayer, I literally fought myself to change my beloved and well-practiced routine. I managed not to cross myself. For the first time in my life, I was carrying a secret. Until now I had been kept a secret from myself, but from now on I am the one who keeps the secret. I imitated Mannie and Gisela and tried to learn fast without them feeling like I was a complete idiot in matters of Judaism.

On the ship was a man, who approached all the children and said that he should be given ten marks, because he was in charge of us and had expenses. Today I understand it was theft. I'd learned the fact that there are robbers and bad, bad people everywhere. I could no longer be innocent and believe that in the Land of Israel everything is wonderful and everyone is good friends with each other, as many who were with me on the ship believed.

Mannie, Gisela and I really understood that from now on we would not have an adult to consult with. Now we were without parents and must conduct ourselves responsibly in our new land.

We arrived at the port of Jaffa. We went on board, watched the rising sun, and stood there, expectant. The sight was mesmerizing. I think the wonderful feeling was not only because of the view, but also because the mood that enveloped me rose and rose. The day opened up like a blooming flower. The sun shone, sending long rays coming to me from the sky, reaching my shoes, as if sending signs just for me, marking my new road with a great light. That's how I felt. I hoped my feelings would not disappoint.

Everyone sang Hebrew songs and I clapped along with the tune. That's what I could contribute to the elation that surrounded us. The ship docked at sea and small boats came and took us to shore.

Now a third language was added: not German, not Hebrew, but English. The officers spoke English. I went through a document check and from there I walked, with my heavy suitcase and handbag, towards the exit. A man stood by the gate and asked in German: "Girl, where are you going?" I immediately read from the note: "Nahalat Yehuda Workers' Farm". The same thing happened with Mannie and Gisela, each in turn. We followed the man to a bus that took us, a group of chatty girls, to our new home – Nahalat Yehuda Workers' Farm, or Nahlat for short.

We lived four girls to a room. Two beds were along each wall, and a nice table sat under the open window. The room was filled with a wonderful fragrance that seemed to entice me to come out. These were the orchard trees of Nahlat whose fragrant scent was brought to us by the wind. The three of us got one room, where there was a fourth girl we didn't really connect with. She was the fourth wheel in the cart that carried us. The table was decorated with a jar holding colorful flowers dipped in water, and next to it a light-blue colored page was waiting for us, with "Welcome" in German written in curly lettering. On one plate, four orange halves were waiting for us. Gisela already knew how to eat this strange fruit. She explained to us that the peel should be peeled off, the segments separated from each other, and to try and not swallow the seeds. I put the new land into me. The taste was sweet-sour and sticky juice dripped all over my hands.

My distance from the Jewish tradition was put into sharp relief the next day. Easter, my favorite holiday, is not celebrated here. Instead, we have Passover. On Tuesday, with a full moon in the cloudless sky, we celebrated the Passover Seder. Oh, it was a long and incomprehensible evening. All fifty girls and all the staff sat around long tables arranged in a rectangle, and covered with white tablecloths made of ironed bedsheets. I didn't understand anything but loved the many songs they all sang together enthusiastically. I enjoyed sitting with all the girls and watching them one by one.

I realized I had a "package deal" here, two words I heard from Max when he spoke to men who came to him: to save myself from the Nazis, I must be Jewish. The fact that I am Jewish is what gave me the permission to board the ship and sail to the Land of Israel. What an upside-down world I was living in: the vast majority of Jews would've been happy to disguise themselves as Christians at this time, if they only could, and to stay in their homes with their families intact.

And so day followed day. I got used to it quickly and even started chatting in Hebrew. How could you not? After all, we had Hebrew classes for four hours every day and I knew how to be a good student when I wanted to. For the second half of the day, I worked in the chicken coop and vegetable beds. I learned the various farm jobs and preferred them to sewing buttons and hemming dresses. I cut my hair very short for comfort, I wore khaki shorts. I folded all the dresses nicely in the wicker suitcase tucked under my bed. I sunbathed and was happy in my lot in life. I loved the Workers' Farm and the social activities with the counsellors Lily and Zipporah. In time, I came to know and understand the Jewish idea of returning to the Land of Israel, an idea that the Jews carried in their hearts and prayed for throughout the years of exile. My ear got used to the Hebrew songs and I began to recognize and understand their words.

I learned to dance and loved dancing with our friend Tirza. She, who was only one year older than me, told me that when she was younger, she was the national German champion in the 100-meter dash for female students, but that after the Nazis came to power, they'd prevented her from participating in competitions. On Kristallnacht their house in Düsseldorf was demolished. Her father was jailed, her mother and younger brother Friedreich were sent to a concentration camp and she and her older brother Julius were left alone. She came to Israel with us. She translated her love of sports into dance and folk dances, most of which she composed. After we left the farm, she married and took the name Tirza Hodes. She was then elected chair of the National Dance Commission and was called "the mother of Israeli folk dance."

I had found myself a home.

ᨓ Summer of 1940 ᨔ

Suppose I prepare a summertime drink: I pour in the Israeli summer heat and the revealing clothing style it entails, add a swimming pool, mix with boys and girls meeting and spice it all up with night swimming.

What do we get?

Young lust.

Now let me add two facts: all the girls and boys are single and in the country without their parents, and the aforementioned pool is being snuck into without permission.

What do we get?

Couples.

I'll pause this story of romance for a moment to say a bit more about my life here in "Nahlat".

I've been living in Israel for nearly two years. I'm eighteen and midway through the last year of my farming classes. My Hebrew is getting better. I can't read Hebrew books and my spelling errors are endless, but I am able to converse. I'll always prefer speaking German and church music, *a cappella* and classical European music.

In Israel my name is Rina.[37]

It was a name suggested to me, and I accepted it since it's similar to Irena and Rennie. I feel like a change of name can signify a change of circumstance and can contain a change in life. Zipporah the counsellor explained to me that it was a special name that expresses joy, and that I would be one of the first "Rina"s in the country. I like my name's meaning. We have two girls here who were given names with a similar meaning: Gila and Hedva. Mannie and Gisela helped me accept that change.

"You'll bring much joy to Nahlat" Mannie giggled.

Gisela kept on with her deep thinking: "Together with your

---

37. A common Hebrew name. It means "joyful singing".

177

family name you're practically a song: joy and singing and peace. What else could anyone need?" We all agreed that would be my name forever.

Mannie, Gisela and I were a lively, popular trio. Gisela's name was changed to Rachel. We were told that this was her name's meaning in Hebrew, and Gisela excitedly told us that there was a Rachel in the Bible. Mannie didn't change her name. So in Israel we're now Mannie, Rachel and Rina.

Mannie and I have a very intimate relationship. She was the only one I told the truth about my childhood. We didn't speak much of it, because immigrants from Germany don't tend to tell personal, intimate stories. *Es passt nicht*[38] that we reveal our deepest secrets. We cover it all up, show a tiny bit and quickly cover it back up and never show it again. *So ist es.*

A year ago, Albert, Rachel's brother, immigrated to Israel and as soon as he came to visit his sister in Nahlat and his gaze met Mannie's, they fell in love. They're a couple. Mannie's heart and eyes predicted her future back when we met on board the ship. Mannie fell in love with his striking appearance, but it turns out they found a shared language, a language that ignited true love. It's enough for me to look into their eyes to understand this.

Now I can tell my story:

I'm in love.

I found the love of my life, my man.

We discovered the Forbidden Pool in Rehovot. Used for storing rainwater, it lies amongst green orchards. We already knew the rows in the orchard that we had to walk through to get to the pool and didn't need to look at the footprints that had already marked the path. On our way we skipped over ditches that led straight to the orchard trees. The pool greeted us with a "no bathing" sign. With the heat of the evening, at the end of a

---

38. It's not the done thing; it's inappropriate (German)

day of work and school, we, a group of giggling girls, walked to this inviting pool. All we knew was that the place was recommended and called "Gotthelf Pool". The sign interested us a lot less than the opportunity to soak our hot bodies and splash water on each other. Between us, when we were beyond the jurisdiction of the rules of the workers' farm, we spoke only German.

One warm evening, as we marched vigorously, chatting constantly, we heard German being spoken from the direction of our pool. The surprise was that those were male voices.

We walked faster.

Five guys were swimming in the pool.

I felt electricity in the air.

Young guys dressed in swimsuits only and talking to each other, just like us, in German.

We undressed in the shade of the red bougainvillea bush that created a closed canopy, stuffed our clothes in the shade out of sight and ran to the pool, all three of us dressed in our swimsuits. The boys whistled in admiration and added cries of "Come, come," "What a surprise" and "We have guests" and also "The water's wonderful." We immediately jumped into the pool to immerse ourselves.

The excitement was great. The pool wasn't very big and we were three girls and five boys. After two minutes we all switched to our mother tongue – German. Suddenly I felt at home. I was flooded with warmth and confidence despite the cool water. Everyone was being very loud; everyone was excited about this miraculous meeting. I was the only one not contributing a single word to the lively conversation. The pool was my playground and after about a quarter of an hour I spoke in a demonstration of my abilities: I exhibited my mastery of swimming styles, rolled over in the pure water, dived and kicked my feet at the sky. I might have seemed distant, but in fact I listened to every word and stole glances at the group.

I started to mark the names of the boys: Jacob, Hansel, Egon, Mickey, and Samuel.

I came out and lay at the side of the pool to gather strength and bask in the evening sun that still gave some warmth. I prostrated myself on the hot concrete and watched the tops of the trees. I listened closely to the background noises, and then the most handsome man I'd ever seen came and sat next to me. He was tall and athletic, with a shock of brown hair. He spoke quietly, very different from the excited shouting emanating from the pool. He spoke to me alone: "I'm Jacob. What's your name?"

I sat up. *Es passt nicht* that I should stay lying down with him beside me. For a moment I hesitated: Do I give my German or Hebrew name? I found myself giving a long answer, perhaps not wanting for this moment to pass quickly: "I'm Irena whose name in Germany was Rennie. Here I'm Rina. I'm Rina." Our gazes said what our words could not. Jacob asked: "Where did you come from?" "From a workers' farm half an hour's walk away. And you?" "I'm a soldier in the Jewish Brigade. Our base is near here."

The conversation flowed of its own accord. We sat shoulder to shoulder. Quite close to each other. Mannie sneaked understanding and encouraging glances at me. Rachel sat with Egon at another corner of the pool. They both sat with their heads bowed toward each other and looked deep in conversation.

It was at that first meeting that I'd learned Samuel was Jacob's brother, though Samuel had red hair; that Jacob had come to Israel before me, in 1938; that he and his brother came to Israel as part of the *Beitar* movement and joined the Rodges group, which was composed only of Germans and Austrians; that they'd then joined the Tirat-Zvi kibbutz for a short while, but very quickly decided to fight the Nazis and found the Jewish Brigade would be their best option.

I told him about my childhood. I held nothing back. Though I'd only just met him, it was clear to me that I had no secrets from Jacob. For the first time since I'd arrived in Israel I had no qualms, the truth flowed out of me. He accepted my story with a compassionate look from his kind, green-colored eyes.

We talked, laughed and shed a tear, listened and shared. I didn't want for it to end. I knew I had so much more to hear and to tell.

Evening fell. We agreed to meet the next day at the pool.

I day passed when I felt the whole world around me existing, the whole world buzzing and moving, the whole world working and laughing, talking and learning, exchanging opinions and dancing. A whole world. And only I am next to it, only I am in a line parallel to the world. I'm in my bubble, closed off from everyone.

A bubble with Jacob and me in it.

And so, the meetings in the pool became more frequent. We felt like we were always together. There wasn't a single moment when we felt embarrassed or ashamed. We flowed in the most natural way that came from within us.

Albert, Rachel's brother, the one from the picture, joined the brigade and the pool. We became a six-piece. The fascinating life on the workers' farm became very unimportant. Every day we three girls waited for the evening to come so we could walk quickly through the orchards to our secret pool. Every evening, if we didn't have a lecture about the Land of Israel or a story from the Torah or folk dances, we cooled our hot bodies in the pool water or in a canopied hiding place in the orchard.

Jacob and I were already a couple. When he got to the pool wearing his uniform with the triangular hat resting on his beautiful head, my heart skipped a beat. The man of my dreams. I have my own soldier. A man to watch over me.

In the water we touched each other. At first casually, as if unintentionally, and later intentionally. I discovered the taste of kissing. We started meeting alone outside the pool. Jacob told me that in the Old Testament, the Torah, Jacob loved Rachel very much and was willing to work for her father for seven years in order to be permitted to marry her. My Jacob, he said, did not fall in love with my friend Rachel, but with Rina. We both laughed at the fact that I had no parents and no-one for him to ask or work to gain permission to marry me, though he does really love me. That's what he said. The thought that went through my head surprised me: I'll tell my children about this moment. He told me the rest of the story of Yaakov and Lea, and I realized I had the chance to be with a knowledgeable man who could hide from the world my ignorance of the intricate world of Judaism. This would be my protector, and I can rest in his shade.

Jacob started visiting me on the farm. In the winter that came, the winter of '41, we officially became a couple. Even the instructors and the teachers knew this. Jacob was mine, only mine. He came to me, only to me. The love between us intensified daily. I also knew his sister Yoland, who lived nearby and was a very accomplished seamstress. I always said she kind of played on a sewing machine like it was a musical instrument. The buttons and hems were sewn by an assistant. The Seifert family's three siblings, Samuel, Jacob and Yoland, lived in close proximity while their parents, Abraham and Karolina, lived in Lisbon, Portugal, where they raised their youngest son, Isaac.

Into our pure love, our life stories were woven. The truth refueled the sincerity of our lives and the depth of our relationship.

Jacob grew up in the district town of Mattersburg, south of Vienna. In the region where he lived, in Burgenland near the Hungarian border, were seven country towns; Jews lived in all of them. He described his town so lovingly that I really saw the place with my own eyes: a town bisected by a flowing stream, located in beautiful countryside where the rolling hills are decorated with rows of vines, wineries, tall mountains on the horizon, lots of greenery, one main street with shops and businesses that are mostly Jewish. He lived with his siblings and with mom and dad. The basic pleasure in its realization, I thought to myself.

Then, just like in the story that Max Oberlander told me when he wanted to illustrate the danger of being Jewish, an immense turning point also occurred for my Jacob. He always augmented his stories with lots of historical background.

"Burgenland was the first Austrian province to come under Nazi rule in March of 1938".

"That was the year I worked in a sewing workshop and knew nothing but my personal troubles," I mused aloud.

"Austrian Chancellor Schuschnigg was very much in favor of Hitler and declared: 'The Jews and the gypsies are parasites in the body of the nation, which should be clean of them, pure.' You can't imagine how our neighbors, the ones I lived with, broke into our homes and took whatever they fancied. My parents' store was emptied. They smashed glass, broke and soiled things. My mother cried for several days. She never went back to looking as I'd known her before. My heart shriveled. Our neighbors, the ones we knew, smashed our lives. My parents and all the Jewish neighbors in the city were forced to declare that they were giving up their property. Can you imagine such a thing? Such looting, such cruelty, such hatred, such betrayal?" My Jacob stared at a distant spot on the horizon and then turned his face to me.

"Yes, I know," I surprised him, "in 1938 – Kristallnacht took place."

"You're right, but by Kristallnacht I was already on my way to Israel and my parents fled to Portugal. Kristallnacht was in November 1938. What I just told you happened six months before, in March. In Mattersburg on Kristallnacht, I learned from letters and stories I heard afterwards, our synagogue, which was right in the center of town, was completely destroyed."

The athlete Jacob was an outstanding student who helped his parents make a living. He kept sharing with me, and I?

I thirstily drank every word that came out of his mouth: "For the three months of March-April-May 1938, when Hitler entered Austria, I worked in a shop under the supervision of the SS. Believe me, for the guy I used to be that wasn't at all simple. I found it hard to restrain myself from getting into physical confrontation. One time, three Nazis came and asked for someone to shine their shoes. I went out to them and found that one of them was my high school classmate. When we were at school I used to help him with his schoolwork. Picture the scene: I tried to laugh and said to the guy: 'Alfred, you deserve a shoeshine. Come on, I'll do it.' He was embarrassed and replied that he'd changed his mind and didn't want the shoeshine, but his friend jumped in and declared that he does want one. I tried to wiggle out of it by saying we had no polish, but then my sister brought me a polish tin. I had no option but to start. Imagine him standing there and me on all fours on the floor, shining his shoes. Then he suddenly says 'You deliberately stained my trousers' and slapped me in the face. That wasn't true, I meant to just shine the shoes. I wanted to punch him in the face, and at the last moment I remembered about Dachau and told them 'The three of you are stronger than me.' They went away. That slap changed my life."

Jacob led me into his world. I understood through that story what made him leave his parents and the town he'd grown up in and come to Israel. At that moment I understood all the Jews in the world. I identified.

I responded with: "I understand the humiliation you went through. I knew humiliations in my life."

He stopped the flow of his story and immediately suggested that I share it. He said a thrilling sentence: "All life is before us. We will find the time for me to tell you," and declared, laughing: "stories of humiliation. One, two, three. Start." He apparently felt that a very rare moment was passing between us, a moment that might pass, where I was ready to bring out of myself another story weighing on me and barring the way for free breathing.

I told him about the beatings and incarceration punishments I'd received at my adoptive parents' house in Zwickau. Jacob hugged me closer and wrapped me in his arms. I rested my head on his beating chest. When I finished, he wiped away my tear. I wanted to keep talking about it and not move our conversation only to me. I mustered my insights and responded: "What greatness of spirit and maturity it took for you to restrain yourself and not get entangled with these three rude Nazis. It is precisely in the small details concerning life and death that we require supreme mental effort. Life is built from small specifications, often hidden from view." Such was the sentence I expressed. I surprised myself. When there's someone who loves me and wants the best for me, I do not blush, but flourish. My senses cooperate.

I curled up inside him like a little girl and felt our hearts beating together. Jacob continued his story: "It's amazing how quickly the entire Burgenland area was 'cleansed' of Jews: within six months, at the end of the summer of '38, there were no Jews in the district. Everyone was deported. Do you understand? They all had to leave! I don't think there was anywhere where ethnic cleansing was done as quickly as in Burgenland. You can imagine the terrible trauma people went through in one quick blow. Families were forced to wander, destitute, and many neighboring countries refused to accept them." "You told me your parents moved to a country called Portugal. How did that happen?"

"Our family was not devout, and we socialized with Gentiles as well. My parents always said that the Jewish religion is wonderful, but what the devout people do with religion has long since ceased to belong to Jewish values. There were many ultra-Orthodox Jews in Mattersburg and we saw many examples. I don't care for the ultra-Orthodox, and generally don't appreciate extremists. My parents chose friends based on whether they were a *Mentch*[39], and didn't care much about religion. My father, Abraham Zeifert, had a friend in Mattersburg, a close friend. They'd often meet for a decent glass of beer. He was a German Christian. See, you're not the only one to hang around with Christians." he laughed.

"That man held a senior position in the Burgenland district and saw some of Chancellor Schuschnigg's papers. He knew what was going to happen to the Jews. Unfortunately, I can't remember that savior's name. I would very much like to write him to thank him when this war ends. He told my dad everything and suggested that we leave Austria. He was the one who raised the option of immigrating to the safety of Portugal. They extracted themselves in the summer of '38, three months before Kristallnacht. My parents managed to sell the house and the shop and left with my little brother and aunt Ida."

The story impressed me. Amidst the sea of evil, a good man with a heart of gold, the person for whom friendship and equality are at the forefront.

"Jacob, we both came from extremist Nazi countries that hate Jews, today I know that, but it turned out that we both also met humane Christian people. You also need luck sometimes," I added to his story.

Jacob did not agree with me about his parents: "The Austrian who helped my father knew him and helped him because my father was his friend. My father did not confine himself only to the company of Jews who, during most hours of the day, carry out all the prohibitions that Judaism imposes on them. He has good friends from all religions. It's not luck. My parents acted boldly: they left their lives and moved to another country. I am proud of their courage and the uncompromising understanding they have shown in it. I'm sure they saved themselves with

---

39. A decent person (Yiddish)

this act. I think we can't imagine what the cruelty of the Nazis might do to the Jews," he said confidently. "I'm sure of it. Those staying in Europe are making a grave mistake. Do you know that the Rodges group helped, seven years ago, teenagers like you who'd immigrated from Germany? I'm so proud of being a part of that! Actually not quite like you, my little Christian, but youth who came from devout Jewish homes. The guys brought these teens into their home, which was nothing but a handful of shacks and tents, and these became an educational institution overnight, all the staff being members of the group. Even in those days of great distress, these youths received better food than the members of the farm and the first concrete houses were for the youth societies. That's Zionism! A combination of religion and the land of Israel and its settlement."

Jacob swept me away with his enthusiasm. With these words, I adopted his views and became a Zionist like him. Life is a winding path. There are many moments when the path is chosen for us. What we have left to choose is the way we go on an unchosen path. But as for our actual path, I think we are fooling ourselves when we think we'd chosen it; it's mostly an illusion. No one chooses the circumstances of their birth. Sometimes, just sometimes, rarely, after we stand our ground, we are at a crossroads where two paths unfold before us and we are given the choice of which way to proceed and we must choose wisely.

I think this time I chose.

"My entire family managed to avoid Kristallnacht, all thanks to that compassionate German. That's the power of true friendship," he said, kissing my lips. "In Lisbon my family has a kosher restaurant and Yitzhak, my brother, whom I call 'Richard', plays soccer for the Benfica team in Lisbon. I haven't seen them in three years, but they will come here when possible. I'm sure. They make a decent living."

It struck me very much that Jacob had a family and that he also doesn't have to worry about them anymore. He is not required to go through the daily nightmare like all my friends at the farm who might never see their parents again. I was glad to find out that it wasn't just Schwester Hilde Rein, Ernest Winter and Franz Kunstlinger who were good Germans, but that among all the evil and incomprehensible cruelty there were a few *Mentschen* to be found. Even then I knew they were few. Too few.

Jacob was absorbed by his story, and I listened as if drinking cool water on a hot day. I remember the details concerning Jacob. I wasn't a good pupil at the Zwickau school, but I discovered that when something really interests me – I digest and retain it very well.

He explained to me the name of the ship that brought him to Israel – "Af Al Pi Hen"[40]. Four such short words holding the entire story of our lives.

Nevertheless.

Our luck as a couple is that for now the brigade is stationed in Israel and is not allowed to go to the front. Jacob says he dearly wishes to fight and take his revenge on the Nazis. I understand him but I am afraid of the day I will no longer see him, and the connection between us will have to surmount many obstacles.

My love for Jacob embraces all the mess in my life. This love fashions some harmony from all the jarring notes of my life. Suddenly all the upheavals I went through drain into one melody. Every memory I have seems to be reworked in light of the circumstances.

We've started talking about a wedding.

I will be a mother and take care of my children. I will establish a family of my own.

What a wonderful summer! The summer of 1941, I will never forget you.

The world smiles at me.

---

40. Nevertheless (Hebrew)

JOHANNA

Our troubles started in the summer of 1941.

My thoughts here in the ghetto, early December '41, help me pass the hours of this long night. My Mia is curled up inside me and we keep each other warm. A little while ago she finally fell into a very deep sleep. What is she dreaming about? About the world we lost, or the terrifying present? Can she even dream tonight?

Next to me in bed my pregnant friend Diana sobs as her two children, Froi'ke and Menash'ke, sleep crammed in together with her. It is now ten minutes past three. We have less than one hour left to report to the meeting point. Everything is ready. We were told to come without any personal belongings. I cannot fall asleep. Even at this hour I hear at regular intervals the footsteps of the Latvian guards as they approach and move away. Sometimes a dog barks, or a short burst of German. An occasional scream pierces the night, but I do not want to speculate on who screamed and why. I can no longer contain evil. I operate like an automaton.

I breathe in the memories' shadow.

Eddie was born ten years ago. After his birth, for a whole year, I wasn't myself. I so wanted to function as a devoted and loving mother, but depression washed over me in waves, emerged and receded and so on and on. I handled little Eddie mechanically. Even when I hugged him, I did it because I knew it had to be done that way, because babies need hugs to grow and flourish. I was very lonely and very bored. It was a great relief on those evenings when my sister Lea would come to visit me and play with Eddie.

I was also relieved when my uncle, Isaiah, who'd always understood me even without words, visited me on weekdays and eased my loneliness. Ever since I was a child, I loved to greet him when he'd return from business meetings in different countries and tell me, in very flowery language, of his adventures. Through him I learned how to look at humans and understand their differences. He witnessed my mental difficulties and was like a father to me. In time I told him about Rennie's birth. I did not volunteer a lot of details; I only gave headlines. There was no need to give him many details. He understood and said to me with a warm look in his eyes, "I am here for you."

I knew and felt he would always be the sturdy oak I could lean on and rest in his shadow if I needed support.

Abram, I think, denied my situation. He never talked to me about it and went on with life as if nothing terrible was happening to me. He loved me and accepted me as I was. He was so happy with his growing, charming son, and that was enough for him. He would wash the dishes, which was a big help on weekdays when I had no maid.

With a lot of effort that took me a long time, I was able to lift my head occasionally and go for a walk with the stroller. I even invited a group of friends to a get-together at my house. Despite everything I'd been going through, I wanted them to see my standard of living, to realize what a rich husband I had bagged. I thought then that visibility was the important thing in life; today I see everything differently. It's nice for me now to remember the days gone by and recreate the nice party I organized.

My mother prepared real golden Teiglach for the get-together. Although it wasn't Rosh Hashanah, I felt the need for sweetness and wanted to pamper and be pampered. I was sure that everyone would be licking their fingers. Over the bright amber-brown Teiglach, my mother sprinkled almond flakes.

When I was a child, I loved to watch as the elongated pieces of dough that she threw into the pot of boiling honey dropped in and then after about an hour rose up to the surface of the honey. I loved waiting near the pot for the moment of ascension and solemnly announcing it to my mother. The smell spread throughout the house, an unusual, sweet smell. Today, when I remember this with the smell of death around me, I cling to the smell of the Teiglach as the smell of childhood, home and innocence.

"Dear friends," I announced as they all gathered in our large living room, admiring the view from the window, "my friends. I decided to sweeten our meeting for all of us and asked my dear mother to prepare a surprise for us. Who can guess what it is? What is the surprise? Anyone?" I waited a second for suspense and then announced with a triumphant shout: "My mother made us Teiglach." Everyone clapped and I hurried to the kitchen to bring the porcelain plate bearing the wonderful pyramid-shaped cookies. Eddie was asleep in a rocking wooden cot beside us, covered in the woolen blanket knitted especially for him by my diligent mother. My friend Hannah stood up and spoke with her mouth full: "Oh, that's the taste of all of our childhoods. Tell your mother, Etta, thanks so much. I'm already a mother and not just me, soon we will all be mothers and it's my wish for us all to be as devoted as Etta."

Diana said that what was special about my mother's dough is that she added brandy and that it's a wonderful idea. Dina noted their airy softness because she was used to these cookies breaking her teeth. Gita reminded us all of the prevailing belief that the Teiglach need the house to be quiet, otherwise they burn, and laughed: "We were always completely silent when mother made the Teiglach." We were all delighted. "Well, of course," Diana smiled, "there was always an excuse like that if the Teiglach were burned. My mother really believed that it happened because we made noise. By the way, I know," she added "that your mother's glaze also contains ginger. That's an addition that makes the taste pop." They all requested that my mother write down her recipe and make as many carbon copies as possible. "Tell her to put in brand new carbon paper," Natasha Laughed. It's so nice to remember all these small details.

Thus I played the part of the happy woman with the perfect husband and baby. I would so like to meet them today and see that they're still breathing. How did I think, before I met Kaminski, that I was the one building the tram lines of my life and choosing the timing of her daily routes? Was it childishness, or is that how everyone develops until reality slaps them in the face?

One day Abram informed me that at the tenants' meeting in our building he got to know the couple who lived above us in the building and that he really liked them. He emphasized that they were Jews and added that he would be happy to invite them to Shabbat dinner.

And so I met my neighbor Ruth, Ruth Gutkin. Ruth became my secret keeper. The one and only Ruth. She reminded me of Ruth from the scroll we read on Shavuot, the one whose words to her mother-in-law Naomi we were asked to memorize: "for whither thou goest, I will go; and where thou lodgest, I will lodge". I laughed in my heart when the quote "And Ruth clave unto her" would come over me in times of depression.

She, too, was raising a baby and we met every morning at a regular time for woman-talk, discussing everything that seemed to men very unimportant and certainly not urgent. I lived for these daily chats.

Our chats took a dramatic turn. Fortunately, the mail arrives in the morning when Abram isn't home. When Eddie was one year old the buried past emerged from its pit and knocked on my door.

I received an envelope from the municipality of Pirna.

I had not been on German soil for about ten years.

I had to sign for the letter's receipt. Registered mail is delivered from hand to hand. I signed like I was an advanced Parkinson's patient. Ruth stood by my side while our babies rattled on in baby language on the rug.

I opened the envelope and the black letters blurred with my tears. The opening officially announced that I, Johanna Friedman, am the mother of the girl Irena Friedman, born on April 7, 1923. The next paragraph said that I must start paying for the custody of the girl in the German orphanage in the town of Gottleuba.

It was a short message that was completely clear in meaning: the responsibility for this girl had passed to me.

We both sat down with the registered letter and began to plan my next steps. To the requirement in the letter was added an unwritten requirement: Abram must not know about it. This presented a very clear difficulty: Abram is the main breadwinner and we share one bank account. An hour after I received the letter, a reply letter to the municipality of Pirna was already ready. The letter was written by Ruth and announced that the official letter had reached me and that I was engaged in finding the appropriate solution for little Rennie. Ruth asked for a little more patience on their part until the appropriate solution was found.

In addition, Ruth also wrote a personal letter to Schwester Hilde at the nursery. We assumed that if Rennie had been moved to another orphanage, Hilde would know how to forward this letter to its correct address. Ruth noted that I was ill and therefore she was handling my affairs. She was interested in Rennie's well-being and expressed concern about her condition. She promised that another letter would arrive in the coming days. And the two stamped letters were tossed together into the mailbox in the square.

The next day the four of us gathered: Dear Uncle Isaiah, Ruth, Diana and me. "A council of Sages," Diana joked. Luckily that week Abram went to Lithuania on business. I opened with a funny story that happened to me exactly the week the official letter arrived: "This week I visited my mother. When I came in, she shushed me with 'Shhhh. Listen, a wonderful opera called "Forbidden Love." Listen for a bit.' I sat down and we listened attentively. 'Now the part where the governor declares a ban, you know a ban of what, outside marriage. Now Claudio doesn't listen to the governor, he does it anyway and is arrested. Oh, sometimes men are a little stupid.' And she laughed lightly. Those words, 'this thing', instead of saying 'the act of love', were familiar to me. We always talked around the subject of bodily pleasures. I listened and wondered if it was the hand of fate that the piece my mother was listening to was called "Forbidden Love"? 'Johannuchka, I love this comic piece. I discovered it tonight. Everything gets complicated there because of that crime. Later in this opera people wear masks. Where there are masks there are lies. You could also say that when there are lies there are masks. Lucky that's not how real life is.' She said this with a kind of disdain that such nonsense happens in other, distant, homes. Hahaha, and now the four of us are here together. "

"You know I believe in fate. It is no coincidence, in my opinion, that your mother discovered this opera only yesterday, when the telegram came. There's a guiding hand in the world," Ruth repeated her doctrine in life. "Well, so be it," Uncle Isaiah concluded. He was one of those people who know how to listen, absorb nuances, plan in their head without saying much, and then, and only then, speak their minds calmly. When their opinion is heard everyone listens attentively. My wonderful uncle.

Uncle Isaiah offered that he would pay for the custody of my child. That way we would gain time to think about the next step. "Remove all worry from your heart. I think you're at the start of another pregnancy. Take care of your family." That dear uncle always reminds me of his brother, my departed father.

And so day followed day. The past, emerging from its hiding place, slowly went back into its place and shrank. This event was to me like a small gust of wind that had passed. Throughout this time, it was clear to me that I was ignoring an inconvenient fact. The fact that my uncle is paying for my daughter's upkeep. I was so busy that I let my responsibility in the matter slip through my fingers.

Two years after Eddie, Mia was born. By that point I'd amassed hours upon hours of telling Ruth about my hysteria at Eddie's birth and the depression that followed. I had the urge to tell, and Ruth had the capacity to listen. Ruth and I made the connection between Rennie's abandonment and my uncontrollable fears after Eddie was born. These conversations were invaluable; Ruth got me on my feet to such a degree that I had a wonderful motherhood experience.

I got my life back.

Abram got his wife back.

Eddie got his mother back.

Mia got a loving mother from day one.

On afternoons the five of us – Ruth, myself and the three children – would take the tram to town. We visited the shops on Main Street, sat in cafés devouring cakes, visited my mother and Lea or Ruth's parents or Diana, mother to Ephraim and Menashe. I learned that my life seems wonderful when I feel wonderful. I savored every moment. Abram kept complimenting me and it was evident a great weight had lifted from his heart. Our path looked like it was heading into the sunset. Oh, such banality...

The place the children would demand to visit again and again was the Freedom Monument built a few years earlier. Eddie was so fond of seeing the woman at the top of this tall tower; in order to look at her closely he had to stand at the right distance from her and stretch his neck repeatedly to see that she was holding up three golden stars. Again and again he counted the five points of each star and again asked me to explain to him that the three stars symbolized the three provinces of Latvia. Again he tried to talk to the two guards standing at the foot of this statue and waited for the changing of the guards at one o'clock precisely. They all ran around in the rambling park by the river. This was the case on every outing. The power of routine is in the sense of security it imparts.

Abram and I also loved going out as a couple for a romantic evening at a restaurant near Liberty Square. We'd invite Ruth's teenaged daughter to look after our two sleeping angels, and watched the blue lights of the monument make the snow look so pastoral. We never tired of this beauty. We were proud of our city. We talked about the significance of this statue, the importance of our freedom and that fortunately the great war had already ended. Yes, that's what we thought then. Who could have known that a second war would break out?

We made nice trips to the Daugba banks, to the statue of Christopher the Great. Mia's first question was, "Mom, why is this man not moving?" Mia didn't understand that this was a statue of a man carrying a child on his shoulders. She believed it was a real man who was put into a small and transparent shack. Alex, Ruth's son, heard and added, "Isn't it heavy for him to carry this child?" The atmosphere was so good and there was not the slightest hint in the air of what was about to happen.

Mia's innocence takes me right back to these moments here in the ghetto, into the shaky bed on which I lie and dream about my past, to this long night that is bounded by four o'clock. My kids stopped being kids in an instant. They said goodbye to their innocence the day we were deported to the ghetto. But I will get to that in my memories. Today I am happy that Mia is embracing her doll and that sometimes she turns on the musical clock, with a ballerina dancing within it, which she has chosen to take in her suitcase.

Ah, the statue of Christopher the Great. It stands there even now, perhaps puzzled that we stopped admiring it... We explained to the children that this statue was built because of the well-known legend about the construction of Riga, whence a man named Christopher saved a baby who drowned in the river Daugba. The optimistic part, like in all legends, comes when Christopher wakes up in the morning to find a box full of gold coins next to him. The gold was used to build the city of Riga. I added that the first house of our town was built where his hut stood. Then came Eddie's questions, which were more elaborate: "Mom, why are there legends?" "Mom, who gave him the coins?" "Mom, if I do a good deed will I also find a box with treasure?" "Mom, do all people build a city with the gold coins they find in a box?"

Until one evening came when my daughter Mia was two years old, in 1936. Uncle Isaiah asked that we meet again to think together at my house the evening Abram was at his billiards club.

And once again we met like a secret spy quartet right out of a thriller. Uncle Isaiah began: "Dear girls, I've been thinking a lot about an appropriate solution to the problem we had four years ago. I thought about how to stop paying for our Johanna's child. I suggest that Rennie move to live with an adoptive family in Germany and then I would not be asked to pay her upkeep. Doing that, we would also accomplish another important goal in life: Rennie will grow up in a family, in a normal home, and not in an orphanage."

Diana responded immediately with admiration: "I want

such an uncle for myself. Your thinking is creative in a way that no one gets to. How did we not think of this before?"

"Thank you," he replied while eating a slice of cake I'd baked, as if saying by that that compliments for him were a common occurrence. "Thank you, Dianuchka. I suggest that I personally take care of starting the process of finding a family when I go to the annual trade fair in Leipzig. After four years of silence on our part we will respond and take the right step."

Uncle Isaiah dictated to Ruth the second letter to Schwester Hilde. Our decision was written in blue on white writing paper. Rennie will move to an adoptive family and Hilde is invited to a face-to-face meeting with Mr. Chaim Yitzhak Friedman in Leipzig. Ruth wrote down the meeting location and the exact time as Uncle Isaiah dictated to her.

A month later we met again on that day of the week, at the request of Uncle Isaiah. He told us he'd met with Schwester Hilde. He surprised us greatly by telling us that Rennie was still at the nursery and reported to me about the great love Hilde had for Rennie. She even offered to adopt her, but he would not hear of it, "because I do not want to trust a peasant woman. I must be sure this story is silenced forever." While the four of us devoured the bonbonniere my uncle bought at the fair in Leipzig, he summed up the report by saying that the municipality was already looking for an adoptive family.

Because our lives were so stable, we started thinking together that I would enroll in college. In the spirit of the new regime my children started to acquire a new language, which we did not use to speak in our house. They started learning Yiddish. In the fall of 1940, a Yiddish theater was inaugurated in Riga. This language sounded so musical and pleasing to the ear when performed on stage, that I began to feel an inner tickle about joining the ranks of this theater.

Oh, those were wonderful days.

Who could possibly have imagined that all this would come crashing down?

Our wonderful family life started changing in June 1940 with the start of the Soviet occupation. Fortunately, none of us had any large businesses or factories because they were all nationalized.

The start of summer 1941, only half a year ago, seems to me like it's a century away. Then, on June 14th, the cracks started appearing, like ice warming up. The Soviets rounded up thousands of Riga's Jews, some of them Zionist activists, including Rabbi Mordechai Dubin, the remarkable leader, and deported them to Siberia. Luckily we're not Revisionists, Bundists or members of the orthodox Agudat Yisrael. This deportation made it crystal clear that we were once again in a war zone. The war we'd experienced twenty-two years ago was not the only war, but the first war. Our future was shrouded in fog. I was tormented by the labyrinth of evil.

Just two weeks after that day, Riga fell to the Germans. I will not forget until my dying day the date when our world turned upside down: July 1st, 1941. Not the day of the beginning of summer, not the day of planning our big vacation, not the day of planning the upcoming trip to Jurmala, but the day after which nothing in the world was ever the same again.

We still lived together in our impressive and comfortable home in Riga.

I was still trying to figure out what was going on.

At noon, on one of the first days of summer vacation, while Abram was at work, two Germans climbed up the building's stairs and screamed: "*Wo ist dein Vater, wo ist dein Sohn, Wo ist dein Ehemann.*"[41] When Eddie heard the shouting he jumped straight into the attic and didn't move. A ten-year-old boy with the senses of an adult.

---

41. Where is your father, where is your son, where is your husband (German)

Mia stood by me as I opened the door. The fat, sweaty Nazi kicked her. This was Mia's introduction to the situation, the taste of the hobnailed boot. She cried and groaned. These damn Nazis opened all the closets in the house and took whatever they wanted.

One Saturday evening in early July the sky was heavy with thick smoke, accompanied by a terrible odor. It turned out that several synagogues in the city were burned down, with worshippers trapped inside. The fire brigade was ordered not to intervene. The Latvian mob was instigated by the Nazis into a murderous act against the Jewish population. Rumor has it that two thousand four hundred Jews were murdered in Riga that night and the following week, and another 2,000 imprisoned.

As a mother, I felt compelled not to defile the innocent world of my children and invented reasons for the smoke and the smell. We'd raised them to ask questions and take an interest in what was going on in the world around them, and now answering their questions felt like climbing up a steep, smooth mountain. I had become a mother who prefers that they do not pay attention and do not ask. I preferred, of course, to turn into a family of birds and fly over the city to another place that is run normally, as it once was. But we had nowhere to run. The prohibitions tightened around us with no way out. Our lives became a nightmare, and death was knocking at our door.

My nightmares and dark moods came back. Abram supported me and wanted very much for our children not to have added burdens, burdens that I would actually impose on them with my reaction to reality, burdens on top of the general difficulties of being Jews in Riga.

I tried very hard.

Inside I was anxious and riddled with nightmares, but tried not to show it to the children. Had Eddie and Mia already realized that we could not shield them from evil?

Several days passed and troubles began to come down on

us one after the other. It beggared belief: binding orders were issued against us, the Jews. Jews were abducted into forced labor, and many were driven from their homes in favor of Germans. I can no longer count the orders, the fences, the prohibitions. No, no, and no upon no, a pile of innumerable injunctions and constraints. This is *Verboten* and that is *Verboten* and more burdensome and strange prohibitions. It's better to forget. I'll spare myself the list just now.

We went through family hell. We had to explain to ten-year-old Eddie and eight-year-old Mia something that logic cannot grasp, that we were subject to insane, restrictive and cruel orders just because we were Jews.

Every morning I had an argument with the opinionated Eddie about wearing the yellow star. I found it difficult to utter to him the words of the prohibition in full which say that whoever violates this regulation will be condemned to death; Every walk from home I had to remind my kids not to step on the sidewalks; We could not travel by public transport, to which we were accustomed: not by taxis, not by buses, nor by convenient tram.

Then a regulation was added to wear the *Judenstern*, the yellow star-shaped badge. I found it difficult to utter to him the words of the prohibition in full, saying that whoever violates this regulation will be put to death; every time we went out of our home I had to remind my kids not to walk on the sidewalks; we could not travel by public transport, to which we were accustomed: not by taxis, not by buses, nor by convenient tram.

Then a regulation was added to wear the yellow badge on the back so that the Jews could also be seen from behind. As the days went by, Eddie the wise had already stopped asking and kept quiet. His silence was convenient, but very disturbing and heavy. I realized that he'd internalized that evil has no logic to it, and that he was the victim. Mia kept asking every day: "But mommy, why?"

At the end of summer vacation my children were not allowed to return to school. All Jews were expelled from educational institutions. But, at the same time, we were banned from entering public places, including city facilities, parks and swimming pools. So what was I supposed to do with my kids? How do you spend time with children who are constantly at home?

We stayed home, all four of us. Proud, independent Abram was forbidden from working. Another prohibition. Abram, talented and industrious, the man who had spent many years in the service of the Latvian army, was forced to sit at home. His dignity was crushed. Despite this he would not give up visiting the synagogue on weekends.

We didn't want to leave the children alone at home and I was afraid to go shopping for food. We were limited to only three grocery stores in the whole of Riga. All three were in the Moscow District, a very poor area that I'd never set foot in, even though I was a native of the city. Abram did the shopping, something he hadn't done since we'd met because it was my job. He returned on foot as he walked along the side of the busy road, without stepping on the sidewalks. My heart ached for him. The food was not enough for us because Jews were allocated only half the amount of food compared to the non-Jewish population. We started starving. Abram and I fell asleep with our stomachs rumbling because we tried to provide the children with their basic needs. Every morning I woke up to a new day with severe headaches.

The most horrible fact, the rumor passed among the Jewish families, was that a special administration for Jewish affairs was established in the Gestapo, which coordinated the investigations and torture carried out in the basement of the building. There were those who said that the detainees were then sent to prison, where they starved to death.

After we learned about rapes, even in girls Mia's age, we did not leave our children's side at all. They no longer met friends and Mia stopped asking "But mommy, why?" We lived in silence with our stomachs rumbling and fear turning into a monster.

We realized that Hitler's plan was to completely "purify" Riga of its Jews.

I managed to find out what was going on with my mother since Abram took more risks by visiting my family every week to bring them food. Once more he had to walk to the Moscow District, carrying the heavy groceries in his hands. Every time he left the house I would stop breathing. I stood at the window, unable to stop looking to the street below. I watched the street and the children watched me.

We had no way of knowing how Tanny and her family were doing. My mother arrived at the hospital seriously ill, but was turned right back out. There was no available Jewish doctor to take care of her. When I asked Abram why she could not be seen by a Gentile doctor, his reply was as unreasonable as the rest of the world around us: Jewish doctors were restricted to Jewish patients only, and only Gentile doctors could take care of Gentiles. With no treatment, mother's condition got worse and on Abram's fourth visit, in early August, she lay dying in her home with Lea, desperate and distraught, at her side.

Mother's funeral was hard to arrange. My sisters and I did not attend. I find it hard to remind myself of the fact that I did not go to my own mother's funeral. Even now my tears come of their own accord. Today I understand that mother was lucky not to have to move to the ghetto and see the bodies strewn by the roadside.

Abram was not built to hang his head down. He was looking to retaliate. None of my admonitions were of any use. I was afraid I'd be left alone with the children. One evening, as I wept softly and looking out the window, time stopped. Abram didn't come home.

Everyone outside was hurrying home, and Abram didn't come home. The moonless night darkened the world, and

Abram didn't come home. Abram didn't come home and I put the children to bed without a word. We were all silent until I broke down and cried uncontrollably. The dams burst and we all cried our hearts out. We cried for hours while my beloved neighbor Ruth came down to wish us a good night. All four of us cried, and, afterwards, all seven of us.

Looking forth through the window became my watchword. The longer it went on, the more my dread grew.

Abram didn't come home.

About a month after Abram's disappearance, and me thinking I'd now been through the worst of it, two Latvians in dark clothes came, kicking brutally at the apartment doors in our house. I heard the command – "SS officer Rudolf Lange orders you to leave your home immediately. Leave all the furniture here and go with one suitcase each to live in the Moscow district. Move!!! You have forty-eight hours" – even before they came to our door, because it echoed in the stairwell. These two were clearly reciting the same words by heart. Their laughter rolled down the stairs and was heard by all the tenants. When they reached our door I smelled the vodka on their breath.

I had two days to get ready, I was alone with two children: it was the end of summer, but soon winter will come. What clothes will the children need? Summer or winter? Summer and winter? How will I carry everything to this ghetto? In those days I dreamed endlessly of Abram coming back. I needed him so badly.

One command from the mouth of that evil Nazi officer and I had to pack our lives and find a plausible or implausible explanation and go out with the kids for this walk. As if it's possible to cancel a life in one place and move it elsewhere. Within a few hours, not enough time, I had to change everything.

Maternal responsibility made me stand on my own two feet. Not to feel sorry for myself, not to dwell in memory, but to be very practical. I can't resist the malicious orders of power-hungry men with absurd theories, certainly not with two children and no husband.

I took many of the cherished photos of my grandparents and parents, of family meetings and get-togethers. I added jewelry, each piece a souvenir of a precious moment which I could perhaps sell in a moment of need.

We packed for hours on end: "I want that," "No, leave it at home, there's no room," "But Mom," "Mom, should I pack this sweater?" "Mom, how many panties to pack? How many socks?" "You can take your doll Monica." I gave the apartment a goodbye glance. I had no way of knowing whether I would ever return. My kids acted like grownups and helped with the carrying. Eddie, at ten years of age, was already acting like a responsible man. He understood that, with his father gone, he was now both the son and the father in our family.

When we finally arrived at the gates of the ghetto, our suitcases were immediately and forcefully opened and anything of value was taken. Luckily, I'd stashed our money between the inner lining and the sides of the suitcase, which was too sophisticated a hiding place for them. They even snatched the children's comfortable and warm shoes and my fur hat. All my neat packing was soiled and wrinkled, with much contempt.

I was so happy to meet the beloved Diana with her two children at the gate. Only half a year ago we would meet them in parks and houses, but it seemed like a different era. She surprised me with her pregnant belly. We arranged so that we would share a small room in a multi-family home. One room with two beds, for six people and one belly.

Two days after the order, on October 23, the ghetto was sealed. There was no going out and no coming in, except for the purposes of forced labor. The number of men dwindled because some were murdered and some left Riga along with the Soviet withdrawal. At every moment I looked up and surveyed the surroundings, hoping to see Abram.

The curtain rose for the fifth or sixth act of my life. I'd already stopped counting. If it were a show (I wish), I would design the decor in blacks and grays, the sky: gloomy and occasionally spluttering; the houses: crowded and shabby; I would instruct the set designers to place a garbage dumpster, its contents overflowing onto the street; I would create a high barbed-wire fence that signifies the end of the world. On the fence I would hang, facing the city, the true wording of the signs "Anyone who passes the fence or tries to come into contact with the residents of the ghetto will be shot without warning". At the ghetto gates I would put Latvian policemen. I would set them as a background, but once in every act of the show, that background would move and enter the center of the frame and kill, as part of a sharpshooting competition, and steal and rape and beat casually while eating, then return to being a background. In the first act I would show the "Jewish Council " striving to maintain order, for health and education, for the daily work of crucial workers, but at the same time I would show the supply of forced laborers to the Germans. I would also include the women trying to be transparent, striving not to stand out so as not to be employed in cleaning and kitchen jobs. I started casting roles. I was debating whether to give Kaminski the role of an ignorant, evil-hearted Latvian, or that of a Christian, looking contemptuously from beyond the fence.

How pleasant to think for a few minutes that I have control over the world around me, to imagine that this is not a world I created from my imagination and that I can move characters at will. How unfortunate that it's only within my imagination.

We shivered in the cold, our stomachs shriveled with hunger. The three of us used to embrace together for most of the day. Just hug and hope that we get the brackish soup and a slice of bread. Hope that Abram would show up and join our family and that nothing else will happen.

"Mom, I'm going. Going."

"Where, Eddie? Where?"

"We are hungry and doing nothing. I need to try to get food. I'd rather die trying to find something to eat than die of overcrowding or starvation."

My only son, ten years old, spoke to me in a mature way about death and his initiative not to give up and choose life.

"How do you get food? How? Do you know?" There was no reason for me to stand in his way. What did I have to offer him? After all, in recent days there'd been a change in the menu and we got meat from a horse carcass or frozen potatoes. Our stomachs rumbled like a broken engine.

"Do not stand at the window, Mom," he asked with a smile. "I'll be back. I promise you. I'm responsible. I'm not alone."

"Are there any more children there?"

"Yes. Yes. And they have experience."

My maternal role remains only in this place, in a place where I have no need or ability to choose an opinion or a suggestion, but only to confirm with a nod.

"I'll bring us food. You'll see."

All day I waited for my two men. I prayed continuously.

In the evening Eddie returned with six slices of bread and three potatoes. Diana and her children also received one slice each. Mia came back to life thanks to her brother. In the circumstances, it was a satisfying meal.

And so it was every day. All this time I was craving for Abram to return, or at the very least to find out what had happened to him. At the same time, I was waiting, tensely, for the hour of each day when Eddie would return. My nerves were raw and exposed. I hoped that time would not just move forward; I hoped that it might bring a change for the better.

A week later I asked Eddie how he gets the food.

Eddie tried to resist: "Mom, it's going to be easier for you if you don't know. How will you survive interrogation if something happens to me?"

"Eddie, if something happens to you, they'll look for us and end us too. If you're going to talk to me as an adult, then let's do it properly and tell the truth we both know."

He agreed.

"You know that the children who are older than me go to work every day, right? I figured out that they work in factories outside the ghetto gate. So I came to them and offered one of them to carry me in his backpack if I promised not to move at all. I explained that while they were working, I could forage for food. At first they all said no because they thought it was very dangerous, but then one of them called Moishe'le agreed. He told me that his sister was already dying and he had nothing more to lose.

"Moishe'le set us a code: When he says the word 'oy' aloud, followed by a short pause where I have to count silently to fifteen and again 'oy oy', this is the agreed sign that I can get out of the backpack safely. If the 'oy oy' doesn't sound I'm not allowed to move. Moishe'le explained to me exactly where the garbage cans into which the remains of the German dining room are thrown, at what time he reckons I can sneak in there and steal the food, where I will get it and where I can hide the treasure until we meet in the evening. He drew me a map and explained it to me step by step. I was given a detailed explanation of where I could hide during the day, how and when I would know to enter the toilets where I'd be put in the backpack again. Moishe'le once again made sure to remind me exactly what the Germans looked like and what the Latvian policemen looked like so I could avoid them."

Mia put her head on his lap; he stroked her hair. Diana sat on her bed and listened intently. Her children played in another room with other children their age.

"Mom, Moishe'le agreed to my offer because I give him half

of the treasure I collect. Moishe'le is already sixteen years old. He is strong and works very hard but doesn't get enough food. Do you understand?

"While he risks carrying me inside his backpack, he also benefits from the deal. He eats most of it in the bathroom before I'm quickly pushed into the backpack. He stuffs the rest under his foot inside the shoe or inside his underwear, where he sewed a pocket, to give to his sister. His whole family is gone. Moishe'le told me yesterday in the bathroom in a whisper into my ear that thanks to me he manages to work and doesn't collapse from weakness."

After he started telling me, he wouldn't stop: "If I were a girl I could hang out outside and get to Riga and steal food. But. You understand? For boys it's harder."

"Yes of course."

Mia sat up straight.

"I didn't want to worry you too much after Dad disappeared."

"Brave boy. My hero," that's all I could say. His blue eyes, so like his father's, had a determined look. How I wanted Abram to be able to be proud of our son too!

Eddie the hero helped us all survive. There were days when this kid even brought us all a slice of cake or a whole apple. He couldn't carry much in his pants. I had already completely calmed down and stopped worrying about him. I realized that he and Moishe'le made an excellent team. We were hungry but less so.

"Amazing. I'm proud of you, my son," I used to tell him every time he returned in the evening and planted a kiss on the ten-year-old man's forehead.

In time I managed to see who Moishe'le and his close friends Moishey and Itzik were. They were three young boys who instead of enjoying their teenage years and running after girls, instead of studying at a proper high school, instead of living with their father and mother, and perhaps even grandma and grandpa, instead of all that they were doing backbreaking work after experiencing the loss of their close family members.

I didn't stop waiting for Abram. I was constantly listening out for any masculine voice that sounded like Abram's. Each day I tried to solicit news from the laborers going out to work outside the ghetto gates, but to no avail. Rennie would sometimes come up in my thoughts: was she living happily somewhere in Germany as a Christian in the bosom of a Christian family, unaware that she's a Jew? Or has her ancestry been discovered and she had been thrown into the ghetto alone?

Perhaps the wars and human cruelty make the moon hide its face during most days of the month? The moon, I noted to myself, carries on as usual. On that first night when Eddie returned home with the food he collected, and on the night I'll come back to soon, on those two nights the moon was full. Eddie has been feeding us for a whole month. The routine of normal life, only six months ago, has been completely erased. All that's left of it is a leafy green tree that grows in the ghetto, the sky above us, the bright sun, children's games and Diana's advanced pregnancy. I clung to this routine, to help me feel like I was holding my head over the morass we are all immersed in.

Two and a half weeks ago, exactly seventeen days ago, Eddie did not return in the evening. This anticipation was far more difficult than waiting for Abram. Though it's impossible to compare heartaches, losing my son was already far beyond my ability. I sat petrified and silent on the bed. I obeyed his request: "Don't stand at the window, mommy". Mia comforted me constantly. Diana wept softly and guardedly, occasionally letting out a heart-rending groan. Every one of these was a sign for us to groan with her.

Night fell. The date was a week before Christians celebrate their Christmas. Snow covered the whole world, the roofs, the paths, the surfaces and the fence that surrounds us. The world was seemingly festive: everything was white and the moon was a shining circle above our heads. The whole world did not interest us, we were encased within our nightmare. I listened carefully, I thought maybe Eddie might be late. Minute followed minute.

I heard the footsteps of the guards' boots, I heard the dogs barking, I heard my neighbors walking down to the building's shared bathroom. I did not hear my son's voice.

Where is my child?

I did not eat or drink anything. Throughout that day I knew time would not move. The next night there was a knock on our door. I jumped out of bed at lightning speed. Moishe'le arrived. He embraced me without saying a word. We sat hugging.

"What happened?" I asked.

"After two hours of work the announcer at the factory announced that we were moving to another location. We got on a truck and were transported to another factory. I had no way of letting Eddie know. We're not going back there anymore. I have no idea where he is now."

"No!!!" A scream escaped my mouth. It cut through the air, and maybe even found its way to God, if he were already done with his break. There are situations that reach God, there must be. Cruelty must have a limit.

Moishe'le told me as he tried to speak confidently, but his voice was trembling: "He's small and quick, he's smart, he's brave. Have a hope that he managed to escape and that you'll meet soon or after the war is over."

We fell silent.

I thought of the time when the outside appearance, the façade, was important to me. My short-statured boy is a giant. A man. A *mensch*.

Now I was waiting for two.

My spirit was bewildered. My mind became unhinged. I was completely confused.

Little Mia sat by me and caressed me non-stop, as if we had switched roles. Now there were just the two of us left. Abram disappeared, Eddie did not return, I'd handed Rennie over. Oh.

Every hour or so, the same sentence would escape me: "Why did I allow him? Why?!"

And so the days and nights passed.

Mia did not leave my side.

Moishe'le visited every few evenings and once called me "Mother." It rattled my soul.

God, what have you done to our children?

Every day passed without the progress of time. One day, one night. Two days. Two nights.

Eddie did not return.

The third day. Third night. Fourth day. Fourth night. Fifth day. Fifth night.

Eddie did not return.

I go every day to probe men and boys. No one no longer works at the factory where he was left.

Moishe'le told me: "Eddie's mother, I want you to know that Eddie saved both me and my sister with the food he stole for all of us. You've raised an i-n-c-r-e-d-i-b-l-e child!" I was proud of my hero. It was small comfort.

Sixth day. Sixth night. Thus passed seventeen days. Slow and mournful.

All able men were taken elsewhere. Who knows where. Diana was approaching her due date. We had no men left. I have no way of finding out anything about Abram or Eddie. It seems there is no chance they will come back here.

A week ago, as first light began to slink its way in, people from another area of the ghetto were assembled on a street in the main square close to our apartment. An endless column of people, guarded by armed policemen, passed by our window.

Young women, women with babies in their arms, the elderly, the disabled and infirm assisted by their neighbors, boys and girls – all marching. Suddenly, right in front of our window, a German SS man started firing a gun at point-blank range into the crowd. People were gunned down and fell on the paving stones. Confusion reigned. People began to trample the faces of those who fell, pushing to be as far away as possible from the SS man who fired wildly. Some threw away their bundles so they could run faster. The Latvian policemen shouted "Atrak, Atrak"[42] and cracked whips over the heads of the crowd... When the horror ended, corpses were scattered everywhere and blood still dripped from the corpses. Most of them were old people, pregnant women, children, the disabled – all of whom could not keep up with the inhuman pace of the march. I stood by the window and watched until noon. I watched motionless, petrified, for several hours. I heard Diana talking and laughing with Mia and I did not even turn my head. I was stuck there by the window.

The next day I heard that the Latvians found a small bundle that turned out to be a living child, a baby about four weeks old A Latvian guard took the child away. We all hoped that child would live.

---

42. Quickly (Latvian)

Schwester Hilde

⋘ 1940 ⋙

My personal pain mixes with my country's pain. It's been nearly four years of Rennie living only in my memories. My life is somehow back on track, but in my heart, every minute, there's a big black hole. My child's absence will never leave me. I have no clue what became of her. Is she happy with the Oberlanders? I wonder if she's already in love. I pray with all my heart that the Gestapo won't find out she's a Jew. Perhaps she's betrothed? She's seventeen already and it pains me to think that she might get married and I won't be at her wedding. My heart aches because Rennie doesn't contact me and I really hope that it's because she isn't able to. She knows my address.

My great comfort is knowing that this Jewish girl isn't living in Pirna, the town our village sits by. These are dark days. There's a rumor going around that Sonnenstein Castle has become a place of murder.

I know it from a source that's one hundred percent reliable. Ernest Winter's adoptive parents, who are actually his aunt and uncle, are highly respected people here in Gottleuba. The woman, Maria Schein, and I keep in touch. Ernest finds in my visits a connection with Rennie, whom he misses so much. I feel that this boy and I have something in common – love for one wonderful girl. His father is a very important engineer at

Sonnenstein Castle. One day, as I was sitting for a cup of herbal tea in their house, Maria dragged her armchair close to me and whispered in my ear, "Hilde, I want to tell you a secret. My husband will kill me if he knows I'm telling you, but I cannot bear the secret. You know, secrets make life difficult."

"Yes, I know. Tell me. I promise you I'll keep your secret. My word," I smiled and crossed myself.

"You see the beautiful castle up there, Sonnenstein Castle. Yes?"

"Of course."

"My husband is a senior employee there and knows all about the secret undertakings there. Three days ago, all the wives of the engineers who work there were invited on a tour, with the thought that we women give a helping hand to the success of our husbands." Maria moved closer and continued: "I know for certain that what is happening there was planned ten years ago and that until now, men and women of all ages, including children and teenagers, have been murdered in the castle, including children and teenagers, all of whom were deformed and retarded."

My eyes filled with tears and my heart was pounding hard and very fast. A scream escaped me: "What, murderers of children? Killing disabled people? Close to us?! God forbid!" And I crossed myself. I wanted to keep talking about the right of all human beings, everyone, even the different and the foreign, to live like any human being born unto this world and the duty to protect those who are born with flaws, but Maria kept talking and introduced the words "racial purity" into our conversation: "My husband is sure that we should stay away from these different people and not allow them to reproduce. He claims and believes that they are defective people. He says that the gypsies and the Jews should also be eliminated. Imagine me hearing, in my house, that if all Jews were murdered then our race would improve. He's sure that the world needs to be organized.

Ordnung muss sein, that's what he keeps obsessively repeating," she said and shrank back in her seat.

I no longer said what I wanted to say. She is suffering and wants to share with me. For many days now I have seen and heard that our area is full of hatred for Jews, and I understand that Sister Katrina represented the opinion of the silent majority when she told us all four years ago: "If there's a Jewish girl secretly in one of our monasteries, it would be good if we passed word of her presence directly to the Gestapo. That's the order. Why should we get into trouble?" I already understood that those who can't reconcile the situation with their beliefs are the ones who keep silent. I've never liked Katrina. How can you differentiate between people like that?

Maria continued: "You're a devout Christian. I know you are a decent and loving woman and you have a lot of compassion. How does Christianity dare to preach compassion while on the other hand there are Christians who cooperate with the Nazis? I'll tell you. I too, am silent in front of my husband. I want to keep the peace." She turned her head to the right and to the left to check that Ernest could not hear the conversation and began to shed tears. "I want to share with you the tour they gave our loyal women, that's what they call us. Do you think Sonnenstein Castle is just a psychiatric hospital? It's nothing like a hospital. The Nazi program is called 4T. There, now you know a secret. Sonnenstein Castle is part of a diabolical plan," Maria whispered to me as if there was someone else in the room. "Since the beginning of the year part of the castle is being used as a murder center. You won't believe it, but in the basement of the men's sanatorium these monsters installed a gas chamber and a crematorium. I saw it with my own eyes. A new brick wall was built, with billboards on it, just to disguise the crematorium smoke. We met workers living in the castle whose job it is to burn the bodies!!! With no shame, even with pride, the showed us how things work there: the victims enter through a gate, the staff separates the men from the women and every victim goes to a room with two doctors. We went into one of these rooms as part of the tour. *Jesus, hilf mir*[43]. I saw the doctors verify the identity of a person with a lame leg from birth fabricating and recording in their neat notebooks, without batting an eyelid, his cause of death. From there we continued to the basement where about thirty victims were gathered. Professor Paul Nietzsche, who conducted this guided tour, told us with a proud smile that 'The victims are taken to the gas chamber disguised as a shower cubicle. They die there the moment they realize that they are not showering, as we told them. We outsmart them. Ah, our ingenious idea.'" Maria had a really hard time breathing. I quoted from the bible: "For ye are all the children of God by faith in Christ Jesus. For as many of you as have been baptized into Christ have put on Christ. There is neither Jew nor Greek, there is neither bond nor free, there is neither male nor female: for ye are all one in Christ Jesus."[44] And added "Oh, Maria. Christ teaches us that religion is equal between all believers, no matter their race, color or class." We both crossed ourselves. We understood that what was happening within the beautiful castle does not fit in with the spirit of Christianity at all.

"I had no choice but to continue with the tour because I already know what happens to those who oppose these Nazis and what will happen to me at home if I give my opinion. After they're killed, the victims' corpses are burned two by two in the ovens. You won't believe it; before they're put in the oven they have their gold teeth pulled out."

Oh, Jesus, hilf mir! I cried. It was hard to grasp. Up there in this ancient castle on the hill, people are being suffocated to

---

43. Jesus, help me (German)
44. Galatians 3: 26-28 (King James Version)

death for the crime of being born lame. We both fell silent, ashamed and miserable.

Maria stared at the floor and asked me to listen to her so that she could voice all her disgust, and maybe that might help her continue with her life: "The ashes from the crematorium are dumped in the sanatorium or straight into the Elbe River. The Sonnenstein office sends the victims' relatives an official death certificate, with a fabricated cause of death and a standard letter of condolence. I can't stop smelling that horrible smell. It permeated inside me and tortures me. Their mechanism is well oiled. I think these dastardly murders will never be discovered."

I did not voice my thoughts: racial purity means Jews' lives are at peril. Maybe Rennie was lucky after all.

From that day on I added a prayer to the ascension of the souls of the victims. I understood Maria and because I wanted her not to feel lonely, I made sure to visit her more than usual. And so I learned from her that in the castle, in addition to the men and women, there were also hundreds of children who suffered from birth defects, chronic diseases and various impairments.

Shame on this world. Rennie had no chance of staying in Saxony. They would have killed her in some way. These are very difficult words, sharp words, but it's really the truth.

The world has gone crazy.

JOHANNA

My night of thoughts is over. My soul's journey is at an end. The end of the night is here.

My little Mia and I stand together at the meeting spot. Winter. Despite my headache and the darkness, I could identify our neighbors' voices. It was so dark, as if the light did not wish to take part in these moments taken straight out of Dante's Divine Comedy, as if the light decided that its place is not in this inferno. The December cold hit us with all its might. Our breath could not be seen. We stood hunched, close to each other to warm our bodies. Nothing is clear, but you cannot ask. I heard it whispered that a few minutes ago Simon Dubnow, the renowned historian, was shot because he was too ill to show up at the gathering spot. What a loss to humanity. Is there a humanity? Is there a world that knows what we're going through here?

My thoughts keep running away to distant sights. I know when a person's life runs through their heads, I understand beyond what I want to understand. The images of my life have run through my head all through this night.

We seem to be marching towards Daugavpils, the big city. I've often taken the train this way. Everyone is silent. There is snow on the path. One of my arms is connected to reality, to my daughter Mia shuffling by my side. Her head is bowed as she stares at the footprints in the snow, the footprints made by the two girls walking in front of us. I hear her whispering to herself: "one two three four. One two three four." Constantly. The girls' long hair dangles from their backs below the tattered fur hats they wear. My other hand hangs in the air as if waiting to be given some sort of task, but it has no use other than wiping my nose with the coat sleeve.

The sound of a girl sobbing sounds like an accompaniment to this march. Our neighbor Olga asks, "Where, God? Where?" No reply. Well, did she think God would answer her? That any of us know what even God does not know? An elderly couple in front of us converse in Yiddish: "Yanke'le, a little more. We'll be there soon. Give a little more. You can." Like that all the time. She tries to encourage him. He occasionally answers her with one word: "Gevald."

I think Diana and the boys are somewhere ahead of us in the column. She is already into her ninth month. What will happen to her?

I try not to look at people falling, defeated, face down into the snow by the side of the road, not to listen to the clubs beating their heads, not to internalize the moans and whimpers. I manage to lift my aching left leg followed by the equally painful right and so on again and again. Step by step. With all my strength. I move. "One two three four. One two three four. One two three four." Mia's little fingers slide into my fingers. Sometimes I change position and stroke her back and then our fingers interlock again. I lack the courage to look her in the eye. I am ashamed in the name of God and in the name of humanity.

We're marching in a long line. All along our way, on both sides, amused Germans in uniform stand and scream "*Schnell. Schnell.*"[45] Here and there, Latvian policemen also wave batons, shouting: "*Atrak, Atrak.*"[46] When they suspect someone is too slow, they beat them.

---

45. Faster (German)
46. Faster (Latvian)

Who'd have thought that my command of the German language would serve me in such circumstances, that I would be able to understand the conversations they have between them? Dogs bark in the distance. How uplifting to throw my thoughts back to the school years, to the wonderful world of a warm home with Dad and Mom and two other sisters. Now I long to return to the childish naivete, and believe that if I want to be pampered, there are those who'd be happy to pamper me.

Where are we going?

Do I hear shots, or are they only echoing from within the depths of my own horror? Mia and I drag our legs through the snow. Darkness still surrounds the world. Both of us are overwhelmed, tired and exhausted. Mia holds my hand very tightly as if she wants to give me strength. Sometimes she says to me, "Mommy, I'm here." With that, I manage to find the strength to continue on this infinite path that I did not choose.

The guards on both sides of the road continue to land blows with their clubs. I cannot understand why a certain person gets a death blow to his head when he was just walking in line as requested. Anyone who stops or even bends down is shot in the head immediately.

Dawn is breaking. I can see the red blood pooled in the white snow. I don't know which is better: to let the darkness remain tonight or let the dawn shine. Once again, I have an image that allows me to survive the sights: I imagine that the reds are works of art at the Museum of Modern Art in Riga. It's only in this way that I can keep this monstrous truth away from me. There's still some advantage to having a weird mind. I'm going to a modern art exhibition with Eddie and Mia and Abram will arrive soon and join us. My right hand is holding the hand of another girl, a black-eyed girl who is looking at me. She just whispers in my ear "Mommy. My mommy." What is going on in my head?

While I was inside my alternate world, I stepped on bodies that fell along the way.

I'm bewildered. Where, God? Where? *Gevald.* One two three four. Sobbing.

Mia grasps my hand tightly and directs me with a glance to the side of the road. Diana, shot in the head, kneeling as if giving birth. The red blood flows and the snow swallows it. Maybe the baby is still fluttering in her womb. I manage not to cry. My empty stomach is heavy and very sore.

My Diana. My friend. My wonderful confidant. You've always been warm and loved life. Rest in peace.

Mia has stopped her counting. We are both silent and continue to drag our feet. After about a hundred steps wise Maya quietly asks me the question I immediately asked myself: "Where are Menash'ke and Froi'ke? Are they ahead? Did they continue on their way alone without their mother and father?" I do not answer her, but clasp her little hand.

At noon we arrive at the train station, which I recognize, Rumbula station. Then everything happens very quickly. We are led with screams and shoves "*Schnell. Schnell. Schnell. Atrak Atrak. Atrak.*" into the forest. What's their hurry? Do they need to carry out their murderous orders before dark sets in? A shriek commands us to undress and dispose of all our valuables. I do everything like an automaton. Mia follows me. What an innocent, childlike, pure and clean body my girl has. I wish I could fly with her from here beyond the treetops. I'm willing to give anything to get my little girl out of here.

The hair of woman standing next to me turns white right in front of my eyes; this is what happens to her the moment she undresses. In an instant. I shift my gaze to the treetops. They, up there, do not know what the human beings at their feet are capable of. They feel the light breeze and enjoy the scorching cold. They are in their natural place.

Now we hear gunshots very close, up ahead. We have no

further illusions about our immediate future. I've given up on attempting not to look helpless in front of my child, I understand that she, too, already knows that this world is not lead by her mother. The world is no longer divided into adults and youngsters, parents and children, women and men, pregnant women and old women; we are all equally helpless. No wand-wielding angel flying about sprinkling kindness and human compassion. There is only a very real devil. The horror inflicted on us is bottomless. All that is left for us is to obey the commands mechanically. Clear thought, guiding thought, critical thought, these are no longer available here.

"I'm thirsty. Water," my Mia whispers. She does not turn to me and does not ask me. She expresses the strongest need I also feel, the tremendous need for water, for a drop of water to moisten the dry throat. One drop. Just one. Thirst drives us crazy and overcomes all the other hard feelings.

We are forced to run through a cordon of guards with only our underwear on, in a cold seven degrees below zero. We have no need to cover our hearts; they are clean, pure and true.

"Water. Water. Water." *Gevald.*

We stop at the lip of a huge pit that looks like an inverted pyramid. This pit is full of naked bodies like ours lying on top of each other and still alive. Bodies bleeding, writhing and regaining consciousness. Here and there I can notice the movement of a hand or head or a moving leg protruding from the pile. Weak moans and sighs. People suffocate under the weight of human flesh. *Gevald.*

Mia stands behind me. She's trying to get my body between her and this most horrible sight.

What kind of mother am I, that I bring my daughter to a place like this? What mother allows her daughter to be shot to death? Abram was saved from this inferno. My Eddie is not here either. Tortuous are the paths of fate. It is beyond my understanding.

I look at the people standing in front of us in line: the two beautiful young girls are trying to sing a hushed song together so as not to be afraid and brave the worst of all. A woman with a baby in her arms cries non-stop. A boy about three years old and a girl about five years old who cares for him like a little mother. A young boy whose gaze is searching for an escape route. The old couple, she no longer comforting him, but him still saying *"Gevald"*. Two three-year-olds already lying on their stomachs, as if shot, looking up in horror and tears at the thugs. A five-year-old boy hugging his teddy bear. An older man shaking all over and peeing in his underwear. Next to us, a man with a long white beard prays and recites *Shema Yisrael*[47] and Mia and I. And after us, many, many more. Too many. Multitudes.

Suddenly I see my grandparents. I see a Shabbat reception at home. Dad wrapped in his tallit. I'm in red lacquer shoes with Dad in the synagogue. I help my mother make Teiglach and stand by the boiling pot. Flora Cohen caresses me. Rennie. Rennie wrapped in Hilde Rein's hands looking at me. Abram and I dancing at our wedding. Eddie and Mia building a tall tower from blocks. Diana, Ruth and I stand at the foot of the statue of Christopher the Great. My beloved uncle Isaiah talking to me in our living room. Abram embracing me lovingly. Our hero Eddie bringing... "Everyone stand in line. Enter the pit. *Schnell. Schnell.*" My thoughts are interrupted. I understand what is perfectly clear: I am about to walk into my grave. I want to encourage Mia with a look in my eyes, but at the same time I feel great shame. I both look at her and avoid her eyes. We walk on top of the bodies. *"Schnell. Schnell."* Then a sudden silence. No one whispers, no one sighs.

---

47. "Hear, O Israel", the first words of a significant Jewish prayer, encapsulating the essence of the Jewish faith. Observant Jews endeavor to say the *Shema* as their last words.

Part of me is in the whirlpool of fate, another part is in the silence that lies beyond.

I am thirty-nine years old. Mia is eight years old. Now I know why I saw my whole life pass before me like in a movie tonight. Today, December 8, 1941, I am going to die.

Crack....... Crack .... Crack. Individual shots, each dropping another person. The old man was shot only once in the back of the neck and joined the pile of bodies.

I'm befuddled. I look at Mia. What does Mia see? I'm already having a hard time seeing straight.

"Mia'le," I say.

"Mommy, I'm here," the little one replies.

"Mia'le, I love you. Maybe our Eddie is alive and maybe Dad too."

"I'm thinking of both of them now, too. Mommy, I love you."

"I love you."

"I love you."

"I love you."

"You ... I ... you ... l---o---v---e."

My blood is pounding so fast that I feel this crazy pounding throughout my body. I try to breathe, but my breaths are superficial. "Air. Air," I plead with myself.

I hear Mia, my little girl who'd grown up in the past three weeks, whisper to herself. I open my eyes knowing this is my last look at the world. I look at Mia and want to smile at her with all my heart and soul, to say goodbye to her with a smile. One last smile. She smiles back at me. What greatness of spirit this eight-year-old girl has. Her little legs are shaking and making her shake all over.

Please God, I ask that we die at the first shot.

Rennie? Where's Rennie?

Mother!!!

IRENA WHO IS RENNIE
WHO IS RINA

⤳ 1941 ⤳

Good things come in pairs.

First: my Hebrew is getting better. I can converse freely, use the right words – sometimes even quite nice ones – and read the Hebrew-language newspapers. But I count and think in German.

Second, and even better: I got married. Yes, 1941 is the best year of my life. A blessed year.

We were married at Café Pinati in Rehovot, next to Yoland's sewing shop. We chose this café, built as an addition to the first floor of a pink-hued two-story house at the junction of two main thoroughfares in Rehovot. We knew the place well and all our friends met there many times. It was simple and narrow, but wide enough to contain all our beating hearts.

On the wedding day, childhood memories came to me. I saw with my mind's eye Schwester Hilde congratulating me. She smiled softly and gave me a hug. I looked at her blue eyes tearing up in joy, at the white nurse's apron over her golden curls, the clean white apron tied behind her back, her tall white shoes. I felt warmth coursing through my body. I wanted to lay my head on her chest, but she faded away. *So ist es.*

I wondered what Ernest Winter would think of me giving him up and choosing Jacob. I was sorry I could not invite my friends from the sewing shop. They would have rejoiced along with me. But my wonderful reality made me content with what I had, my good friends who were so happy with me, Manny, Rachel and Inge and a few other girls from Nahlat. All of our guys, including the groom, wore the Brigade uniform. I married a soldier, but I knew what he had under that uniform. I knew well the warm heart, the heart hidden from all, the heart I married.

For the first time in my life, I put on a little make-up. When it comes to make-up, I'm a nun. Rachel gave me red lipstick and applied it. I felt beautiful and happy in the white dress and veil I received from Inge, Hansel's wife from the Brigade who got married before me. I held in my hands a bouquet of white carnations, with a single white lily among them. The flowers perfumed the air with a delicate scent that carried me up to the realms of happiness and freedom.

The smell of flowers brought to my mind my sheep Laura, me feeding her in a meadow somewhere in Germany. "Laura in my suitcase is white. So suitable here. She was born solemnly. I would weave a colorful chain of wild flowers around her neck," I thought, but it was not to be. "No bride brings her favorite doll to her wedding ceremony," I scolded myself.

"With you, my dear Rina, I am filled with song and joy" Jacob said with loving eyes and brought me back to the ground of reality. This became one of the most beautiful sentences said in connection with me, one of the sentences that would provide welcome sustenance during gloomy moments later in life.

Throughout the wedding I was enveloped in a warm pleasantness, as if I were in a womb. A womb that desires me, and not an abandoning womb. I felt protected and embraced, wrapped up and wanted. I was inside a pure drop springing from a peaceful eternal spring, a drop in no hurry. A drop next to its friends, enjoying the pleasant rays of the sun and the sounds of the woods. Jacob was with me in that drop as we embraced with our entire being.

I felt a light bride, a bright bride, floating bride. A bride dancing the dance of life. There were moments in our ceremony where in my imagination I was standing at the top of a mountain, my hands spread upwards with all my fingers spread out. A strong desire came over me to let out a scream with all my might and watch as it shakes even the blue mountains, faded across the horizon.

At my feet stood one white sheep.

✥ Summer of 1944 ✥

I tasted the honey for three years.

We lived in a rented room in a family's house in Kiryat Haim. The Brigade helped us find the place. We moved to the north of Israel and thus I moved away from my good friends. I tried to accept things as Jacob accepted them.

I was lucky that I attended "Our Kitchen" classes at the vocational school in Zwickau. I managed to impress Jacob here and there with my cooking: schnitzel expertly fried, mashed potatoes, Spätzle fried in breadcrumbs on which I sprinkled cinnamon and sugar. I baked cheesecakes and even managed to make strudel dough with apples and raisins. Jacob consented that I buy Shpak and Ham at a Haifa deli. The frying ham with egg on top made me feel giddy. The tastes of childhood and their intoxicating aromas.

I managed to be a proper wife.

The Brigade remained stationed in Israel, so we decided that it was time to make our child. The time for waiting was over.

When the fruit of our love growing inside me was only three months in the making, The Jewish Brigade announced it was preparing to enter the war against the Nazis.

Once again I am abandoned by those who are supposed to protect me. Rennie the deserted, Rina the abandoned. Dear lord, when will this world work the way nature intended it to? I'm wracked with worry. Jacob is going off to fight and I might stay a widow with a child. What would I do alone in this world? During these moments of worry, alone, I had to stop myself from crossing myself.

Jacob enlisted and left for North Africa and I was left without him, the baby developing within me not waiting for my man to return. The rhythm of life inside me will not match the rhythm of the war men wage.

I got a very nice room and a lot of love from the Ostrov family in Kiryat Haim on Alf Street, close to the railway tracks. Their two older daughters were like sisters to me and this whole wonderful family relieved my loneliness and longing.

Relieved, but did not dispel my loneliness.

Relieved, but did not alleviate my longing.

Relief, but Jacob was within my soul twenty-four hours a day, seven days a week.

Christmas Eve increased my loneliness. I did not want to join the Ostrov family like every evening. I closed my eyes. Deep inside the blanket, in the darkness, the wonderful Mass at the Gottleuba church came to my ears. I heard the clear voices of the church choir in my head, harmonies lifting to the sky. I tried to guess the exact timing of events so I could be with them. I saw Schwester Hilde beaming with happiness and me jumping around in new clothes around the tree we decorated. I became an unburdened child. I wept with longing, while humming and tapping my belly to the beat of the bells ringing in the song of a sleigh flying through the snow, the belly within which Jacob's and my baby had been growing for seven months.

Communication between my lover and me was only via postcards. Each such postcard released handfuls of oxygen into my soul, oxygen that revived me for several more days until it was gone and I needed the next postcard to arrive. Jacob told me they were in Benghazi, in Libya, and a few months later updated that they were moving to northern Italy. He always signed that he was faithful to me and that I was the love of his life. It was a consolation that filled my whole being.

⫷ 1945 ⫸

On my last visit to the doctor, he informed me: "You're ready for childbirth. The contractions could start any day," and they did. The labor pains started with a frequency that announced that the birth was fast approaching. The Ostrov family did everything for me. I was in a taxi when Mrs. Ostrov joined me. Close to the Heroes' Bridge in Haifa, my moans of pain and Mrs. Ostrov's encouragement concatenated: "Rina, you're the hero. We're nearly there. Take a deep breath. You're wonderful."

I was taken straight to the delivery room. "When you feel strong pain, push out." I screamed: "It hurts all the time!" and pushed. The baby would not move towards the exit and into our world. I squeezed breathed right tried not to scream the pressure was terrible I breathed I hurt I hoped and nothing happened.

"What's your name? Rina? Good. Mrs. Rina, push harder. What's wrong with you?" The nurse scolded me. Again and again and again and again. I'm doing my best, and the nurse scolds and is not satisfied. About two hours later, me completely exhausted by now, the doctor arrived. He checked and this time the one who was reprimanded was the nurse: "Can't you see that the baby's head is lying diagonally? What did you want from her?" He brought forceps and within one second my baby was out.

Her crying released my crying. Such relief! The moment had finally arrived. Even in the moments of my birth there was a misunderstanding and I suffered insult and humiliation, but the feeling that prevailed was the amazing fact that I was a mother. How happy Jacob will be, what a shame he's not here, I told myself. I sent him kisses and lots of tears. Mrs. Ostrov stood by my side and said to me in tears: "Rina'le, you have a daughter. Congratulations." "A daughter or a son, it really doesn't matter to me. The main thing is that she'll be healthy and that Jacob would come back soon." A nurse showed me my baby, wrapped in her arms. So small and so mine, I was happy.

The labor pains and the pains of childbirth itself were forgotten when I realized it was my dream closing the gap with reality and touching it: this will be my baby. I will take care of her, the baby that will be mine only and we will never part. I wondered about the woman who gave birth to me: perhaps she, too, was alone when she gave birth, without her husband, and I really could not understand how she gave me up after I'd grown inside her for nine months. A strange and insolent woman. I hugged my beautiful baby, looking at me with her black, intelligent eyes. I held her with a sense of triumph. I loved the moments she would look at me closely and as if telling me, "Mommy, we're together. Forever."

Every time I put her to bed I sang my lullaby to her softly, and heard Schwester Hilde join in.

Guten Abend, gut' Nacht,
mit Rosen bedacht,
mit Näglein besteckt,
schlupf' unter die Deck':

Morgen früh, wenn Gott will,
wirst du wieder geweckt.

I always finished the song just for me and for Schwester Hilde, because my little baby always fell asleep before the end.

I chose a new-fangled Hebrew name for her, not after Jacob's grandparents, nor a name that brings all the dead of Europe into our young home, but a name that I chose on my own – Nurit[48]. Giving the name was my only advantage to Jacob not being there, I was given the opportunity to decide for myself. It was my little feeling of victory: I stand on my own two feet; I have an opinion. I love the name Nurit, a modern flower name that symbolizes for me the blossoms in my new country. So special. I loved this flower even back in Germany, where I enjoyed its colors and we used to decorate the entrance hall of our orphanage with vases. What's more, my girl was born when the Nurit blooms, in the spring.

I found it natural to take care of my Nurit. I enjoyed every moment. After all, for thirteen years I specialized in caring for babies ...

The fact that I now had my own family, a family that no one will take away from me, that fact gave me great hope.

❧ 1955 ☙

MY man came back from the war. He returned straight into my arms late in 1945, ten years ago. Nurit was already making her first steps and was babbling a little. The young man who was her father didn't find it simple to connect with such a small creature added to our life without being a part of the wondrous processes of her growing inside me and coming

---

48. Buttercup (Hebrew)

out into the world. I understood him, but more than that I found the situation painful. I thought that landing from that manly world of war straight into a home with a wife and daughter might take some time. I knew the best cure for the soul's hardships was time. I wanted to be patient. My dream flew over reality and did not touch it.

Jacob and I went through intimate moments when he tried to hold our daughter in his hands. He tried. He hugged and patted. I became a little nervous. I lost the required patience and said things I shouldn't have: "What's the problem?" "If you love her, she'll feel it and return your love. That's what babies are like." "Bitte schön,"[49] "She's your child too," "Halten sie ihr baby nur eine halbe stunde am tag,"[50] "Enough! It's time you'd be able to help me raise our child. An hour a day, half an hour, ten minutes, anything. J-a-c-o-b. Bitte schön."

At such moments, I couldn't fulfill my promise to myself to speak Hebrew as much as possible. The German language flowed out of me. I'd been waiting for this triplet of togetherness for too long. While Jacob was away at war the images of the three of us as a close-knit family passed my hours of yearning, and when reality barged in, I began to lose my patience. In my more reflective moments I knew that Jacob, too, did not expect to come back to such an angry, demanding spouse.

When Nurit was one year old, we moved to our house in Gev-Yam, a house of our own, not a room rented from a family. This time, too, we received assistance from the Jewish Brigade. The house was sunk into the dunes that reached as high as our room window. I became an Israeli housewife, a housewife who loves her husband and waits for him every day to come back from work. A housewife who meets her many neighbors at the

---

49. Please (German)

50. Hold your baby for half an hour a day (German)

grocer's and slowly discovers that they also speak German like her and enjoy little chit-chats.

As time went by, Jacob began to take pride in his daughter, to stroll along the streets with her and enjoy talking to her. Not a day went by that I did not revel in hearing him put Nurit on his lap and playing *Hoppe Hoppe Reiter*.[51] Cute, smart Nurit would roll with laughter. Despite this, something began to crack inside me and memories of the past grew within my mind during the day and became dreams at night.

I felt torn between two identities, between the mountains with one sheep, and dunes of yellow sand scattered in the wind, between two religions, between two types of scents, between being an orphan and having a family, between the dull sky and the bright and burning color, between being secretive and revealing the truth, between shame and openness, between the sturdy pine trees in the mountains of Saxony and the only two short pine trees I planted in our yard, between German and Hebrew, between Rennie and Rina, between Friedman and Seifert. I was torn, and Jacob was always by my side to heal me. The need for my healing, gentle work for Rina, became an everyday task. Jacob knew how to do this with love, understanding and listening.

Despite all my inner dichotomies, I was a fortunate woman.

Then I decided, with Jacob's encouragement, that it was time to write to Schwester Hilde and tell her of my whereabouts. I got a very quick reply, considering the fact that all of Saxony where I grew up was now behind the Iron Curtain, in East Germany. It seemed like Schwester Hilde had been running for the postman every day in the ten years that had passed since we said goodbye, and looked forward to this letter. She seemed

---

51. Go go rider (German). The first words of a very well-known German children's song. The small child is bounced on the adult's knees.

to have sat down to write her reply as soon as she'd finished reading. She wrote to me in Old German, *Sutterlin*, which is the historical form of German script, an ancient and different script whose use ceased before I was born. A form in which the letters of the alphabet are completely different. I couldn't read it at all, but my smart Jacob could; he'd attended a normal school. I bring here its opening and closing:

Dear, sweet Rennie (short and sweet name for Irena)

It is all still clear in my memory when we said goodbye in those days in Zwickau. You cried and I was very unhappy. It took me a long time to get my peace of mind back. I miss you very much. I watched over you for thirteen years. You were nine days old when I first held you at the hospital in Dresden.

I met your mother then and we have not met since. When your father also disappeared, you were transferred to Zwickau. Perhaps your mother is no longer alive because she was very ill then —

Thank you very much for your letter, I was very happy to receive it. Please write to me soon and tell me everything in detail, why did you leave Zwickau?

Gottleuba, 8.11.46

This moving letter revealed to me what was hidden from my tear-covered eyes that I shed like a tap left open in the garden: for Schwester Hilde, too, this separation felt like a rupture of a living organ.

I came back to the letter many times. I came to know it by heart. And still I found myself opening it and reading it over and over again. Sometimes I got up at night and took it to the bathroom. I wanted to be with myself and with the letter for one more minute. Schwester Hilde told me of all the people I knew there. Her letter threw my entire being into the depths of Gottleuba, into the vanished world I loved so much. I read and mourned the deaths of several people, the illness of others; I was happy to read about marriages and children born. I also read about Ernest Winter, who was still single. Schwester Hilde wrote that she gave him my address in Israel.

When I arrived in Israel, I thought I would be at peace here, but the reality was different: when my Nurit was two and a half years old and I was in the fifth month of my second pregnancy, a war started here as well. My ridiculous fate caused labor pains on the most inopportune day. Jacob ran to the only phone in the area to order a taxi to take me to Haifa, to Molada Hospital, but instead of a taxi, an armored vehicle arrived. We couldn't understand why an armored car was taking a woman in labor to the hospital, but the answer was, "That's that. It's an order." Only the day after the birth did we learn the truth: my daughter was born the day the *Haganah*[52] learned that the commander of the Arab forces in Haifa was going to bring ammunition and explosives, as well as money to pay the salaries of the Arab fighters in Haifa. The *Haganah* ambushed the convoy at the entrance to Kiryat Motzkin, an ambush so secret that even the tenants who lived there didn't know about it. A decisive battle took place in which many were killed, a battle in which the *Haganah* achieved what it wanted and therefore later succeeded in taking the city of Haifa. Devorah came into the world as if already saying: "Hey, I can't set my schedule by your wars."

Devorah was the name of Jacob's grandmother. He insisted on the name and explained that he must stay true to his family tradition and name his daughter after her. I tried to resist, but Jacob was right as usual and his wish prevailed. Thus, the essence of my two daughters' names stands on the two sides of

---

52. The Jewish defence organization in Mandatory Palestine, before the State of Israel was founded.

the divide that runs across my life: a new, springtime name versus an old name from the diaspora. A name I'd chosen versus a name Jacob had to give. A name that says that I have the choice and a name that speaks of family expectations and tradition.

I raised my two daughters as best I could. Yoland, Jacob's sister, sent them beautiful, original identical dresses from Rehovot whenever she had the chance. Making them my beauty queens, two princesses with clothes that looked like the ones in *Stern* magazine that I subscribe to. Nurit and Devorah'le were good friends and I, to the best of my ability, was content with that.

To the best of my ability.

Every morning at exactly 11am, after the house was washed and lunch was ready, Edith Shalgy, my German-speaking Czechoslovakian friend, and I would meet for our daily get-together, either at my house or at hers. I was reminded of Francesca's routine. We rode our bikes. We talked about cooking, cleaning, shopping and especially about the children. We never discussed our past or heartaches and arguments, as befits two keepers of the German tradition. Edith, my close friend, knew very little about my past. *So ist es.*

Kiryat Yam was full of ex-Germans. On Saturday mornings everyone would go forth and meet friends, hordes of Germans wandering hither and yon. *Spazieren.*[53] In the summer we'd all meet at Galia beach by our homes. On Sunday nights we'd play Canasta with the beloved Ilka and Lippa who rode their bikes over from the nearby Kiryat Shmuel.

The routine gave me solace and peace.

One fine day as I returned from my shopping with a full basket, debating in my head whether to start making the soup or roasting the meat, I rested my bike on the wall and saw, in

---

53. A walk, particularly on Saturday mornings (German).

the box devoted to the mail and the milk bottles Kaminka the milkman would leave us, an envelope with a stamp from East Germany, but the address was not in Schwester Hilde's handwriting. I was surprised that there was, in that faraway place, someone except her who did not forget me.

"Strange," I remarked to myself and could hardly wait to get into the house and open the envelope. The handwritten letter said:

"Dear Rennie,

I got your address from Schwester Hilde. There's not a day in my life that I do not think of you, my friend. I would like to come and visit you at your home. I will arrive via Romania. Rennie, will you agree to reply to me quickly? Thank you.
I really miss you and want to hear all about you. After you answer me, I will send you a telegram from Romania , in which I will tell you exactly when I will arrive.

Yours,

Your childhood friend, Ernest Winter."

Ernest promised me we would meet again. Unbelievable, he actually intends to stay true to the words he said to me in the moment of our parting.

Jacob and I discussed the matter. Jacob thought that Ernst might be feeling guilty about the actions of the Nazis and that therefore he felt the need to visit Israel. I thought the contents of the letter said everything and that there were no hidden motives: Ernest missed me. I also wanted to see him, but Jacob and I were concerned that he might not know that I was a married woman and a mother of two daughters.

I also wanted to see him, but we only had two rooms in the

house and there was no place to spend the night in the whole of Kiryat Yam. I was intrigued to see him but at the same time I was really afraid that a window would open to the past that would flood me and that I would not be able to return to the blessed and relaxing routine I had laboriously achieved. I was afraid that this portal would make Rennie overcome Rina, the Christianity I had buried deep inside me would overcome the Judaism that doesn't really speak to me, and especially that I would be overwhelmed with longing for Schwester Hilde, who raised me.

In the immediate return letter I told Ernest all about the accommodation problems, and the fact that there were no cafés in Kiryat Yam, and added that he should write to me when he arrives, I am always available. I signed with the words "Your childhood friend, Rennie, her husband and two daughters." Jacob suggested this so that Ernest would know for sure that I wasn't single. I was Rennie again. The landscapes came back to me, the walks in the snow, the house where he grew up, Patrice the shepherd and the ringing of the bells, Fronella, our first teacher. I was awash with memories of Ernest and myself, and the deep friendship we felt for each other.

Ernest stood at the door of our house in Kiryat Yam with a bouquet of white roses in his hand. In the days before his arrival I cleaned the house thoroughly, tended to the garden, bought a new coffee service, traveled to Haifa and tried on many dresses until I found one I liked. I greeted him looking very carefully coiffed. Behind me stood Jacob, with Nurit and Devorah'le peeking from behind us. The four of us greeted him as I faced him.

Ernest and I looked long at each other. I noticed Devorah'le asking "Who's the spiffy-looking man?" as we shook hands warmly, as we did back then. We carried on talking as if twenty years had not passed and we were still in Gottleuba, telling each other all our secrets.

Excited, we sat down in the living room. From that moment on, any fear I had of the encounter vanished, and joy and curiosity flooded me. Jacob was a gracious host. Ernest liked the coffee, served in the impressive new service, and the apple strudel. He was almost as handsome as my Jacob. A tall, thin man with a small mustache that he did not have as a child...

I tried to see my house and my girls through his eyes and get inside his thoughts. I imagined he thought the girls were beautiful and well-educated, and probably calculated that they were younger than we were at our last meeting. We were thirteen years old.

Ernest told us that he was a journalist, and that his offer to cover the young state of Israel in an article was welcomed, despite or perhaps because of the heavy weight of the past in Germany. He said that he was staying at the Zion Hotel in Haifa and that the next day he would interview Mayor Abba Hushi. He has already interviewed passers-by on the Haifa streets and noted that it was not hard to find German speakers in Israel. He was single and happy in his life. The first article about the State of Israel to appear in a German newspaper will be his, but the real reason for its writing will be told only here, only here between these four walls, he said.

"I was worried about you. I know very well the horrific history that took place on German soil. Rennie, I was always worried about you. I was so happy when Schwester Hilde told me that you wrote to her and that you were sent to Israel. I had to hear your story from you." He fell silent, looked down at the floor and repeated one word – "had".

Ernest looked at Jacob and suggested that he and I recount our experiences in the nice lobby of his hotel in Haifa. "We have a lot of people to go over, people you don't know. I promise you I'll watch over her. I've made enquiries before arriving in Kiryat Yam and there's a nice quiet café in my hotel that's open till midnight. I promise you, Jacob, that I'll keep her safe and return her by taxi to your front gate."

And so it was.

We had a sumptuous dinner at the spacious restaurant next to the bar, with a string trio playing in the background, a meal of the kind that Jacob and I could not afford. We were happy and nostalgic at the same time. Ernest told me that he had moved to Dresden, which was heavily bombed during the war, and that fortunately he was recruited to a lowly clerical position in a warehouse in Berlin and had no part in the Nazi war machine. I told him about the Oberlander family and especially about my escape to town hall, and about coming to Israel. I told him about Manny and Rachel, my friends, and about meeting Jacob at the pool in Rehovot.

"Rennie, Rennie. Your memory is very fresh inside me and I not a week passed in my life without my hoping we would meet again." He sounded forthright as usual. He hadn't changed. I have a real friend. A friend all of my own. The borders in this world and twenty years had failed to blunt the bond between us.

He drew closer and whispered in my ear: "Rennie, the main reason I came here as quickly as I could, I mean the earliest I could travel to Israel, is that I wanted to tell you a secret. You first of all. My secret has already intensified inside me and is hard for me to bear. With every day passing, I felt that my secret wanted to reach your ears and see how you would react. It's a strange and difficult secret. Unusual. When I was a child you were the girl who heard my secrets and reacted well. After all, you are the one who helped me deal with my orphanhood." His eyes teared up.

"Ernest, what's this secret? Are you terminally ill and not taking care of yourself? Do you have children out of wedlock? You ran someone over and did not report it to the police? What?"

" Rennie, now is the moment I'll tell you. Will you still be my friend?"

"Always," I replied, feeling ten years old again.

"Rennie, when I started growing up, around the time you left, I found out I liked boys. That's the truth. I am attracted to men and not to women. I'm not married and happy that way. I love children and I would so like to be a father, but that's impossible for me," he said with a pained look.

"Dear Ernest, for me you are the same Ernest. I heard about this, I know there are people who are attracted to members of their own sex. But you know, obviously Adam was not like you, but today there are many more like you in the world. That's what I think."

Ernest trembled with excitement. "Oh, you're so great. As for Adam – you're right." And he fell about laughing. We laughed together.

"Rennie, it was worth it for me to get as far as Kiryat Yam to hear your reaction. You are the one and only for me. A real friend," he said, grabbed my hand and pressed it warmly.

"I've felt like this for twenty years. At first I suffered a lot because after all in Germany *Ordnung muss sein* and men loving men is not the correct order of things. Rennie, do you accept me as nature made me? I came as far as Israel because it is the most important thing to me in the world that you accept me and understand me. My heart hasn't changed. Believe me." His eyes sparkled and the sincerity was evident in his face. And suddenly the taps opened and we began to cry together, weeping over the various painful truths, the fate that rules us, his secret and our friendship that will soon have to end again. I took his hand and told him: "Ernest, I accept you as you are. It's really unusual, but I believe it's your nature. I have no arguments with nature. "

He smiled and added, "Your Jacob need not worry at all now," and we burst out laughing. As it was when we were children, when Ernest laughs a lot he starts crying, when he cries I can't stop laughing and we both end up holding our stomachs. Then we both say together "Oh, it's so good to laugh!"

With this personal statement of his Ernest cracked the shell of secrets that enveloped my world and made me tell him in great depth and detail about my life, not just the headlines. I knew we would soon say goodbye so I dared to tell him secrets that even Jacob did not know. "I pay a daily price, D-A-I-L-Y. I experience so many moments of loneliness and impatience. I constantly struggle to swallow my nervousness and anger." He listened intently, as if he knew our time together was running out and he had to treasure every word and every sight of mine. "I'm cross with my younger daughter for being rambunctious, but I know I'm worse than her, but it doesn't seem so from the outside because I am very, very, very restrained. I swallow, deep inside me, all my memories of the past, the dreams I had and my longings. I keep everything inside. I have constant pressure coming out of my sore stomach and climbing up my throat. Inside me is a heavy stone. When I'm alone, in the morning hours, I sit and cry to myself. In these moments I hear you call me 'Rennie' and I run along mountain paths with you. " Ernest brought his chair closer to mine and hugged me. I started crying. He wiped my tears away one by one. His gesture increased my flow of tears.

I felt heard: "I'm insecure. All these housewives who grew up in a family and could see how a wife and mother functions within a family. I never had a personal example. I'm constantly afraid I'm wrong. Most hours of the day, when I'm out of the house, I walk on eggshells. This is how I feel. My insecurity comes out of me in many situations, especially in moments when people bring a lot of information to a conversation and roll out their opinions. In such conversations I take a step back and send Jacob forward. There are many moments when I prefer being transparent, invisible."

"Rennie, you were always an example of bravery and courage in my eyes. When I wanted to do well interviewing for a good job I saw you in my mind's eye and poured your determination and courage into myself. You, insecure?! Is that what life has done to you?! Woe to us."

"Breaking away from Schwester Hilde and Gottleuba made me feel like I was divided inside. I was torn inside, and not in a gentle way, but with a rough and painful pull. I'm still bleeding."

He said one word – "trauma".

"Jacob is a real find.' I need you to know that." I noted so he wouldn't think I was just a poor woman, constantly suffering.

We sat silently together, hugging each other.

"Do not envy me for moving to a different culture and such a different country. Ernest, it's not easy for me to be Rina and speak Hebrew." He listened and I added, "And live with the flying sand that gets into everything. Really."

"Rennie, you are so talented. You are a brave and strong woman. I know the truth about you. You've been through trauma and I'm glad you're now telling your little secrets. I knew, I felt, I thought I should come here to visit. I hope that tonight you will return home to your family lighter and more whole."

He said the word I use about myself, without hearing it from me. "Whole. I am whole. You are whole. They are whole. The whole world is whole!" I burst out laughing.

When I entered the house at the latest hour I'd ever come back home alone, Jacob was sitting with an ashtray full of cigarette butts and grabbed me in a crushing hug. I immediately said, "Jacob, you won't believe it, Ernest told me he likes men. He's not attracted to girls." I somehow felt the need to start reporting on the spirit of the meeting with my friend, to dispel any possible concern.

Ernest Winter. My friend. childhood friend. How good you came. I miss you already.

"Jacob, stop! That's enough!" I stood in the girls' bedroom pleading for their souls. When Jacob decided that one of the girls needed to be spanked, he would not listen to me at all. He was in his own private world, very determined to carry out the punishment. He hits the girls occasionally, sometimes very roughly. My girls are like me, they never cry out or weep, even after they are limping from the pain. I could never understand parents beating their children, but I find it ten times more difficult to witness my husband doing that terrible thing to my girls. I'm ashamed of it, but I'd never managed to stop him. Sometimes, during those moments I stood there and cried. All the tears that did not come out at the Oberlanders' come out now, when I'm the mother. I begged Jacob, told him I was an abused child and that his beatings cut my soul apart, but he never listens to me during these times. At least I'm not like Francesca, I was never silent when they were beaten, I always tried to stop it, as hard as I could. Jacob was sure he knew better because he'd grown up in a family and I hadn't. He always replied: "That's how you educate children. You can't educate with namby-pamby. It takes a strong hand." Even now I have no way of knowing if that's the way it is in all families, how they teach their children. Though this hurts me so much, I don't discuss it with anyone else, not even with Edith in our daily chats. This dirty laundry, you do at home.

With experience gained from the workers' farm in Nahlat and the tea herb garden in my old nursery I cultivate a large garden. The trees have grown tall and bear fruit: the custard apple tree by the garden tap; over to the right, by the hop-bush hedge, are two rows of vines curling around the trellises I made for them and providing bunches of grapes all through summer; the two guava trees we all adore; the feijoa tree whose fruit we eat with a spoon. The mulberry tree is at the far end of the yard, but whatever mulberries remain after the neighbors' kids are done gorging themselves we find, black and sticky, on our porch where the birds had left them. Every day I tend the grass by the porch and sweep out the pine needles from the porch.

I'm most proud of my vegetable patch. I grow leafy greens and love seeing Devorah'le eating parsley right off the plant. The tomatoes and cucumbers provide our morning salad. I covered the strawberries with a net so the birds won't get at them before we do. The radish is growing pretty well but the carrots were small and inedible. Perhaps they don't do well in the sandy ground. The white lilies have spread by the sides of the veggie patch and intoxicate us with their scent. Their blooms always remind me of my wonderful wedding and of my friend Ernest's visit.

Opposite this patch I tend a flowering patch. Before every summer and every winter, I plant seasonal flowers: asters, marigolds, chrysanthemums, African daisies, low-lying verbenas and portulaca bushes. I plant tubers of hot red amaryllis, dahlias in a variety of colors. The fiery flowers of Indian cress spread out leisurely and paint the garden in passionate colors. When I grew sunflowers, my girls and I would look on in amazement as all these yellow flowers turned their heads towards the sun sailing through the sky.

Devorah'le once discovered a tomato plant on the edge of our front lawn, between the vegetable patch and the flowers. She tended it and watered it. It grew and grew but gave no tomatoes. Today it is a large and shady white cedar tree...

We don't lock our doors. Everyone knows everyone in our little town.

Our house is in a very convenient location, almost exactly in the middle of my world: the girls just have to cross the road to be in kindergarten, and it's five houses further to elementary school. The grocery store and the greengrocer are two houses away from us. In the center of town is a larger grocery store –

Brahad's – and Pincus's toy store, a hairdresser's and a butcher shop. Greenspon the cobbler is Edith's neighbor, and Adler's shoe store is on the main road that crosses between Kiryat Yam and Kiryat Shmuel.

There's just one telephone in town, at the Friedmans'. There's no sidewalk on the road by our house. It really does not matter to us because no one in Kiryat Yam has a car, so we can walk in perfect safety on the sides of the road and sometimes in the center as well. We all ride bikes. Even Jacob rides a bicycle to work in Haifa Bay. Summer or winter, scorching sun or hailstorm, always on his bicycle. Every day he rides home from work at three-thirty with a block of ice for our icebox strapped to the bike.

A *ma'abara*, a temporary camp for immigrants, was set up around the elementary school. It houses Jews who'd escaped Europe and who'd finally managed to reach Israel. The new immigrants are destitute. They live in the sands in barracks that used to be a British army base. We call it the "Kamp". Their fences are old iron beds. Devorah'le told me that Rachel Hershko, her classmate, lives in a shack whose floor is old carpets and the walls are a hodgepodge of wooden beams and hot corrugated iron. But, she noted, the house is very clean and tidy.

In light of the circumstances, I thought I was lucky.

Jacob was promoted at the "Even Va-Sid" factory where he worked and was even sent to Europe for study. The number of card nights a week increased and we were both paired with great bridge players. The parties of our German gang are fun: we dress up every Purim, fool around playing games and take much pleasure in dancing. Most of the parties take place in our house because our living room, which used to be a restaurant for British soldiers, is unusually large.

"Mom, where is your family? Are you an orphan?" This was what Devorah'le asked me one evening. Nurit was already serving in the army and Jacob was having his afternoon nap, so the two of us were alone in the house.

I didn't reply. How could I tell her? What would she understand? I'm so used to living with my secret.

But she insisted: "Mom, tell me. Please."

I couldn't understand how come she'd never once before asked me about my family, and now suddenly this.

"Mom, this is important to me. Truly. I need to know," she started nagging me. I gave her a little information. The truth is that I didn't know much more myself. My anger at my mother manifested itself by these words: "If I ever meet my mother, I'll kick her."

This seemed to take her by surprise, but she tried to hide it and said "I understand how you feel. But remember that this woman is my grandmother. Do you have childhood photos? Documents? Anything?"

"No. I won't have it. We won't start with this business."

She fell silent but came back a few days later while we sat on the bench under the kitchen window. "Mom, I ask you to reconsider. It's my right to know who my grandmother was. That woman isn't just your mother, she's also my grandmother."

Thus she hammered on for quite a while. Her persistence formed a crack in my secret. She cares. I started thinking about this secret. Maybe, in spite of my great shame in being abandoned and my mother forgetting all about me, maybe it really was my daughter's right to know?

Until one day, when Devorah'le asked once more, I untied

my apron (not quite suitable attire for such moments) and took my drawer out of the white bedroom wardrobe. I laid it on the table and declared: "Here you go. Pry away."

First, she found the postman's photo from one of my birthdays. It really wasn't the best thing to start with. The April 7th celebrations were a great joy when I was little, but starting her journey in the middle of my story would just confuse her. I wanted her to understand and told her: "I was born to a woman who abandoned me when I was a few days old and handed me over to an orphanage in Germany. That woman doesn't interest me in the least."

And my younger daughter has never since stopped searching for traces of my family.

EPILOGUE – DEVORAH

Dream

An undefined location. A universe without borders. Anyone who was a person on this earth is a tiny soul that resembles a firefly. Everyone is now equal in size and light. They are all eternal.

No plans, no future. No body, no weight and no gravity. There is no religion. There is no competition. No jealousy.

We all soar lightly.

It doesn't matter what we were there for: man or woman, young or old. It doesn't matter how our lives ended, whether naturally or prematurely. It doesn't matter at all what our faith was or whether we attached ritual to it.

Anyone who'd intentionally harmed others back there isn't here. Maybe they'd burned.

Here too God is not seen, his spirit might be hovering over our infinite universe. Perhaps.

Some say that God is within us, that this is the light that shines and illuminates our path.

∽ 2004 ∾

The long-awaited envelope has finally arrived. One moment that combines over forty years of searching.

My curiosity has fueled the fire of the search since I was seventeen. I tirelessly checked with the tools that were available before the Internet. I met many people throughout Israel, wrote letters, published an ad in the newspaper, spoke on a radio program, inquired at Yad Vashem[54] and was invited by them when a Righteous Among the Nations award was awarded to a person from Riga, I went to a psychic who sees through photos, phoned every Gerson family in Australia, looked for Kaminskis in Argentina, recruited one of my daughters to the search as part of her 'family roots' program at school. I tried everything. I felt a tremendous need to understand what my life was made of.

The incentive for me was a daily event I experienced in our home: Every day at two o'clock in the afternoon, my mother would return from work and bring to her ear the radio receiver for the "Relatives' Section." I was intrigued and realized that the truth is complex: she says she will kick her mother and yet she longs for her mother to look for her. She needs a mother who wants her child. She imagines and waits for the moment when her mother, despite the abandonment, will return to her and want to connect with her child. She misses a state of survival that she cannot remember: to be a daughter, to have a mother. I was overwhelmed with compassion. I am the daughter and granddaughter, but I am beginning to be in the role of the caring and inclusive mother. The duality in her treatment of her biological mother spurred me to help her and me, and to understand what happened before she was born.

---

54. The World Holocaust Memorial and archives in Jerusalem.

The breakthrough happened when the Internet age transformed our world into a single village. As the Iron Curtain fell, channels of communication with Riga and East Germany became possible.

Time continued to move forward, as time will do, and left its mark on us all.

When I thought I had already discovered everything, Barbara Kirchner arrived and it all started anew, but now in a very professional manner. The angelic Barbara, a German woman I didn't know, introduced through a friend, supported my hands as I held the loom and wove the full image together. Barbara carries within her a huge need to support us Israelis, and so she volunteered to help me with my search. We worked every day, tirelessly. She wrote, telephoned, traveled, thought, poked and prodded, and enlisted the help of local officials.

Barbara and I looked under every rock. We started with the official form that my mother showed me first. That form gave Barbara her first entry point: my mother's mother is named Johanna Friedman; when my mother is nine years old, her mother is a married woman living in Riga. Irena Friedman, my mother, is in an orphanage in the village of Gottleuba, south of the city of Pirna in Saxony, Germany. On that year the municipality of Pirna appeals to Johanna demanding that she pay the upkeep for her daughter in the orphanage. To this I added the information my mother told me she remembered Schwester Hilde told her, that her father's nickname was "Friedland" or "Friedlander." I added that the orphanage was a nursery and that I understand how Hilde couldn't bear saying goodbye to the girl she was raising. She fell in love with her.

We went through every photo and every letter in my stash of documents, which had moved out of the drawer of the white wardrobe of my childhood home and into a drawer in the wooden dresser of my own study.

Together we examined, with thousands of miles separating

the two of us, the photograph in which my mother looks about ten, her hair cut in precise bangs, very serious, her gaze melancholy beyond her years with no glimmer of mischief in her eyes, holding a baby in her arms while sitting on a rug and not on the grass. Around her are toddlers and also one blonde woman with a nurse's apron on her head and her clothes all in white. The woman sits on a wicker chair; in her arms, two babies who look like twins. It's clear that this is the orphanage my mother spoke of. "That woman is Schwester Hilde. That's obvious," I said to Barbara. In the background are fruit trees and flowers. A nice, well-tended spot. The strange fact was already clear to me: that all the children in this photo are babies and only my mother is a pretty mature girl. On the back of the photo was handwritten German in a script that I could not decipher because the letters were all connected to each other. I could only read one word – 1930. That is, my mother is seven years old. This is her chronological age. The writing notes her age as seven, but she looks much older. Barbara, too, could not read the text because Hilde had written in German letters in *Sutterlin*, which hasn't been widely used in Germany for many years.

In the next photo we saw Schwester Hilde lovingly holding a baby and once again the only word we could read was the year – 1942. By this time my mother had already immigrated to Israel and married my father. In the third photo, the nurse is sitting in the garden on a wooden bench and holding two babies, and on the back it says 1963. I was already in the ninth grade of high school by that time. It was easy to figure out that my mother had kept in touch with Schwester Hilde for a long time.

If that were so, then of course Schwester Hilde would also have received photographs, from those taken annually by Stanitz the photographer. Once a year we would dress in our finest clothes and our parents would put us on their bikes and ride to have our family photos taken by Stanitz in Kiryat Motzkin. I liked the trip not because of the time freeze in the filming nor because of the "musical moments" I experienced in the studio, because only there did I find myself "playing" the accordion and the recorder, not even because of the beautiful clothes we had to wear. I liked the moment when the photographer would look at me closely and I would give him a searching look right back. I always wondered how it was that one of his eyes was blue and the other green. Because of watching the riddle of his eyes, I was always very willing to be photographed.

Barbara's creativity, assiduousness and willingness knew no bounds. She checked different theories and pieced the puzzle step by careful step. Most important was her deep knowledge of East German culture, her familiarity with the place where my mother grew up and the various local authorities and agencies. With her help, I was granted a Latvian passport as well as my mother's birth certificate, and a declaration that the record shows that my grandmother Johanna stayed with Flora Cohen and Gustav Arnold in Leipzig while pregnant. The Kaminski name was suggested by Barbara: Walter Kaminski, who was my grandmother's age, was also known as "Friedlander" and his family lived close to Pirna. They immigrated to Argentina. I remembered Ernst Winter's visit well. The apartment neighboring my grandmother's apartment in Riga houses a family by the name of Gutkin.

With the help of dear friends, some of whom I met only via my computer screen, people who understood me, I finally managed to find my grandmother's name, Johanna Gerson. I wrote to the Riga Archives, and a large white envelope arrived in the mail.

Greek mythology introduced me to the goddess Hecate, whose name means "she who comes from afar". The distances are those of time and space and my Hecate is Johanna. Hecate, goddess of crossroads, had three heads, each looking to a different way heading out from the crossroads. I like the idea of Hecate being a unification of three goddesses representing the grandmother, the mother and the daughter, the feminine chain of a family. I thought Hecate embodies my grandmother, my mother and me, my own intergenerational family chain, the three of us intertwined and interconnected. Hecate, depicted on an ancient Greek coin as holding a loom, helps me weave my own path. I agreed with the ancient Greek belief that, in the place where a person must choose their path and feels uncertain, their feminine ancestry can help, especially the grandmother.

The envelope from Riga contained two A4-sized passport photos of Johanna, a family tree going several generations back, and photocopies of the birth certificates of Yedidia-Elias Friedman, Johanna's father, and Johanna herself, a photo of her husband, Abram Gerson, and a photo of her aunt.

Johanna's square chin is so similar to mine that I immediately accepted her into our family. I see a well-groomed and elegant woman in the shades of my mother, my sister Nurit and mine, as well as Nurit's daughters: brown eyes, dark hair. In the second photo she looks older, her eyes look melancholy. I saw sad eyes echoing deep grief. Does everyone see Johanna like that, or is it me, ascribing her with constant pain about her separation from her daughter and the heavy secret she carries?

Her date of birth is in March, in which many of our family were born, and the exact date of her birth is my grandson's birthday.

I was overwhelmed with excitement: I was given a family. Admittedly a two-dimensional family, in black and white, inside an envelope, but I can start walking towards the light. My mother is no longer alone in the world; she belongs.

Somehow.

Unfortunately, by this time my mother was already in a state of advanced dementia. She could not recognize me, saw imaginary figures and would talk to them. In her moments of loneliness, she would not ask for her mother as we all instinctively do, but called out "Schwester Hilde". It was simultaneously amazing and exciting. Schwester Hilde was her mother when she was a child and remained so even in this state of primordial survival. My mother would not call out "mother"; she never had one. I understood that when she left the orphanage, my mother had to say goodbye forever to the woman who loved her.

On the day I received the letter I met with a spiritual friend. "What should I do?" I asked him. "My mother deserves to know her family tree, to see her mother's face." He did not hesitate at all and replied: "Tell her everything. Her soul will understand."

The very next day, on as the heavens opened and dropped buckets of rain over the entire north of the country, I drove to her nursing home in Kibbutz Ramat David with the envelope. Mother was nearing the end of her earthly journey. She was usually closed within her inner world, which could only be penetrated by the music tapes we prepared for her. Dementia had devastated all remnants of communication between us.

My mother was sitting in a wheelchair, wearing a diaper under big blue sweatpants, her eyes glazed and her head down, her hair woven in white and black was disheveled, and she was surrounded by people seated, open-mouthed, in wheelchairs. Here and there a family member sat next to one of these detached people. The odor that dominated the hall space was that of urine mixed with disinfectant. My aversion to this place was constant; I could not free myself from knowing that the day might come when I, too, would be in this situation.

I sat down in front of her, in the corner of the hall. "Mom," I addressed her as if a conversation between us was a routine act. "Mommy, I'm holding an envelope I got from Riga. In it is the answer to the question I first asked when I was six." I took no heed of her disengaged gaze and kept on: "I found your family." I wept as I told her of the chain of events that led to this moment. A nurse who passed by remonstrated: "You shouldn't cry next to your mother, she has troubles of her own."

I opened the envelope and showed my mother the photographs of her mother Johanna. I could feel her reluctance to know fading. She looked on with as much interest as she could muster. I saw tears in her eyes. I felt encouraged when I saw her watching me, reacting, her glassy stare changing to an alert, understanding look.

With my mother by my side I felt more comfortable analyzing the results, so I showed her the family tree. We read it together:

"Your mother," I told her, "Is undoubtedly Jewish. She's the youngest of three daughters, and your grandfather had three older sisters. You know, that's nice to know because Nurit and I also had three daughters each but Nurit, as a bonus, also has a son. You had a brother and a sister. Perhaps someone from your family survived the holocaust. They might be alive here in Israel with a family."

Her posture was less droopy than before. I couldn't stop weeping. There were a few things I didn't dare mention. I didn't say that my mother was not part of the Freidman family tree. Johanna, according to the Riga archive, had only two children. My mother was also stricken from the official genealogical list. In fact, "stricken" is the wrong word; my mother was never included in that list.

I also didn't read her the part that said that her mother was murdered together with her eight-year-old daughter Mia in the forests of Riga as part of the horrific Rumbula Massacre. I didn't want to tell her what I knew about the Rumbula horror, a horror that took place in the forests before the death camp showers were invented. Johanna and Mia were listed among those murdered and I hoped they died quickly and did not have to undergo the nightmare described by the three women who had managed to live through it. I hoped they didn't have to walk, naked and wounded, until the next day, begging for help that would not be given, knowing the pain of being transparent, not considered a creature born in God's image. I hope neither of them was still alive, groaning and whimpering into the night, suffocating under the hundreds of bodies on top of them. I thought a lot about little Mia, walking alongside her mother, not letting go of her hand on the way to the killing pit. About Johanna, helplessly watching her little girl as she was killed. I made myself part with the disturbing thought that perhaps the eight-year-old girl might have been separated from her mother by force while they were divided into groups of eleven, each group forming a line which the Nazis would shoot together and let fall into the pit. I never even touched on the fact that my mother, owing to the vagaries of fate, was spared this massacre. It was enough that my mother knew that she has a family tree, that her mother had a face.

I keep hearing, in my mind, my grandmother Johanna's personal cry, merging with the cries of so many other innocents. I see an image of cries rising to the skies as a single bundle and encountering a cold, opaque ceiling. This monstrosity brings me to ponder fate, the evil in humans, the illusion of choice and free will, the danger of theories and ideologies, including the practice of ritual.

We parted about two hours later and I drove away with the heavy rain obscuring my vision.

The moment I came in the door, my shoes overflowing with water, a phone call came from the aged care home: "An ambulance took your mother to the Afula hospital. She had trouble breathing and even turned blue." My sister Nurit was very worried, but she was living in Arad at the time, many hours away.

My car was still warm. After about two hours of driving, with water pelting down on the road and the wipers working at their fastest setting, I found my mother sleeping in the hospital bed at her ease.

The doctor, who was sitting calmly behind a table, greeted me with "I examined your mother thoroughly and found nothing."

"I believe you are right," I replied quickly and he raised his head and seemed very attentive to hearing this strange statement.

"I find it is puzzling that she turned blue and suffered from shortness of breath, as her caregivers at the nursing home reported. This is a condition indicative of great excitement."

"The excitement of a person who has received weighty information, for example?" I asked.

"Indeed yes. Maybe," he replied to me and whispered to himself, "how strange." and added: "I won't give her any medicine. There's no need." I agreed immediately, without hesitation. An hour later, an ambulance took her back to the nursing home.

To my amazement, it happened just as my friend believed it would. My mother seemed so excited to hear the story that she had difficulty breathing. The human shell that my mother had been in for a long time was filled with human warmth and a remembering, sensitive heart. A spirit entered her and brought her life. It was the first and only time I realized that there were things in our world that are hidden from our understanding. I experienced the soul understanding even as the brain cells were being erased. In those moments, fate was good to her. I hope my dear mother left our world more reconciled.

On the way home I visited her again at the aged care home. I found her sleepy and relaxed in her bed, listening to the tape we made for her, a collection of classic tunes and songs she particularly loved. "Little Drummer Boy" played in the background. In my childhood years my mother was always excited to hear it played on the radio. Today you can find countless versions on

YouTube. I only recently learned that this is a Christian song sung at Christmas. Perhaps the ecclesiastical *a cappela* style made her love cantorial music, to which she also listened with great excitement. There is an atmosphere of holiness in these songs that moves the worshipers deeply. My mother loved music that nourished her soul.

I looked at her in her solitude and remembered a conversation I had about two years earlier, when living alone without her beloved caused her to deteriorate and become demented. Still, every week, four friends continued to meet for a game of bridge. Though my mother could not always recognize me, they continued to meet regularly. One day I asked her good friend Edith, "Edith, how can it be that Mom plays bridge? You have to remember a lot in this game."

"Devorah, my sweet, she hasn't been able to remember the rules of the game for a long time. We come because we love her. We want to give her pleasant moments. She thinks she's playing."

The tears welled up in my eyes, back then, and even now as I write this. My mother had friends who agreed that, to give her two hours of pleasure, they were willing to play pretend. My beloved mother earned this by right and not by grace. The girl abandoned at birth was not abandoned by her friends. Life did reward her, after all.

The long drive back home was a good time to listen to Smetana's *Moldau*. In the past, every time I listened to this piece, my thoughts would harken back to the grandmother I never knew, Johanna. I never knew why. I thought this uncontrollable connection was due to the landscapes she'd grown up in. This time, after talking to my mother, there was no doubt it was the music I would choose to listen to in this hour.

I listened to the mountain spring, flowing and gurgling it until it becomes a brook that becomes a tributary, then a stream that flows like a river and empties into a river larger than itself. It made me think of my search for my grandmother that began with one little question as a six-year-old girl.

I listened to the melody and relished the flow. I pictured the green pastures of Europe, with the ancient villages sitting on the banks of the rivers and on the slopes of the mountains. I could almost feel the noise of the water, running and rippling. Sometimes I saw the river bouncing along playfully, cheerfully, and sometimes flowing dramatically and seriously, sometimes rushing and gushing and sometimes very calm and wide.

The wanderings within this melody, its incarnation, are like my own family's wanderings and like the wanderings of the Jews. During the various ceremonies in Israel as I stood for the playing of "Hatikva", the national anthem, I recognized the small motif that is also found within the *Moldau*. I thought then that it was musical theft, and I didn't like this fact. I thought that our anthem was not all ours. I had a hard time understanding why this non-original tune became part of the national anthem.

Now I already knew that Smetana was not being wholly original either. The origin of the melody is a Sepharadic *piyyut*, a Jewish prayer song from early fifteenth-century Spain. The source passage is Jewish: this is the spring. This prayer wandered and rolled along with the wanderings of the Jews expelled from Spain. There is a clear source here that has returned the flowing, meandering river back to its route. It is a magical and mysterious thing, the connection that this piece makes between an ancient Jewish prayer and the national anthem.

The European, civilized grandmother who gave birth to my mother, the grandmother whose cards were dealt on European soil, the grandmother whose fate played out so that she had a descendant, the grandmother whose fate brought her daughter on a winding and unusual road to Israel, even if the flow was sometimes blocked by stumbling blocks, flotsam and jetsam, that grandmother eventually reached the source of the water, the beginning of the meandering river. Her daughter had returned to her roots.

I understand that Johanna's tormented soul had passed on to her descendants and had not disappeared from the world. Despite the circumstances, there is hope.

My grandmother has a family. Fate contrived to leave some remnant of her family.

I wonder how much choice we have even in times of peace when we seem to be the masters of our lives.

A secret seems to me like an oil painting. You can paint over an existing painting and cover it completely. Ostensibly, the painting in the hidden layer was never there at all. But only ostensibly. The painting exists below the covering layers. The many layers can make the painting heavy, thick and very opaque. A secret is passed down from generation to generation even if it is not visible to the eye. It exists somewhere in the hidden depths.

Revealing a secret is like painting in watercolors. Each layer blends in with the one in front of it and can easily flow beyond its boundaries. The beauty of the painting lies in the transparent layers, onlaid upon each other. All of them together make up the visible painting. Every color that touches the paper belongs to the painting and builds it.

I learned that what happened to my grandmother and mother in the past were layers that form an integral part of my painting. It's a part of me, like in a watercolor painting. The transparency allows to see further, allows to feel relief and lightness even if these layers were painted more than a hundred years ago. The hands of my clock show the present time and the moment of abandonment of the baby and the great love that connected my mother and her caregiver and my mother's escape to the Zwickau town hall and the birth of my daughters and grandchildren and my divorce from my daughters' father and the deep friendship between my partner and me. That is the way with our time, it can never be just here and now.

During my mother's decline into dementia, we often needed to dig through documents at her home. I came across a package of postcards that my daughter, Maayan Keret, sent to her from around the world, from places where she worked as a model. I arranged them all in an album and gave it as a gift to my daughter. On the first page I wrote: "It seems that just as you kept in touch with Grandma, I longed to find my own grandmother. Now we are all granddaughters and we are all mothers. A cycle is complete."

In her response, full of gratitude and excitement, Maayan said to me: "Mother, I am sure that in your grandmother's last moments, when she stood in front of the firing squad in the Riga forests with her eight-year-old daughter, she thought of the nun Hilde with whom she had to leave her baby, and was comforted by knowing her daughter might have been spared the fate of Europe's Jews. Every mother thinks of her children."

To be a daughter and granddaughter, to be a mother and grandmother.

My mother was not raised by her mother. I was raised by a derelict girl. One link in the intergenerational chain had opened and the next one cannot be hung on it with confidence. Any slight tremor might drop the one hanging on the open link and slam it into the ground. The link, my mother, hangs on the edge of the precipice. I hang on her.

The intergenerational path paved in our family is discontinuous. It's sometimes hidden or blurred by the forces of time, and requires deep breaths while climbing to its heights, and attention while gliding down a steep slope that can come to the edge of an abyss.

The rupture of our family chain left a void within me that cried out for words. The break in the link is also a fracture of life that has not passed over me; it has seeped into my own motherhood. To this day I long to be a mother who gathers her chicks under her wing. I long for it but cannot persist. It does happen that my motherhood is one of abandonment. If only I knew how to be a proper mother. My amazing girls experience it to this day, much to their, and my, sadness. All three are wonderful, loving, dedicated women and mothers. But I, the mother and grandmother, sometimes I'm not there for them.

The life-puzzle that is this book, I put together like the haiku written by Hokushi in the seventeenth or eighteenth century:

The moon in the pine
I hang it on, remove it
Step back and observe.

I left the moon be once I was satisfied that it was in its right place.

The miles of my journey are complete. I've come a long way, and a long way has come within me. I hold the hope that this journey has soldered and strengthened the links of our intergenerational chain and that every link in it will hold, fulfilling its destiny: to hang on to the next links in the line.

FINAL NOTE

I hope that this book might help find my family, the off-spring of:

Abraham, son of *Sheftel Friedman*, born 1830, and his wife *Itte*.

Their children: *Hanna* (1862), *Hode* (1867), *Shifrah* (1869), *Yedidia Elias* (1872), *Haim Itzik* (1875)

The three daughters of Yedidia Elias Friedman and his wife Etta, the daughter of Mark Leib Brick: *Tanny* (1899), *Lea* (1900), *Johanna* (1902)

May it be so.

Acknowledgements

Shaike Shafrir, my wonderful friend and partner, whose image should be beside the term 'true friend'.

Shaike, love of my life, without your wise and creative words this book would not have been what it is.

My three beloved daughters – *Rottem, Maayan* and *Reut* – who always encouraged me in my quest to search for my grandmother and find my root. Each in her own way.

My dear beloved sister *Nurit Aviram*, who always lent a hand when I asked.

Barbara Kirschner, who came to my assistance with great energy and assiduousness o that I could advance my research.

Barbara, it is because of you that I managed to link together this chain and understand the whole picture.

The websites *Tapuz Shorashim* and *JewishGen* who provided an excellent starting point to my research, in particular *Dr. Eran Re'm, Rony Golan,* and *Dr. Hadas Hannany* who devoted their time and skill and made it possible for me to take the crucial first step of the journey. The active sites *"Jews of Latvia"* and *"Hopa Hopa Reiter"* whose participants always replied to my questions.

The wonderful *Manny Kornitzer*, born 1922, who first met my mother on the platform in Trieste and became her best friend.

Dear Manny, your memory is astounding and your joie de vivre is a wonder.

Dolly Modai, my friend, who introduced me to *Tovit* and *Tamar*, German-Jewish contemporaries of my mother, both lucid and energetic despite nearing a hundred years of age.

Ken and *Barbara Feinberg*, *Beth Huppin* and *David Bennett*, *Yatzok Azuz*, *Israela Or Erlich*, *Ditza Lahat*, *Dr. Bracha Elhasid Groumer*, *Esti Haviv*, *Gita Vider Schlick*, *Niva Alush*, *Gershon Belhorn*, *Paz Hischman*, *Irit Aviram* and many more friends and family who answered my questions and listened to my process over many years – sometimes the help was extensive and sometimes short but significant.

The wonderful poet *Nurit Zarhi*, who gladly allowed me to quote her poem at the start of the book.

Writing this book was a fascinating, enriching experience thanks to you all.

Thank you.

Printed in Great Britain
by Amazon

46557215R00152